D0801557

TIME OF THEIR LIVES

TIME OF THEIR LIVES
THE DIONNE TRAGEDY

A true-life fairy tale
by
John Nihmey and Stuart Foxman

NIVA Publishing

First published in Canada April 1986. Distributed by Macmillan of Canada.
A selection of Literary Guild Canada June 1986.
First published in the United States September 1987.
A selection of Literary Guild America January 1988.

Canadian Cataloguing in Publication Data

Nihmey, John
    Time of Their Lives

    ISBN 0-921043-00-7

1. Dionne quintuplets — Fiction.
I. Foxman, Stuart. II. Title.

PS8577.I44T44 1986   C813'.54   C86-090097-5
PR9199.3.N44T44   1986

The authors are grateful to Warner Bros. Inc. for permission to quote lines from *Anything Goes*, words and music by Cole Porter, © Copyright 1934 (renewed) Warner Bros. Inc. All rights reserved. Used by permission.

NIVA Publishing
800-180 Elgin, Ottawa, Canada K2P 2K3

Printed in Canada

Authors' Note to the U.S. Edition

Time of Their Lives is a novel based on actual events surrounding the first eight years in the lives of the Dionne Quintuplets. All of the incidents described in the book occurred. All of the outcomes are true.

The book's main characters—Oliva and Elzire Dionne, their children, Dr. Allan Dafoe, Premier Mitchell Hepburn, and *North Bay Nugget* reporter Mort Fellman—are real. Most of the other characters—the extended Dionne family, World's Fair promoter Ivan Spear, child psychologist Dr. William Blatz, and many others whose names you will immediately recognize—are also real. A few supporting characters, namely the ministers in Mitchell Hepburn's Cabinet, several nurses in the Dafoe Hospital, and Oliva Dionne's lawyer Martin Poulin, have been created to represent the actions of a number of people who occupied those positions between 1934 and 1942.

During our three years of research into the Dionne story, we made frequent trips to Corbeil, Callander, and North Bay, the book's main settings. There, we visited the Dionne farmhouse and Dr. Dafoe's house, both museums now; the Dafoe Hospital, today a private home; and the site of Quintland, now a fenced-in field. During our visits, we spoke with townspeople who witnessed the various events described in the book. Their reminiscences helped give authenticity to our descriptions of people, places, and situations.

Our research included reading hundreds of magazine and newspaper articles dating from 1934 to 1942, including every issue of the *Toronto Star* and the *New York Times* from that period. We also viewed dozens of Pathé newsreels and listened to the many radio broadcasts featuring the quints and Dr. Dafoe. These provided a fascinating glimpse of how the quints and their doctor were perceived by the public. Equally revealing were the three Twentieth Century-Fox films—*The Country Doctor, Reunion,* and *Five of a Kind*—whose mythical depictions of the book's main characters reflected prevailing public opinion.

Many books, accounts, and studies were written about the quints during their heyday. Works such as the midwives' *Administering Angels,* the nurses' hospital diaries, and Dr. Blatz's psychological texts were particularly helpful in capturing the professional and personal views of some of the prominent figures in the quints' lives.

As well, government records and commentaries such as "Infant Industry" (*Harper's*, Nov. 1938) were invaluable to our understanding of the magnitude and importance of the Dionne Quintuplets during the Depression. Later works, notably the quints' autobiography *We Were Five* (co-authored by James Brough), Pierre Berton's social history *The Dionne Years—A Thirties Melodrama*, the Canadian Broadcasting Corporation's documentary *The Dionne Quintuplets*, and Barry Broadfoot's oral history of the Depression, *Ten Lost Years*, provided us with interesting perspectives on both the quint phenomenon and the period in which it occurred.

We are indebted to many people for their valuable recollections, and for making available to us important documents and artifacts. In particular, we would like to thank the staff at the National Library and Public Archives of Canada for locating rare documents; the Public Film Archives staff for repeatedly letting us see their reels "just one more time"; the people in the Ontario Public Archives' Government Records Section for looking into those "missing" files; Jimmy Rodolfos of the Dionne Quint Collectors' Club in Boston for lending us his cherished collection of quint memorabilia; Senator David Croll for recalling with candor Mitchell Hepburn's Cabinet; and Leo Voyer for telling us what it was like when the world dropped into Corbeil, and stayed for eight years. We would also like to thank those people who spoke to us under the condition that their names not be mentioned.

We extend special thanks to Mort Fellman, the reporter who covered the Dionne story for more than forty years. His desire that the truth behind the facts be told is reflected in the many hours he spent sharing his memories with us, and in his agreeing to review our manuscript for historical accuracy. We are also grateful to him for helping us to meet Elzire Dionne, who died eight months after we presented her with the Canadian edition of this book.

Finally, thanks must go to our editor, Ann Fothergill-Brown, for helping us to write a book that aims to be true to the spirit of what happened to the Dionne family.

John Nihmey
Stuart Foxman
June 1987

To Elzire

Contents

Prologue

The words flashed onto the screen in big black letters. *Attendance Sags At Chicago World's Fair*. Shots of the worst-hit areas of the fair followed: vacant ticket wickets, boarded-up exhibits, closed pavilions, a trickle of people wandering aimlessly about the desolate midway.

Ivan Spear shifted in his seat. Joe had been right. This would do wonders for the fair's image!

Joe had called after screening the newsreel in the fair's theatre this morning, and said that the report didn't make them look too good. But Spear, optimist that he was, had no idea that it was this bad. Even the clipped voice of the announcer sounded more ominous than it had during countless matinees before, as he spoke now with certainty of how last year's hit had turned into this year's flop.

Then, Spear himself was on the screen, leaning back in his chair, and looking dapper in a double-breasted suit. His demeanour did not betray his fears. He had been in the business for thirty-five years, a small-time hustler turned big-city promoter. During that time, he had mastered the art of downplaying a bad situation. And this one was *very* bad.

"You have to understand something," explained the black-and-white image of Spear, his voice brimming with false confidence. "People are fickle. They grab hold of something, squeeze what they can out of it, and drop it, just like that." For effect, he clenched his fist, then opened his fingers all at once. "Especially these days," he continued. "You've got to give people something new. Something exciting. Something to help them forget their problems." He paused, waiting for a reaction from the hidden interviewer, even a simple grunt of agreement; but nothing came. "We'll give them what they want," he concluded. "I'm not worried."

Of course, he was. Last year, the crowds had lined up for hours to get into his fair. Every day, people had waited patiently to see the Adler Planetarium, the golden-roofed Lama Temple, the Transportation Building, the General Motors assembly line, the Sky Ride, and Sally. Especially Sally.

They had lined up six deep outside, waiting for the doors to open, just to see some unemployed thirty-year-old silent film actress from Missouri named Helen Beck. Spear had changed her name to Sally Rand, given her a couple of huge white ostrich feathers, told her to strip – and presto, a star had been born. The civic-minded authorities had been horrified, but Spear loved it. For every arrest on lewd and lascivious conduct charges, ten thousand more people had flocked to see her provocative fan dance. What did Sally care? It was the Depression, and she was getting rich. So was Spear. Bar none, Sally Rand had been the best racket of his life.

But that was last year, and the newsreel's final image – Sally on stage before a sparse crowd – proved it. Spear should have planned for it, even expected it. When the gates had opened three weeks ago, the public, not hearing word of anything new, stayed away in droves. The newsreel announcer now summed it up best: "The novelty of the greatest world's fair ever has simply worn off."

Dramatic music swelled as the last image flickered away and the screen went white.

"Okay, okay. Hit the lights," Spear hollered up to the projection booth. He stood up, rubbing his temples. Not yet eight o'clock in the morning and already he had a headache.

The lights went up in the empty theatre. Spear blinked. "Just what we fucking need." He turned to Raymond, his young assistant, who had been sitting next to him during the newsreel.

Raymond remained silent, afraid to speak. He had learned to keep quiet until his boss cooled off. It was Joe, on Spear's other side, who spoke up first.

"What do you want me to do, Mr. Spear?" he asked.

"Don't show it, of course," Spear exclaimed. "It's taking everything we've got just to get anyone to come here in the first place. That shit would be enough to make them leave."

"I'll lock it away in my office," Joe said.

"Good. Thanks, Joe." Spear turned to Raymond. "Come on. We have a lot of work to do."

The two men left the theatre and walked across the fair grounds, empty now because the gates hadn't yet opened for the day. But Spear knew that even when the gates did open, the grounds wouldn't exactly be full. He had to do something. And fast.

"I talked to Reynolds this morning," Spear told Raymond as they walked into the Administration Building.

"Yes?" Raymond followed Spear down the long hallway.

"We're down twelve per cent from last week. And that was down seven from the week before." He pushed open the door to his suite.

As they stepped through the door, a woman of about twenty-five, dressed smartly in a brown cotton skirt and a beige high-necked blouse, looked up from the pot of tea she was preparing for herself. "Good morning, Mr. Spear," she called out cheerfully.

"No calls," Spear grumbled, heading straight for the inner office.

Raymond followed, closing the door behind him. "It's still early in the season," he speculated, trying his best to sound optimistic. "Sally's bound to get them back."

"Sally's dead." Spear's voice was flat as he glanced at the framed photo that hung on the wall behind his desk. Two seven-foot-long feathers with a pair of shapely calves and spiked heels sticking out below, and a head of free-flowing hair with an alluring smile popping out above. "We've got to come up with something new." He sat at his desk, as Raymond settled into the chair opposite. "Get your pen ready. We're not leaving here until we come up with something." He looked into yesterday's teacup. "Arlene," he called out. "Get us some tea."

Spear started by giving Raymond a lecture on how to milk human nature. Then throughout the rest of the day, and long into the night, the two of them threw ideas at one another, Spear desperately trying to conjure up a fresh attraction to draw the crowds, and Raymond dutifully writing everything down, then giving his opinion. Some ideas were better than others – more rides, a life exhibit, a *Streets of Paris* replica, a Hall of Science – and Raymond almost jumped out of his chair with enthusiasm over some of them. But, each time, Spear told him not to get too excited, for there were no guarantees that any of them would work. He likened ideas to numbers on a wheel of chance. All you could do was place your bet and wait to see if your number came up.

Part One

The world has gone mad today,
And good's bad today,
And black's white today,
And day's night today....

— Anything Goes, Cole Porter, 1934

1

Home at Last

It had been the third pew for as long as Ernest could remember. That wasn't very long, but he figured his mother had been kneeling in that same spot for at least a hundred years.

Ernest fidgeted, but beside him his mother was perfectly still. Eyes closed, head bowed in silent prayer, thick hands wrapped around a rosary – Elzire Dionne was a picture of serenity. Even the statues that stood on either side of the altar, whose fixed stares humbled many who entered the house of God, could not make Elzire feel uneasy. She was content with her life and at peace with God.

After what seemed an eternity to Ernest, his mother finally opened her eyes, dropped her hands, and started to rise. That was all the boy needed. He jumped up from his seat. Now, at last, they could go to Voyer's for some candy. She had promised.

Elzire had trouble getting up. One hand on Ernest's arm, the other on the back of the pew in front of her, she carefully raised her very pregnant self to a standing position. She winced as she straightened up, then forced a smile for Ernest, who was on tenterhooks ready to go.

The eldest of her five children, Ernest was also the most impatient. Becoming more and more like his father every day, Elzire thought, cupping his face. Knowing how anxious he was to get his candy, she told him to run ahead. "I'll be there soon."

Ernest was off like a shot.

"And get something for your sisters." Elzire's loud whisper echoed against the walls of the small but empty church, as she turned to watch Ernest leave.

She watched as he banged from side to side down the length of the pew, and then as he sped down the centre aisle, where he made a quick half-turn to bend his knee and make the sign of the cross, before bounding out through the big wooden doors and onto the steps outside. Elzire smiled, then covered her mouth before a chuckle got the best of her. It pleased her to see Ernest so carefree. When she was his age, life had been quite different.

When Elzire was nine, her mother had already been dead for two years, and she was well on her way to assuming full responsibility for a farmhouse and a family of eight. The chores that Elzire inherited instantly transformed her childhood. She went straight from playing with dolls to sewing patches on overalls and cooking and cleaning for her father and six brothers.

By the time she was twelve, Elzire was getting up every morning at five to make a big breakfast for her father, who afterwards disappeared into the fields with his implements while she started to milk the cows. Then, she fed the chickens and collected whatever eggs there were before cooking another big breakfast, this time for her six brothers who had their own chores to do. School followed, but for Elzire, it was more a rest period than an exercise in learning. At least there, her mind could drift off to strange worlds outside her own, before she had to run home to get supper ready for everyone.

In the evenings, she darned the boys' socks and sewed sheets from flour sacks while she soaked the beans and waited for the bread and pie to bake for the next day. Then, it was up to bed, where she often fell asleep with a book open on her chest, only to jolt awake a few minutes later to turn out the lamp and say a prayer for her father and for the brothers she looked upon as her own children.

Elzire now wondered what the future would hold for her *real* children and she said a quick prayer for the five of them as she moved along the pew. On her way out of the church, she stopped to dip in the face of the altar and make the sign of the cross. Then she said another prayer, not for health or salvation this time, but for rain. It was *les rogations*, time to pray for future reapings, and there had been no rain in weeks. Then, before leaving, she added another prayer, one for her new baby. The one that was giving her so much more pain than all the others had. The one that seemed ready to come into the world right now, though the anticipated confinement was still two months off.

Elzire stepped outside and looked down the narrow dirt stretch that passed for main street in Corbeil. Ernest was nowhere in sight. All she could see was the barren road and Voyer's General Store, the structure that, along with the church, marked the heart of the community. They were Corbeil's meeting places. Nourishment for both the body and the soul, Elzire liked to think.

Beyond Voyer's, she could see the log farmhouses of Corbeil. Many of these farms had been in the same family for generations, and Elzire knew all the wives and children. Other houses lay scattered on the horizon, nicer ones than those in their community, but Elzire knew few of their owners. They belonged to another town, Callander, and to another parish. That was the way things were in Corbeil. Your neighbours were your family, but the sign-post where their road met the Ferguson Highway marked the end of the world.

As Elzire approached Voyer's, she noticed how badly the paint was peeling off the outside of his store. She looked up and also saw that the eaves were beginning to rot. It disturbed her to think that with so many people out of work, Léo couldn't get someone to fix up his place. After all, when the lumber mill had finally closed last winter, men from all over had come to the Dionne farm looking for work. Oliva always found something for them to do. And if he didn't have the money to pay them, they were certainly satisfied with a bowl of Elzire's hot vegetable stew and a basketful of potatoes or turnips to take home to their wives. They had all had better years than 1934, but Elzire was grateful for whatever they had, and was always glad to help others less fortunate. She would suggest that Léo do his part too.

As she opened the door to Voyer's, Ernest was standing just inside, with plugs of black licorice and other pieces of candy poking out of his fist.

"Maman, can I have these?"

"I think you already have," she laughed, eyeing his black lips and teeth. "Just save some for Daniel. And for your sisters. They'll be home from school by the time we get back."

The words were barely out, when Ernest thrust a caramel into his mouth and turned his attention to the sugar sticks and peppermints in the showcase, carefully surveying the selection.

Elzire smiled to herself. She could remember doing the same thing, when Léo's father ran the store. Things had hardly changed at all since then. The room was fragrant with the same aroma of tea and spices. The shelves heaved with the same assortment of groceries and dry goods. The wooden floors creaked with the same creaks. Even the calendar behind the cash register hung in the same spot on the wall. Only the year had changed.

"Léo," she said to the tall, stocky man behind the counter, "you'd better get a coat of paint on before the wood dries out."

Léo nodded politely. "Have you got the money for it?"

"You don't need money. Oliva's got some paint in the shed." Elzire gestured in the direction of the sacks in the far corner of the store. "Give someone some sugar or a tin of tobacco to do it."

"Don't worry about my paint," he said, pointing to her bulging stomach. "Look at yourself. You look like you're ready to have the baby right here."

Elzire didn't comment.

Léo studied her anxious face, and knew right away that this wasn't a good time for humour. "Are you feeling okay?"

Elzire wiped her neck and brow with the sleeve of her smock. "This heat is something," was her answer.

Léo hoped that that was all it was. "You know, I have a feeling it's going to be a boy this time." A glimmer came into his eyes. "Don't ask me how; it's just a feeling."

"It's not up to…." She tightened her jaw as a contraction gripped her, exerting a downward pressure that burned her legs from hip to ankle.

"Are you all right?"

She nodded. "I will be, when I get home." Pain crept into her reply. "We were just at church. The kneeling is getting to be too much."

"Your weight doesn't help much, either."

Elzire pooh-poohed the lecture that she knew was coming about her weight. "You and le docteur."

"Speaking of le docteur, didn't he tell you to stay at home?"

She exhaled hard, then waved her hand in disregard for the doctor's orders. "If I listened to le docteur, I'd be in bed all the time. My children would starve."

Léo came around the counter, dragging a stool with him. "Here." He pushed it in front of her. "Sit for a while. You look terrible." He tried to force her onto the stool, but she resisted. If she sat, she knew she wouldn't be able to get up.

"No, no. I've got to get home." She looked over at Ernest, who was sitting on a crate by the door, absorbed in a funny book. "How much for the candy? And give me some gum, too."

Léo passed her a box of Chiclets but didn't say a word. He had gotten used to seeing most of his customers come in without any cash in hand. If they didn't have butter or eggs to trade for flour and sugar, they would just take what they needed and turn over their relief vouchers to him when they got them. Léo knew that the Dionnes were one of the few families not on relief, but he still said nothing. Just in case.

Elzire looked up at him. "Six… seven cents?" She reached into the pocket of her smock and pulled out some coins. Then she opened the box of Chiclets and held it open to Léo. "Do you want a chew?"

Léo shook his head. "A nickel is fine."

She tossed two pieces of gum into her mouth, then plunked five dull coppers onto the counter in front of Léo. "I better go." She turned to face the door. "Come on, Ernest."

"You get some rest now, Elzire."

"I will," she assured him.

"And give my best to Oliva."

If she were to do that, Oliva would know she had walked all this way. She remained silent.

"You're not saying anything." Léo wagged a finger at her in mock anger. "Oliva doesn't know you're out, does he?"

"Goodbye, Léo," she said, smiling as she edged toward the door. "Ernest?"

He didn't move.

"Ernest!"

He slowly rose from the crate, his eyes still glued to the page. "Can I take this, Monsieur Voyer?" he asked out of habit.

Léo squinted, making the request seem greater to consider than it actually was. "If you bring it back," he finally said, knowing that Ernest would. All the children did.

It amused Léo to see children of Ernest's age ask to borrow the funnies. That was the common procedure now. No one had bought a magazine in his store since the beginning of the Depression. And before then, Ernest was too young to read, so he knew of no other practice. Léo didn't mind. They were the only items in his store that he could get on consignment, and the loans made all his customers happy, especially the children. So what if their parents spent only a few cents when they came in? Most of the time, that was all they had.

Elzire hobbled out of the store as fast as she could, pulling Ernest along, and hoping that Léo wasn't watching her too closely. If he was, he would be bound to notice her enormous legs – right now swollen to the size of two small tree trunks – and he would tell her there was no way she could walk two miles. So she pushed on, hearing his voice rattle as the door shut, but not answering as she lifted one throbbing leg after the other down the steps, stopping at the bottom to take a breath before starting her long journey home.

She knew Oliva would be angry to see her out, especially struggling like this. As it was, he had been the one to finally call le docteur, despite her assurances that the swollen limbs caused her no pain. After le docteur had seen her, he had scolded her for being up and around when she was as big as a cow. He ordered her to bed, and insisted that Oliva tie her down if he had to. Anything to keep her off her feet. But keeping Elzire down was easier said than done. Her own personal well-being always took second place to the needs of her family. She believed that she had been put on this earth to be a good wife and mother, and anything she did to that end was simply part of her role. As for the welfare of her unborn baby, that was completely in God's hands, regardless of what she did.

Elzire stood on the road, thinking about the distance she would have to cover. She started to tell Ernest to run ahead, then changed her mind. If something happened, he would be needed to run for help. This had been the most difficult of her six pregnancies, and in the back of her mind was the word *twins* that le docteur had squawked about. She didn't want to find herself lying on the road, halfway home, giving birth to two babies without Tante there to take care of her. She wished that one of the neighbours would ride by in a buggy, or even better, that Père Routhier would happen to drive by in the parish car. He would not only give her a lift home, but would, at the same time, reassure her that she had not done wrong by taking a mid-week walk to church in her condition.

In the two miles between Voyer's and home, there were five farms to pass. These were not the sprawling farms with big houses and huge barns that dotted the landscape along the Ferguson Highway.

Rather, they were strips of naked land that, although consisting of several hundred acres, were mostly unsettled and uncultivated. Even in the best of times, the soil was not rich, but the severe drought this spring had only made things worse. The law of the land had become self-sufficiency, and all that was needed for that was a small hayfield, a vegetable garden, some chickens, one cow, a small barn to store hay, and a root cellar to keep potatoes and turnips through the winter.

A pegged sign announcing each family's name sat at the edge of the road, just in front of each small, one-and-a-half-storey log house. A broad porch, overhung by the sloping roof of the building, extended across the front and along one side of the house, ending at the big summer kitchen, whose steps led down into a yardful of girls doing the wash in big steel tubs, and other, smaller children playing about. If papa wasn't out in the field with his sons, he was probably working in the barn, or chopping wood to store in the shed for winter. Maman could be anywhere – hanging the clothes to dry, picking beans for supper, churning butter, plucking a chicken, or setting the table in the summer kitchen. Only the grandparents, *pépère* and *mémère*, were allowed to sit idle, usually in rocking or straight-backed wooden chairs on the front porch, waiting for neighbours or the occasional immigrant clothes peddler to come by and while the time away.

As Elzire and Ernest passed, neighbours called out *bonjour* and *ça va?*, but Elzire did not stop to chat. She just smiled, said *bonjour* and *ça va* back, and kept walking. Unlike some of the other wives in the community, Elzire had never been one to stand around for small talk when there was work to be done. Especially not now, with pain weakening her knees to the point of collapse.

She only stopped once, and that was to spend a moment with Monsieur Bélanger, the ninety-five-year-old father of the community, who was also one of the prime suppliers of its population – eight children, twenty-two grandchildren, forty-three great-grandchildren, and four great-great-grandchildren. Elzire would never forgive herself if she failed to say a kind word to the old man, only to find out the next day that he had died during the night.

At the next house a woman of Elzire's age, Gaëtane, was outside hanging laundry on the line that stretched from one end of the porch to the other. She called out her concern over the way Elzire was walking. Elzire shrugged off her childhood friend's concern, then pointed respectfully to the sky.

Before Elzire struggled by, Gaëtane offered to go and prepare dinner for Oliva and the children, thereby giving Elzire a chance to rest.

"You've got enough to take care of," Elzire called out, laughing to herself. She was thinking of Gaëtane's husband and seven children, who would surely complain if there was no supper on the table at four o'clock. Oliva and her five certainly would.

"You're sure?" asked Gaëtane.

Elzire nodded, offering one of her childlike, almost angelic, smiles as goodbye. She and Ernest then continued down the sloping road, past friendly Madame Lebel's house on the right, and on for another few hundred yards into the small valley where, on the left, their own farmhouse stood. Home at last, Elzire thought, hoping to make it to the back room before she dropped.

Ernest spotted his five-year-old sister, Thérèse, playing out back near the woodshed, where their father was chopping blocks in the shade of a big tree. He tore off to meet them.

"Don't tell your father where we were," Elzire called out weakly, but Ernest was gone.

As Elzire left the road, she heard the dog barking at Ernest's arrival. She quickened her step, hoping that Oliva wouldn't look up, then slowed down when she knew that she was out of sight. She trudged up the dirt path that led to their front porch, only to meet the sight of the steps with the grimace she had been desperately holding in. The prospect of climbing the three steps seemed to drive her into the ground. But she was determined. Holding her breath, she climbed one step at a time, bending when she reached the top step to pick up a small shovel and a doll.

Oliva was about to lay axe to another block, but looked up from his woodpile when he heard the screen door slam. His shirt sleeves were rolled up, and both arms glistened with the sweat that had also soaked his back. He had been splitting wood for the past half-hour. Before that, he'd been out in one of the fields, replanting an area where the seeds planted a month ago had dried out before taking root.

"Where have you been?" he called out to Ernest, some of the frustration of *no rain again* apparent in his voice. "I let you stay home from school to help me, not to go flitting off."

Ernest was quick to the defence. "I went with Maman to church." He was even quicker with the news of the best part of the trip into town. "Then we went to Monsieur Voyer's." He flashed the funnies in the air.

Oliva swung the axe and split another block. "That mother of yours," he said, wiping his brow with his forearm. He positioned the next block for splitting, then put only enough power into his stroke to wedge the axe firmly into the wood, straightening out his short but wiry frame at the same time.

He started toward the back door, prepared to give Elzire a lecture for going out when le docteur had given them both strict orders, but he stopped after taking a few steps. What was the point? I'm fine, Elzire would say, don't worry. But he always did.

In fact, he had felt protective of her since their very first meeting at church ten years ago. Elzire Legros had been only sixteen years old then, with the face of a child and a youthful innocence about her that gave no hint of the hard life she had already been leading for years. Oliva had been an intense-looking, wilful man of twenty-two, still helping his father on the farm, but already planning his own life and determining what means he would need to support a family before he even had one. Shortly after he met Elzire, he knew he had found a wife. Here was a woman of good farm stock, who didn't shudder at hard work, who had the grace of God in her bones, and who had a love for children that few women twice her age could admit to. A brief courtship followed, and they were married.

Oliva knew of Elzire's hard upbringing, and also knew how ready she was to work hard the rest of her life. But rather than take advantage of that, he was always trying to make things easier for her. Leave some things for tomorrow, he would tell her on a particularly busy day. Go lie down and rest for a spell, he would suggest after she had run herself ragged with the chores and the children. But she never listened to him. Or to anyone, for that matter – except God, who seemed to give her enough strength and determination for *three* lifetimes.

Oliva continued toward the house, not now to pointlessly scold Elzire, but to check on baby Pauline, who was sleeping soundly on a big pillow that rested on the ground next to the steps leading up to the summer kitchen. He looked up when he heard a noise from inside the house, but couldn't see Elzire through the window. He thought once again about going in, then decided he had better not. This was no time for an argument. When he finished splitting the wood, he still had to haul a load of gravel to North Bay for the

Government, a job that paid three dollars for each day he was needed. Elzire thought it was too much work for him, what with farming their own land and accepting all the other back-breaking jobs that no one else would take. But Oliva didn't mind. To support his family, no job was beneath him or too much to handle. They needed the money, and anything was better than going on relief.

"Where's Daniel?" Oliva called out, walking away from Pauline and looking about for his three-year-old.

"I don't know." Ernest left Thérèse with the funnies, and scooted past his father to the far side of the house, where seven-year-old Rose was intently studying a butterfly that had landed on a big rock. When Ernest reached her, he waved the remaining candies from his visit to Voyer's in her face.

"Where'd you get those?"

"Monsieur Voyer's," he said smugly, enticingly waving a sugar stick just beyond her reach.

"Can I have one?"

Ernest held his hand out, then pulled it back as she grabbed for the candy. With his other hand, he tugged on her hair and ran off into the back yard again.

Rose started to cry and ran toward the house, banging up the steps and waking Pauline, who also started to cry.

Ernest just laughed and ran past the hay press, and on toward the big maple tree behind the barn. He was determined to reach his treehouse before he got into trouble for teasing Rose. But as he shot by, his father grabbed him.

"How many times do I have to tell you to keep your hands off your sister?" He kept a firm grip on Ernest's arm. "Every time you walk by, you have to touch or poke or pull."

Ernest bit his lip and shrugged sheepishly as he looked up at his father.

"Do you do it to bother her or me?"

The tongue-lashing would have lasted longer, but a child's scream from the kitchen cut the air.

Oliva dropped his hold on Ernest, and started running toward the back door. The dog followed, barking as if to sound an alarm. Then came the children: first Thérèse; then Daniel, appearing from the barn; and finally Ernest, far behind, sighing with relief. He was off the hook for now.

2

Nightfall

O liva couldn't understand why Tante was talking about getting le docteur. She had assisted in the deliveries of hundreds of babies, including Elzire's first five. But he knew not to argue with her. Not only was Adouilda Legros one of Corbeil's two midwives, she was also Elzire's aunt and *Tante* to the entire community.

For the past eight hours Tante had also been custodian of the back room – called that simply because it was at the back of the house, next to the summer kitchen. The function of the back room was never quite certain, since it served as both a sewing room and a pantry. Today it also served another purpose, for it was where Elzire lay, on a narrow wood-frame bed fitted with sheets and a light patchwork quilt. To one side of her was a small pine table, upon which rested a tiny oil-lamp. To the other side were rows of shelves filled with jars of preserves, bottles of oil, and tins of flour, barley, sugar, and tea. A solitary crucifix graced the wall above the bed.

Elzire had often commented that whenever she walked out of the back room, she could see her whole world – everything that mattered to her. Looking to the left from its doorway, she could see into the summer kitchen and through its screened windows to the barn and the hayfield. Immediately to her right was the door to the root cellar stairs. Straight ahead she could see all of her kitchen, the main room of the house, with the black wood stove at its heart. And if she leaned far enough forward, to look to the right beyond the central stairwell, she could also catch a glimpse of the boys' bedroom, as well as the view through the glass in the front door.

Oliva had put the bed in the back room only three weeks ago. What with Elzire's condition, and the fact that she spent most of her time in the kitchen, Oliva didn't want her to be climbing stairs every time she had a few minutes to rest. He had no way of knowing how useful that bed would prove to be – and how soon. When Elzire had collapsed in the kitchen this afternoon, it had been all Oliva could do to lift her arm over his shoulder, and drag her into the back room before sending Ernest to get Tante.

Oliva was outside, on his way to the well to fill a pail, when he heard the back door open and slam shut again. Heavy footsteps pounded down the steps and toward him. He turned from the pump to see Tante almost on top of him, panic in her eyes.

"Oliva, get le docteur for me right away."

"You mean you really need him?"

"Oliva, Elzire is very sick." Her voice quavered. "I'm afraid she's going to die."

Oliva's eyes searched Tante's face for a brief, frightening moment; then, letting the pail fall to the ground, he darted off toward the house.

He took the three steps to the summer kitchen in one leap, then tore into the house. The first thing he saw was Ernest, lurking just outside the back room and poking his head through the open doorway. Oliva swept by him and into the dimly lit room, but the sight of Elzire brought him up short. She lay eerily still, bathed in sweat, and moaning loudly. Her face was almost blue, her eyes puffed and closed.

Tante returned with a full pail of water, handing it to Ernest and instructing him to fill the pot that was on the stove. Then she stepped into the small room, almost bumping into Oliva, who stood over Elzire's bed. She turned to face the table and wrung out a cloth from the basin of cool water that stood there. She took the cloth and started to sponge Elzire's face and neck, glancing up a couple of times to see Oliva's anguished face. "Oliva, go," she finally said. "Please. You can't do anything for her. We need le docteur."

Oliva reached out to touch Elzire's hands, but they didn't move. He noticed the black rosary beads rolling between her swollen fingers, and touched them in prayer for her. Then he leaned over to kiss her forehead, pausing uncomfortably as he lifted his head away.

Elzire opened her eyes slowly. They were glassy, with tears running out at the corners. She lifted her head, and started to mumble something, but Tante gently pushed her back down.

"Save your breath, Elzire."

Elzire moaned loudly. "Ma tante," she struggled. "I don't think I can make it." She gritted her teeth, tightened her face, and let out a deep wheezing sound. "Oliva, get Père Routhier."

Oliva looked helplessly at Tante.

"Just hold on, Elzire." Tante looked up at Oliva, whose dark face was now almost as pale as the damp, crumpled sheets on the bed. "Oliva, we don't have time to waste. Please, go. And get Madame Lebel on your way."

"But I'm getting le docteur."

"I know, but I don't think the baby's going to hold off long enough for him to get here. Stop on your way. I'd like her to be here."

Oliva backed out of the room, unable to take his eyes off Elzire.

Ernest, who was back at his post by the door, jumped out of the way just in time to avoid getting his head knocked by his father's retreat. He walked around to the foot of the staircase, and sat on the bottom step, next to Rose. His sister had been there for what seemed like hours, a worried look on her face, her elbows propped up on lifted knees.

Oliva joined the two children. He knew that their mother's loud and pained cries had kept them awake. He could also hear Pauline whining upstairs, and expected to see Daniel and Thérèse emerge from their rooms at any minute.

He observed how frightened Rose was. "Don't worry, sweetheart." He leaned over and kissed her on the forehead. "Maman's going to be fine."

Papa's words didn't comfort Rose any more than Tante's earlier reassurances had. And no wonder. It was Rose who had run into the kitchen this afternoon to find her mother propped up against the stove, trying to stand on legs that were so weak and painful that she collapsed at each attempt. "Papa," she whimpered, "why is Maman so sick?"

"Maman is just having the baby, that's all," Oliva wished aloud. "Now I'm just going to get le docteur, and everything will be fine."

Seeing his father occupied with Rose, Ernest got back on his feet, and crept around the stairwell to peek into the back room, only to pull his head back when Tante caught him.

"Take the boy with you," Tante called out. "He's prowling around here like a cat."

Oliva followed Tante's voice to just outside the back room. "Come on." He grabbed Ernest around the waist. "You're coming with me."

"Aw, Papa," Ernest objected. "I'll miss everything."

Oliva was in no mood for discussion. He hoisted Ernest up under one arm, grabbed the keys to his truck off the top of the icebox with his free hand, and exited out the front door. Rose ran to the front window to watch them leave. As she stood there, still in tears, Daniel came out of his room, half-asleep and rubbing his eyes.

"Where's Ernest?"

Rose just looked at her three-year-old brother, whose birth was the first she could recall happening in the house. She didn't want to say where they had gone. And she was too afraid to say why.

On the way to the truck, Ernest voiced his complaint again. "I don't want to go there, Papa," he pleaded. But it was too late. In seconds, he found himself deposited in the front seat of the truck, next to his father, who was strangely shaking as he tried to fit the key into the ignition.

The truck stalled at first, as it always did, but Oliva didn't panic. He was glad to have a vehicle, especially at a time like this. It saved him from riding Pépère's horse, or running all the way. He would normally have done that, even to summon help, in order to save the precious fuel for when he needed the truck for work; but Tante's urgency, the fear in her voice, the uncommon way she was trembling in handling her own niece, her words – all of this told him he had better get le docteur as fast as he could.

The truck finally started. Oliva switched on the headlights, only one of which was working, and turned right from his property.

"We're going the wrong way," commented the know-it-all son.

"We have to get Madame Lebel." The truck sputtered along for a few hundred yards, then Oliva pulled up in front of a farmhouse similar to theirs. "Hurry, run in. Tell her Maman's having the baby. Quick."

Oliva watched as Ernest ran up a path that was like theirs, climbed the same three steps to the porch, and knocked on an identical-looking door. A few moments passed before the door opened to reveal a sturdy woman dressed in an oversized nightdress with her husband's woollen cardigan draped over her shoulders. Ernest spoke to her, and she quickly disappeared from the doorway. Moments later, she returned with an armful of towels and a bag clanking with the sound of both glass and metal. The woman galloped over to the truck, hopping in even before Ernest could catch up with her. Ernest followed, squeezing into the little remaining space as his father, who had already half-released the brake, lifted his foot the rest of the way and accelerated back the way they had come.

"How is she?" Madame Lebel knew that Elzire wasn't due until the end of July.

Oliva looked straight ahead. "She doesn't look good. Tante wants le docteur too."

Even in the dark, Madame Lebel could see the worry on his face. "Any time that it's early like this, Oliva," she tried to reassure, "it's better to have help. Tante just wants to be safe."

"Is Maman going to die?" Ernest asked, the bluntness of his words not hiding the fear in which they were uttered.

"Not if I have anything to do with it!" Madame Lebel's certainty heartened both of them. "I've had eighteen of my own and I'm no stronger than a Legros woman. Maman will be fine."

They reached the house. "Stop!" Madame Lebel ordered, just as Oliva pulled up. She hopped over Ernest and out of the truck. "Now, hurry."

Oliva continued, revving the motor as hard as he could, but not getting very far. The tires spun in the loose dirt, forcing him to take his foot off the gas and continue at a slow pace.

The potholes and bumps forced him to slow down even more. It was frustrating, especially now. With so many people out of work, he reasoned as the truck rattled along, the road should have been fixed long ago. If a few of the unemployed would only volunteer, everyone, including he, would gladly chip in and give them some food or a little cash. The road could be repaired in a week's time. Simple things were always so complicated, he thought; and forgot again when, a few minutes later, they crossed the highway and the road smoothed out. That was a sign that Callander was near.

Closer to the city of North Bay than was Corbeil, Callander was also the more sophisticated of the two small towns. Poles carrying the wires for electricity and telephone lined the streets. These were luxuries that, in addition to waterworks, Corbeil lacked. The road was still dirt, but it was packed, and had a raised shoulder of loose soil and gravel to separate the road from the private lawns that lined it. The houses that sat in the centre of each lawn were visibly nicer, too. Most were made of brick instead of log, and many had stone paths and gardens full of daffodils and crocuses in front of them.

Oliva stopped in front of the nicest: a two-storey red brick house surrounded by a white picket fence. He jumped out of the truck, slid open the gate, and rushed up the path. Ernest followed reluctantly behind. Gripping the heavy knocker above the metal plaque that read *ALLAN ROY DAFOE, M.D.*, Oliva banged several times. When no answer was immediately forthcoming, Oliva knocked a little louder and longer.

"I'm coming, I'm coming," grumbled a woman's voice from behind the door. When it finally opened, it disclosed Mrs. Henderson, Dr. Dafoe's silver-haired housekeeper, standing in robe and slippers and wearing an irritated look on her lined face. "Mr. Dionne, what are you doing here in the middle of the night?"

"We need le docteur," he said urgently, pulling Ernest into the house with him. "Elzire is going to have the baby."

"The baby?" Mrs. Henderson's irritation turned to surprise. "She's only...."

"The baby?" a weak voice trailed through the air.

All three of them looked down the hallway that ran the length of the house to see a stumpy man with an oversized head come toddling in from the living room. He was fully dressed in suit trousers, white shirt with grey tie, and a woollen vest. He held a pipe, together with an open book, in one hand. With his free hand, he took off his eyeglasses and folded them into his shirt pocket.

"She's not due for another two months." The voice was matter-of-fact, but curious. "Did you ask Mrs. Legros to come and look at her?"

"Tante is already there," Oliva interrupted, resenting the assumption that he would waste fuel for nothing. "She's the one who wants you. Elzire is very sick."

"Hmm." Dafoe rubbed his bushy grey moustache and put his pipe to his mouth. "We'd better go, then." He turned to Mrs. Henderson. "Would you get my bag, please?"

The housekeeper walked quickly down the hallway, running every few steps, in the direction of the doorway from which Dafoe had just emerged. Before she reached the parlor, she turned right and disappeared into the doctor's examining room.

"I think it's under my desk, Mrs. Henderson," Dafoe called after her. Though they had lived in the same house for the eight years since his wife had died, he had always called her Mrs. Henderson. Intimacy was not something that came naturally to him.

Ever since his arrival in Callander twenty-five years before, Dafoe had nurtured a distance from everyone – especially his patients. Mostly French Canadians, they knew him as *le docteur*, the kindly doctor from a faraway town they had never heard of, who had actually chosen to practice here. Dafoe revelled in the status his position here gave him. He felt himself a good doctor, available at all hours, and prided himself in knowing the first names of all his patients, even the hundreds of children. But he had never shown any interest in becoming a real part of the community's social fabric. He declined all of his patients' dinner invitations, never showed up at community events, and refused to learn any French. After all these years he was still, by choice, an outsider.

Mrs. Henderson reappeared from the small waiting room that adjoined the examining room, only steps away from the front vestibule. "Where did you leave it?" she asked, empty-handed.

"It could be upstairs, you know," he thought aloud.

"Why didn't you tell me?" She tightened the frayed cord around her robe and started up the stairs.

Dafoe laughed. "Sometimes I wonder who's working for who."

Oliva was too upset to joke. "Tante said Elzire could die."

"Calm down, Oliva. Mrs. Legros is a midwife, not a doctor." He leaned over to address Ernest, who had been hiding quietly behind his father. "You'd better stay here with Mrs. Henderson, Ernest."

The boy looked grim. Everything was so tidy and neat here. It made him afraid to touch anything. "Can't I stay with Oncle Léon?" he asked hopefully.

Oliva pulled out his watch. "It's after midnight, Ernest. We'd be waking them."

"Oh, I'm sure some milk and cookies will make Mrs. Henderson's company bearable for a while," Dafoe added.

"Don't you listen to him," Mrs. Henderson barked as she descended the staircase, carrying with her Dafoe's black satchel.

Dafoe straightened up. "I'll go with you," he told Oliva. "You can pick the boy up when you bring me back." He opted for Oliva's old truck over his new Dodge; not for comfort, but with the cost of fuel these days, taking two motor vehicles to the same destination was unheard of. Especially when there were only three in the whole community.

Oliva noticed Ernest's pout. "You be good, Ernest." He turned to Mrs. Henderson. "Don't let him stay up."

"I certainly won't. After midnight, goodness!" She was still rattled about being awakened when her calendar had no births scheduled this week.

Dafoe grabbed his bag, took his suit jacket from the coat rack, and followed Oliva out, tousling Ernest's hair as he passed.

Ernest flinched. He hated when le docteur did that, but knew that he would be scolded if he protested aloud. So he kept his mouth shut, and resigned himself to spending an unpleasant time in the stifling house where all the walls were the colour of a cloudy day; where all the windows had thick curtains to shut out the light; where the dishes on the fancy tables never moved; where the pictures of strange-looking lakes, towns, and houses hung perfectly straight on the walls; and where the cool air smelled of the museum in North Bay he once had visited.

He followed Mrs. Henderson into the kitchen at the back of the house, ready for cookies, but hoping all the while that his father would be back soon.

Oliva took one step into the back room and froze at the sight before him. Tante was standing at the foot of the bed, holding in her hand the tiniest baby he had ever seen. It was impossibly small, with arms and legs like small twigs. Madame Lebel was at the table placing another baby, just as small, into the butcher's basket Oliva had fashioned into a cradle one or two babies ago.

Dafoe moved past Oliva to Tante.

"Docteur!" Tante motioned to the cradle with her free hand. "We have two others like that. And I think a fourth is coming."

"Fourth?" Oliva was ashen, his eyes still fixed on the baby that Tante was holding. He didn't even notice Elzire, who was breathing raggedly and trembling as her body worked hard in the grip of her fourth set of expulsive contractions.

Dafoe squeezed by the midwives in order to look into the cradle. "Are they breathing?"

"Barely." Tante carefully placed the baby she was holding into the cradle next to the others.

Oliva's eyes shifted to his wife. "Elzire," he muttered, but couldn't get any more words out. She kept moaning, pushing, breathing, curling her body forward; and all the while, praying, gripping her rosary over and over.

"Oliva, get out of here!" Dafoe shrieked. "Mrs. Lebel, come here!"

"Are they alive, Tante?" Oliva pleaded. There wasn't any crying like he remembered from the previous births.

Tante pushed him through the doorway. "Oliva, it's no place for you in here now. Just wait outside." Her voice was shaking. "Everything is going to be fine."

"But four...."

"Close that door," yelled Dafoe, trying to be heard above Elzire's straining sounds and the anxious urgings of the midwives.

Oliva watched the door close. At first the door stuck and wouldn't shut tight. That was no surprise to Oliva, for it had never been closed before. But Tante gave it a good shove from behind and it thudded into place, firm and secure. Oliva stared at the closed door for a moment, then looked around for the children, who were nowhere to be seen. He figured that Madame Lebel had probably come in to find them all up and had scared them back to bed and to sleep. Having eighteen children had given her that kind of know-how and authority.

Inside the room, Tante and Madame Lebel worked frantically, following Dafoe's every order. One at a time, in turn, Madame Lebel massaged the babies with olive oil. Afterwards, she handed each baby to Tante, who wrapped it tightly in a blanket heated by flat-irons, and placed it next to the others in the cradle. Dafoe dropped warm water on their lips through eye-droppers from which the tips had been cut off, and told his two helpers to watch the babies constantly and to let him know if any one of them stopped breathing. Then he moved over to tend to Elzire. Long after the last of the babies had been born, she was still moaning and trembling atop the bed, her prayers and utterances barely coherent. In great pain, and convinced that she was going to die, she also kept calling for *le père*. Dafoe finally gave her a needle to relieve the pain and she soon fell asleep, her rosary still held tightly between her fingers.

Madame Lebel left the room a few times, but said nothing to Oliva. She just went about nervously reheating the flat-irons on the stove and bringing them back to warm the blankets in the cradle. Dafoe emerged once, but only for a moment to tell Oliva that they were all girls. How could it be, Oliva asked, when he heard the final tally? But Dafoe had no answers. He simply told Oliva to try to get some sleep, then returned to the back room, closing the door behind himself.

Oliva felt helpless. He wanted to see Elzire and the babies, but the door to the back room stayed shut. He wanted to get Ernest and bring him back home, but Mrs. Henderson would have already put him to bed. He wanted also to tell his father, as well as his brother, Léon, what had happened, but it was too late to visit anyone. All he could do was stand by the door to the root cellar and press his ear against the door to the back room. He strained to pick up any comforting sounds: the babies crying naturally as they entered the foreign world outside their mother's womb; Elzire praying to God with thanks; Tante choosing among her favourite old-fashioned names; le docteur finishing up to go home. But no such sounds came. Only quick footsteps, sharp orders, and the clinking of basins and bottles being passed around. And occasionally, a faint murmur, much like the cry of a newborn kitten.

After a while, Oliva left his spot by the door and went to check on each of the children. First Pauline in his and Elzire's bedroom; then Rose and Thérèse in theirs; and finally Daniel, who was spending the night alone in the big room downstairs. He watched them as they lay peacefully in their beds, all sleeping soundly. Their breathing was the only familiar sound in the house tonight.

3

Five

I t was another slow day at the *Nugget*. The same old stories of soup kitchens and more people on the dole coming over the wire; the odd notice of a community social being sponsored by the few who could afford it; and the usual political press releases filled with promises of more jobs. Certainly nothing to keep an editor and three reporters occupied. But then, only one of the reporters was being paid. The other two had been laid off for over a year now, but they hung around the tiny news office anyway. There was little else to do.

Right now, Mort Fellman didn't have anything to do either. He thought he would die of boredom if something – anything – didn't come in soon. The highlight of his agenda for May 27, 1934, had been an interview with an evicted widow who was setting up home for her family in front of R. Monsour's Dry Goods in Mattawa. Tomorrow's would be one with Mitchell Hepburn, the Liberal candidate for premier in the upcoming provincial election, who would be in town campaigning for votes. Today, there was nothing.

He searched around the pile of old newspapers on his desk to find his mug. There it was, half-full with yesterday's tea and resting on a stained press release – some Liberal propaganda, weeks old, crowing about less government interference in the lives of the *little fellow*. Mort grabbed his mug and looked across the dusty room. His colleagues were speaking with Bob Knight, the *Nugget* editor.

"Hey," Fellman called. "We short on tea today?"

One of the reporters looked over. "Take it easy, Mort. It's on."

Knight poked his head out from between the two men. "I guess you're too busy to put the water on," he joked, "eh, Mort?"

They all laughed, Fellman included, then returned to what they had been doing – various forms of nothing.

The telephone rang, breaking a silence that had just started. All three reporters raced to the telephone near the door, but Fellman got it first.

"*Nugget*, can I help you?"

The other two reporters looked on jealously. They would sometimes talk on the telephone for an hour when someone called, even if there wasn't a story to get. It passed the time.

"Yes, this is the *North Bay Nugget*," repeated Fellman. "Can I help you, sir?" After a long pause, Fellman's placid face registered surprise. "*Five?*" He sounded incredulous. "Is this a joke?" Obviously being chastised by the caller, he pulled the receiver away from his ear. "Okay, okay, you're the uncle. I just have to make sure."

The other reporters moved closer. They could hear a faint stream of words from the other end of the line.

"I'll have to check on that.... Are you kidding? Nobody gives away nothing for free any more." Fellman looked to his colleagues. He cupped the mouthpiece on the telephone and gestured toward his head, implying that the caller was crazy. "Yeah, sure.... Why not?" He tried not to laugh at the gestures his colleagues were returning. "Yeah, I know where.... Uh-huh.... If it pans out, I'll see what I can do."

As he hung up the receiver, the other reporters leaned forward expectantly.

"Now I've heard everything," remarked Fellman.

"Who was it?" asked one of the reporters.

Fellman smiled, and headed to Knight's desk. He wanted to share this tale. "Hey, Bob. I have a good one for you."

"Yeah, what?" asked Knight, not bothering to look up from the *Time* magazine he was reading.

"Some farmer from Callander called. Says his brother's wife in Corbeil had five kids during the night."

"Farmer, eh?" Knight's eyes were still on the *Time* cover story. "Are you sure he wasn't talking about his pig?"

They all laughed.

"I almost believed him, until he asked if a birth announcement for five would be more than for one."

They laughed harder.

"And if we still give out baby packages." Fellman chuckled. "I'm lucky if I get paid."

"At least *you* do," one of the other reporters added sarcastically.

Knight looked up. "Take a run up," he suggested. "You never know."

"Come on." Fellman discounted the possibility. "I've never heard of five kids being born at once. Not around here, anyway."

"What have you got to lose?"

That was true enough. The only thing that could fill his otherwise empty plate today was a piece on cattle feed prices that he had been falling asleep over for some time. No research was required, but it had to be long enough to fill a few columns on another day when nothing else turned up.

"Well, nothing else is happening," he admitted. "I guess it won't hurt to look into it."

"Sure," Knight agreed, pleased at doing his share of a good day's work – getting his reporter out to cover a story. "But take the camera. Even if it is his pig, we'll still have page one."

They all laughed again. Knight went back to the *Time* story on Colonel Edward R. Bradley, while Fellman headed out the door with the camera. The other two reporters settled back in their chairs, talking about the merits of communism and waiting for the telephone to ring. Maybe the next call would bring a *real* story.

Léon Dionne held the telephone receiver for a few seconds before hanging it up. He reflected on the conversation he had just had with the reporter. Then he looked at his wife, Marie, who was standing next to him, waiting anxiously for the verdict. He looked over to the table where his brother, Oliva, and their father, Olivier, sat, also waiting for some hopeful words.

"He doesn't believe you," Marie concluded from the frustrated look on her husband's face.

"He thinks I'm a crackpot." Fellman hadn't come right out and said it, but Léon could tell.

"I knew it." Oliva rose from the table. "Nobody's going to believe it."

"Wait..." Léon began.

"Why should they?" Oliva continued. "I don't believe it myself." Although the dazed look he had been wearing since last night's ordeal suggested otherwise.

Olivier gave his son a gentle tug to sit back down. Oliva looked terrible, and Olivier had told him so when he had driven up shortly after dawn to tell him the news. He had never seen Oliva so upset, slurring his words as he recalled the night's events, and rambling about how he could possibly feed twelve mouths. *You will* had been all Olivier could offer to console him, as they headed to Callander to tell Léon and Marie the news.

At first, Léon had thought it was a joke, but Marie could tell by the circles around Oliva's eyes, the unshaven face, the wrinkled shirt hanging out of his trousers, and the awkward way he moved, that something serious had happened. Olivier confirmed it, sending Marie into a mad dash about the house to pick up things that Elzire might need. She had been half-way out the door when Léon suggested that they telephone the newspaper office in North Bay.

And now, Oliva was wishing they had never made the call. He didn't like people laughing at him.

"Now, hold on, Oliva," Léon said. "The man said he would come over."

"To the house?"

Léon nodded.

Olivier took a long drink of the tea Marie had made when they arrived. "What about the baby gifts?"

Léon went to sit with Oliva and their father. "They don't give them away any more."

"That figures," Olivier acknowledged. "No one gives anything for free these days. Except the Government."

"And so they should," Léon snorted. "It's their fault the whole country's in this mess in the first place."

Olivier gulped down another mouthful of tea. "It's just as bad in the States, Léon."

Oliva wasn't listening. He just looked down at the plate of uneaten, and now cold, fried potatoes and eggs that was on the table in front of him. "What are we going to do?" he repeated his incessant question to Marie, who was standing by the kitchen cabinet, tearing a flour sack into pieces just big enough for diapers. "You should see how small the babies are."

"What we're going to do," Marie announced, "is go to the house and help Elzire. There's no sense wasting any more time here." She glanced at Léon and Olivier, then winked at Oliva. "That is, if your brother and father have finished discussing politics."

"We'll get Ernest on the way," Oliva decided, getting up from the table.

"Why don't you get him now," Marie suggested, packing the pieces of cloth into a bag, "and bring him back here to stay with Michel. The kids will just be in the way with all the fuss."

"We've got to get Tante Alma," Olivier reminded them, getting up too. "She would never forgive us if she was the last to know."

"Let's bring the whole town," Marie quipped, removing her apron and throwing it across the table. She moved to the back door and opened the screen. "Michel. Annette."

Olivier squeezed Oliva's arm as he passed. "Everything will be fine, Oliva. God provides."

"I hope so," Oliva answered, going out the door.

Within minutes, Oliva was back with Ernest, who announced his arrival by hopping out of the truck before it could come to a full stop and racing into the house to proclaim the news that Maman had had five babies all at once. Seconds later, he was in the back yard telling his cousins what they, too, already knew.

"Hello, Ernest," Marie laughed, then jumped to attention as the horn on Oliva's truck honked. "Let's go," she said, lifting a rhubarb pie off the table and urging Léon and Olivier to follow. She threw the bag that she had packed into the back of the truck, then jumped into the front seat with Oliva, placing the pie on the seat between them. Léon and Olivier hopped into the back.

As they pulled out onto the road, their attention was diverted by an accident at the junction with the highway. They stopped for a moment to make sure that no one was hurt. When they saw that no one was, they continued, with Olivier questioning how anyone could possibly have an accident when there was no traffic.

"It's like they waited for a car to come by," Marie commented, "and then ran right into it."

Olivier seized the opportunity to break some of the tension they were all feeling. He leaned forward and shouted into the cab: "Must be one of those women drivers from North Bay."

"I think I would be as good a driver as any man," contended Marie.

"Just keep thinking," Léon yelled up. "I don't think Oliva's going to let you show us. Are you, Oliva?"

Oliva remained silent, barely suppressing a grin.

"Are you?" Léon repeated, this time even louder.

"Well...."

"You're stalling, Oliva," Léon prodded.

"You mean, you wouldn't let me drive if I could?" Marie asked in mock amazement, turning to Oliva.

"I don't know," Oliva said, as his laughter finally got the better of him. "Keep me out of this."

Marie turned and smacked him on the shoulder.

That made Oliva laugh even more openly, and forced everyone else in the truck to replace their downturned mouths with uplifting smiles.

Olivier was glad for the humour. He was also relieved that whatever private fears were passing through all of their minds were being left unsaid. In fact, the moment there was a lapse of silence, he became worried and off the top of his head came up with a comment about trying to find five silver dollars to give as a gift for the new babies. This sparked Marie, who went on about the problem of knitting five identical outfits every Christmas and birthday.

When they stopped to pick up Tante Alma, the merriment didn't cease. After she got over the shock of the amazing news, she climbed into the cab between Oliva and Marie, carefully transferring Marie's pie to her lap, and joined in the joking. How could she bake a cake big enough for everyone? Olivier replied with a story of how Maman's cakes had always become pudding when he threw another stick into the stove. After this, even Oliva made a contribution. About how cold it would be in their home next winter – especially after he used all the firewood to make five new cribs for the babies.

They arrived to find Dafoe looking weary, sitting alone on the living room sofa. Their entrance seemed to break some deep, worried thought.

"Well, it's about time," Dafoe said, eyeing Oliva with annoyance. "Where were you?" He nodded briefly to the others as they followed Oliva into the house. "Olivier. Léon. Mrs. Dionne. Ma'am."

"Why is it so hot in here?" asked Olivier, inhaling the musty air and looking toward the back of the house, where the door to the summer kitchen was firmly shut.

"We closed all the windows," Oliva explained, beating Dafoe to the answer and feeling for a moment more useful than he had in the last twelve hours.

"Why?"

"The flies," Dafoe said. "The mosquitoes, too. I don't want any more germs in here than there are already." He rose and moved toward the front door. "Let's go outside. I don't want to wake Elzire."

The men started to follow Dafoe, but Tante Alma and Marie immediately headed toward the back of the house.

"We should leave the babies right now." Dafoe's voice was firm.

"Why?" Marie asked, setting the pie down on the kitchen table.

"Where are all the children?" Tante Alma added, looking around the room.

"Outside; I don't want...."

The door to the summer kitchen flew open.

"No they're not," Tante Alma said, a big smile blossoming on her face as Thérèse came running out of the summer kitchen and straight into her arms. "Bonjour, Thérèse."

Olivier reached out to take her. "Bonjour, sweetheart."

"Bonjour, Pépère." Thérèse gave her grandfather a big hug.

"Close the door, Mrs. Legros!" Dafoe called in the direction of the back room.

"No kiss for me?" Marie asked, childlike.

Thérèse leaned over from Pépère with a kiss for Tante Marie. Then another one, for Oncle Léon, who was keeping his eyes glued to the comings and goings at the back of the house.

"Bonjour, Tante Adouilda," Léon called as he saw her come out of the back room and close the door to the summer kitchen that Thérèse had left open. She didn't seem to hear him, since she returned to the back room without a word.

Dafoe watched Léon nervously, as if he expected the babies' uncle to barge into the back room at any minute. "Let's go outside," he suggested again, this time more loudly. He looked in the direction of the back door, hoping that no one else would appear there. "I've got to get a lock for that," he mumbled, thinking about the rest of the children out back, who were no doubt ready to charge in, too. He shepherded everyone through the front door ahead of him, closing it sharply behind himself.

"How is Elzire?" asked Marie. She lifted Thérèse away from Pépère.

"She'll be fine," Dafoe assured her. "It's the babies I'm worried about."

They stood silently, waiting for Dafoe to continue. The pause lengthened as he stood, breathing deeply and staring blankly at the empty field across the road. Then he paced the length of the porch, appearing ready to keep doing so.

"Well?" Tante Alma couldn't wait any longer. "Tell us. How are they?"

Dafoe looked at first to Oliva, then to Alma. He was still wondering how the babies had even made it through the night. "To be frank, I think we should get your Father Routhier to come up."

Tante Alma choked. "What?" Were things really that bad? She signalled to Marie, who was still holding Thérèse.

Marie put Thérèse down, giving her one last hug. "Go play in the back, sweetheart."

Thérèse ran down the porch steps and disappeared around the corner of the house.

"I'm doing everything in my power," Dafoe emphasized, "but they're very weak. And small..." he held out his hand, palm up, "... you have no idea."

"How is Elzire?" This time it was Oliva who asked.

"I have her sedated now, but she'll be fine. But those babies," he repeated, shaking his head. "Their breathing is very irregular."

Olivier was becoming frustrated by the gloom in Dafoe's every comment. "There must be something...."

"There's only so much I can do," said Dafoe. "And I have to stay here. I had wanted Oliva to go into town for me this morning," he added, turning a perturbed eye to Oliva. "But you were gone."

"Well, we'll go now," Olivier offered. "What is it you need?"

"First, stop at my house and tell Mrs. Henderson what has happened. Tell her to call my brother in Toronto. I need an incubator right away. It's our only chance."

Both Oliva and his father looked at Dafoe with puzzled faces. They had never heard of an incubator, let alone actually seen one. Or know what it might be for.

"Just go," Dafoe said. "Mrs. Henderson will know." He immediately recognized their ignorance and didn't want to take the time to explain. He sometimes found it frustrating being the only *cultured* man in town, with no one around to rival his wisdom or to engage in an intelligent conversation. He often wondered why he stayed. "We'll need a nurse, too," he added. "Tell Mrs. Henderson that the one from the Red Cross in Bonfield will be fine if we can get her." Dafoe watched the men's puzzlement turn to confusion. "She'll know who I mean," he explained.

But that was not what had confused them. "What about Tante Adouilda?" Oliva asked. "And Madame Lebel?"

"They're still here, but I need a real nurse. And more supplies too. Clean towels. Blankets. Cotton. Some baby oil. Alcohol."

"We have all that," said Oliva. "And if we don't," he said, gesturing down the road toward the only visible house, "Madame Lebel does."

"And I brought some things." Marie noticed Léon was empty-handed, so she signalled him to go over to the truck to get the bag she had brought.

"*Clean* supplies, people. I don't want to risk the babies getting any more germs than they've already been exposed to. They're too weak to get sick." It was a convincing argument, he thought, given the right audience. But these farmers? He remembered one time when Ernest was sick and Oliva had asked to see the germs.

"I want to see the babies," stated Oliva. "And my wife."

"Okay, but not for long. I need those supplies right away. And I'm not going to be able to do anything if I don't get an incubator here soon."

Olivier started down the steps. "Come on, Oliva. Alma and Marie will look in on Elzire. This is more important right now."

"I'll stay here and keep an eye," Léon offered.

"On what?" Dafoe asked, wishing that they would all leave.

"On you," Léon joked, then went around the back of the house to see the children.

"Get as much as you can," urged Dafoe, watching Oliva and his father as they climbed in and started the truck.

Hearing the truck rumble to a start, Thérèse returned to the front yard, with Daniel following right behind.

"Can we go?" Thérèse asked.

"Can we go?" Daniel echoed.

"And try calling the *North Bay Nugget*," Dafoe called out, his voice barely audible over the motor of the truck. "I know they used to give out gifts when you put a birth announcement in the paper."

"We already called," Oliva shouted back, as he lifted the two children into the truck between himself and Pépère. "They don't do that any more. But a reporter is coming over anyway."

"Oliva, the one thing we don't need right now...." He stopped before he got angry. "Okay, just go. Maybe they can spread the word for help. And like I said," he added delicately, "you may want to stop at your priest's house."

Marie cut in. "Never mind le père," she said firmly. "They're going to be fine." She turned to go into the house, looking back at Dafoe. "You must be hungry. I'll fix you some breakfast."

"I'm more tired than hungry," he said, turning to follow her as the truck pulled away. "But I suppose...." He stopped abruptly and spun around. Facing the billow of exhaust fumes, he yelled to the departing truck as loudly as he could: "If we don't get that incubator, the babies are going to die!"

He didn't know whether they had heard him, but Marie must have, because she fixed him with an angry stare. Alma must have heard him too, judging by the cold look she was also giving him. But what could he do? He needed the incubator, and these people didn't understand anything unless you hit them over the head with it.

Mort Fellman at first cycled right past the Dionne home. It wasn't until he saw the sign reading *DIONNE* at the far corner of the property that he knew he had reached his destination.

At first, the placement of the sign made no sense to him. But then it occurred to him that Dionne was a French name. Their sign would naturally be on the Corbeil side, the direction from which most of their friends and family would come.

Fellman turned around in a wide circle to face the farmhouse he had just passed. He was unimpressed by the simple, quiet, and infertile surroundings, but the small house intrigued him. He had often heard that most of Corbeil's houses – *shacks* was what everyone in town called them – had families living in them with upwards of fifteen children. How did they all fit, he wondered, glad for the opportunity to find out. At least the trip wouldn't be a total waste.

He got off the bike and left it lying on its side near the sign-post, just off the road. He straightened his back after the twelve-mile ride, and used his handkerchief to mop up the sweat on his forehead and neck. He hoped they would offer him a cold drink. This heat was too much.

He opened the creaky gate, and walked along the dirt path and up the plank steps. Wiping his face with his handkerchief one last time, he rapped on the door.

"Yes?" Madame Lebel asked, eyeing the strange young man with the camera slung over his shoulder and a notepad stuck in one hand. His was an unfamiliar face.

"Is Oliva Dionne here?"

"No."

Figured. The whole thing was probably someone's idea of a big joke. "What about Mrs. Dionne?" he asked cynically. "She gone too?"

The midwife looked at Fellman suspiciously. "Madame Dionne can't see anyone right now. She's just had a baby. Who are you?"

"Mort Fellman. *North Bay Nugget.* I'm trying to get some information." He hesitated before offering the words of doubt. "I heard she had five babies last night."

"Wait here." She hooked the screen door and closed the inner door with a thud.

Fellman walked the porch. He tried to peer into a window, but a lacy curtain obscured his view of what seemed to be a bedroom. He turned to go the other way and followed the unpainted wooden planks around the side of the house, where he heard muffled sounds coming from a window draped with flowered curtains. When he reached the end of the porch and the back of what seemed to be more an oversized playhouse than a proper residence, he looked through the screened window of the summer kitchen. He noticed right away that the door that led to the main part of the house was closed. Unusual, he thought, for such a hot day – especially in the country. He looked at the young girl and boy playing in the backyard, but they didn't see him. He wiped the back of his neck and gazed out toward the barn. Two cows grazed in the field beyond, reminding him of the story on cattle feed he still had to finish.

As he walked back up the porch, he heard the sound of a door opening. A voice yelled back into the house that no one was there. Fellman rushed around the corner and over to the door to face a chubby man who was peering out through the screen, one hand holding the inner door tightly to his back.

"I'm Dr. Dafoe," the man announced curtly. "What do you want?"

"Mort Fellman, *North Bay Nugget.*"

"Yes, yes. So what do you want?"

"Did you deliver five babies last night?" he asked, half expecting the doctor to laugh in his face.

"Yes."

"I don't mean from five different patients," Fellman specified.

"I know what you mean. I already answered you."

Fellman met Dafoe's eyes. If this was true, it was far, far better than yesterday's story on the squatter, or his little gem on cattle feed prices. "You mean Mrs. Dionne had five kids at once?"

"Yes," Dafoe said impatiently. "Now, what do you want? I'm busy."

Fellman flipped the cover of his notepad, and poised his pencil to write. "This has never happened in these parts, has it?"

"Not in my twenty-five years here."

"Can I see them?" Fellman patted the camera. "I mean, this is page one news." It was likely also the only news the *Nugget* would get that day.

"No one can see them right now. There's enough germs in here as it is."

Fellman wanted a picture. Desperately. "Just one shot. People are going to have to see this to believe it." His own doubts wouldn't be completely erased until he saw five real live babies himself.

"Young man, I don't have time for pictures right now." Dafoe glared at Fellman. "I'm trying to save some babies' lives, if that's all right with you." He began edging back into the house.

"I've got a story to cover, Doctor," Fellman apologized. "If this is true, I have to...."

"What do you mean, *if* it's true?" asked Dafoe angrily. "I'm not in the habit of lying, sonny."

Fellman didn't respond.

"Look here, a picture in your paper won't save these babies' lives, but some proper medical supplies might. If you want to write something, ask your readers for help. We desperately need an incubator."

Fellman nodded and took notes, but obtaining supplies wasn't his job – getting the story was. "Do you know when Mr. Dionne will be back? I'd really like to talk to him."

"No, I don't. And he can't tell you anything anyway. Now, good day." He started to close the door.

Fellman stood his ground. "Doctor, when was the last time this happened? I mean, anywhere?"

"How would I know?" And with that, Dafoe firmly closed the door.

Fellman walked toward the road, trying to think of an angle. There wasn't one, but it was still a good piece of local news. Before hopping onto his bike, he snapped a picture of the house. It would help fill the page.

Fellman rode back to North Bay, glad that he had been the one to get the phone when it rang. People liked that kind of news. Especially these days, with all the problems. He just hoped the babies wouldn't die before he could run the story.

*   *   *

Ivan Spear read the five-line story on the back page of the *Chicago American* for the tenth time that morning. This time, he read it aloud to Raymond. "Can you believe it?" he asked, positively exultant over the news. "We've got our life exhibit."

Raymond was also excited, but more relieved. Spear was a wreck after weeks of trying to come up with something to keep the World's Fair from disaster, and he had made Raymond a wreck, too.

"Think we can get them?" Raymond asked, dreaming that if they did, he would get a Friday night off for the first time in a month.

"Of course we can get them," Spear declared. He looked through his desk for a map of Canada. He had maps from all over, but couldn't find one right away. "Arlene," he bellowed.

The door to his office promptly opened and Arlene stepped in. "Yes, sir?" She walked over to his cluttered desk and automatically started organizing the potpourri of trade magazines, trophies, and knick-knacks that appeared out of nowhere and piled up day after day.

Spear tore the story from the newspaper, and handed it to her. "Here. Find out where in hell *Cor...*" he strained to pronounce the name of the town, "... *be-il* is. And book me on a flight there. Or somewhere close, at least. Charter a plane if you have to."

"When would you like to go?"

"Right away. Yesterday."

"Yes, sir." As she left the room, Arlene took with her a full ashtray, some magazines, and a couple of empty Coca Cola bottles she had retrieved from the top of Spear's desk.

Raymond was glad Spear would be gone for a few days. "I'll check the papers while you're gone to see if there are any developments. You can call when...."

"What do you mean? You're coming with me."

Raymond frowned, but Spear was too excited to notice.

"Arlene," Spear hollered, "we'll need two seats." He leaned back in his chair, feeling like his number had just come up. "Incredible. I don't think this has ever happened before."

Raymond shrugged and made a note. "I'll check." He was wondering what on earth he was going to do up in Canada. Go fishing? Trap bears?

"Five identical baby girls." Spear drew out every word, lingering over the reality of it. "*Quintuplets*," he cackled. "What a stroke of luck. The crowds will be lined up and down the grounds for this one. Can you picture it, Raymond? Right here at the Chicago World's Fair. Nowhere else in the world. It'll make last year's profits look like peanuts."

"If we can get there before someone else does."

"We will," Spear assured him, then looked toward the door. "Arlene," he prompted, "please hurry." He turned back to Raymond, his promoter's mind already spinning with possibilities. "Of course, we'll have to have continuous showings. Maybe build a small house, you know, instead of a tent. Make it look on the up-and-up. Like they were born there." He picked up a scrap of paper from his desk and started to sketch a house with a string of people lining up outside it. "This has to be a class act all the way. I mean, we don't want anyone to think we're running a freak show."

4

The Set-up

Peering out the front window, Oliva felt like a prisoner in his own home. He had rarely seen such a commotion, and certainly never in their small community, where you could count on one hand the outsiders who passed by in the period of a week. Now his whole front yard, small as it was, was packed with reporters. He thought of sneaking out the back door to escape facing them, but he figured they would catch him sooner or later. They were everywhere.

It hadn't taken them long to arrive, either. When news had spread that his and Elzire's tiny babies were the first surviving quintuplets ever, the cream of the North American press corps had descended on Corbeil en masse. Since then, others had been coming at a steady pace. Each hour brought a fresh batch of reporters and photographers from Toronto, Montréal, New York, Chicago, Detroit – even London, England. And the babies were only three days old!

About fifty reporters were there right now, filling the tiny front yard to capacity. A few were gathered, chatting off to one side, and occasionally sneaking looks behind Oliva's truck to see if anything was happening out back. But most just stood around the front porch. Waiting.

Some of them, mostly the American reporters, had come up yesterday and camped in the field across the road all night. Others, reinforcements from the Toronto and Montréal papers, were just now parking their cars, covered with dust from the long ride on dirt roads, along the narrow roadside. Even neighbours from right there in Corbeil, and townspeople from Callander and the surrounding communities, were coming by to see what was happening. Some hadn't even heard what the news was – just that there was a big crowd hanging around the Dionne farm.

As Oliva watched, another car pulled up, then another. As each person got out, he stared at them with both disdain and curiosity. On one hand, he resented the intrusion of his land and home, but on the other, he was captivated by the sight before him. It defied comparison with anything he had yet encountered in his life. Eyes glued to the window, ears pricked to hear the foreign sounds, he was so intent on what was going on outside that he didn't hear the footsteps come down the stairs or notice his father join him at the window.

But his fixation with the goings-on in front of the house was only partly to blame. There was a lot of commotion inside the house, too. Dafoe and his new nursing staff were, at this moment, standing over the kitchen table heatedly discussing something. The raised voices easily smothered the sound of an old man's footsteps crossing the wooden floor.

Olivier rested his hand on his son's shoulder.

"I just heard one of them say that one of those newsreel companies is coming in today," Oliva said, as he pressed his head against the window in order to see the far reaches of his property.

Olivier strained his neck to see where Oliva was looking. He spotted some men unloading equipment from a truck. "Craziness," he said, remembering how he had had to sneak in the back door himself when he had come over earlier. "The kids should be ready soon," he said, trying to lead Oliva away from the window. "Don't watch, Oliva. It will just upset you more."

Oliva let the curtain fall and turned. "I appreciate your taking the kids, Papa."

"This is no place for them right now," Olivier said, as a movement outside the window caught his eye. Another car had pulled up, followed by a horse and buggy loaded down with a bunch of people, mostly children. "Are you sure you don't want me to take Daniel and Pauline too?"

"They'll be fine with Tante Adouilda. And Léon and Marie offered too. You'll have enough on your hands."

"Nonsense. I love to have them. I just wish your mother were alive to see them."

"I know."

"Talk to Elzire, Oliva. She should go and stay with Léon and Marie until she's better. Or at least until all of this dies down."

"You know she won't leave the babies," Oliva said, certain of that.

Olivier leaned closer to whisper. "Yes, but le docteur won't even let her see them," he mumbled, careful that Dafoe didn't hear. "And that nurse is even worse."

"You're telling me." Oliva agreed wholeheartedly with his father's quick assessment of Louise de Kiriline, the domineering middle-aged nurse from the Red Cross post in Bonfield, who was more than a match for Dafoe's bossiness. "But Elzire won't leave anyway. Come on, let's have some tea in the back before you go."

Oliva turned to face the rear of the house, where, at the table, Dafoe was now sitting. He was giving the new nurse's helper specific instructions on the proportions of milk and corn syrup to use in the babies' formula. Nurse de Kiriline was leaning over his shoulder, reversing some of the instructions.

Dafoe looked up as Oliva approached. He started to give one of his *now what do you want?* glances, typical of late.

But Oliva, who had been prepared to slip past and into the summer kitchen without a word, avoided him. "Don't worry," he mumbled, grabbing his father's arm and turning him around.

Olivier saw the rage in his son's eyes. "Take it easy, Oliva."

They were heading back up to the front door, not knowing exactly where they would go next, when the door swung open.

"Close that door," Dafoe bellowed from the table, assuming without looking up that it was Oliva on his way out.

Instead, three male strangers walked in. Obeying the stern order, they very quickly shut the door.

"Good day," said one of them, face-to-face with Oliva, while the other two, each carrying several small boxes, nodded politely. "You're Dr. Dafoe?"

Oliva looked to his father, who just shrugged, then back to the man who had asked the question. "No, I'm not!" He blocked them from going further into the house. "Where do you think you're going?"

"We're from the county Board of Health," said the leader, pulling a folded piece of paper from his pocket. "We have instructions from Toronto to drop these off for Dr. Dafoe."

"Did they tell you to barge in like...."

The sound of a chair's legs dragging along the wooden floor stopped Oliva. "I'm Dr. Dafoe," came the high-pitched voice from behind. Dafoe had risen and was motioning from the table. "Come right in."

"You know them?" asked Oliva, annoyed by how easily these men were being given freedom to wander about his home.

"Not personally," snapped Dafoe, who couldn't see what the problem was. "But I knew they were coming." He turned to the three men. "Right in there," he said, pointing to the summer kitchen, whose door, like that of the back room, was firmly closed. "Put them on the table back there, then leave by the back door." He looked at Oliva as if daring him to countermand the order, then gestured to the men to go ahead. "It's mothers' milk," he told Oliva. "For your babies," he pronounced, then followed the men as far as the doorway and closed the door after them. Then he disappeared into the back room.

Oliva and his father listened as the door to the little room, which until this week had not been closed once in the ten years since the house had been built, shut yet another time. Each time it shut, it became clearer to both of them that the back room was no longer Elzire's cozy pantry. It was now Dafoe's private ward. *My nursery* he had called it from the moment he started the transition from warm and homey to cold and clinical.

He had begun by barking orders at everyone in sight: Oliva; his father; Elzire's father, Moise; her brothers; Tante Alma; Léon and Marie; Madame Lebel and Tante Adouilda; the children. Especially the children. None of them was allowed to enter the room, for fear of infecting the babies with germs. He had made that clear the very first day. Later the same day, when Elzire was strong enough to be moved, he asked Madame Lebel to help her upstairs and out of the way, and instructed Tante Alma to take care of her. Then he ordered Oliva to get rid of the bed and to go into town to look for a sturdy table. "Clean it up before you bring it over," had been the abrupt instruction. It would be needed to support the incubator his brother was sending from Toronto.

Germs was the watchword from then on. On people, on clothes, in the air, everywhere. Madame Lebel had been instructed to remove all the preserves and other foods from the shelves in the *nursery* and to scrub the whole room spotless, from top to bottom. She had over-looked removing the sack curtains covering the window – they had looked perfectly clean to her – so Dafoe ripped them off himself and asked Marie to make new ones out of plain white cotton. Then both she and Madame Lebel were dismissed.

Tante Alma, who had been spending most of her time tending to Elzire upstairs, had offered to help le docteur in any way she could. But as Dafoe brusquely told her after most of the work was done on the second day, the fewer people around, the better. Even Tante Adouilda, the great matriarch of the Legros family, had been useful only for a while. Because of her steady hands, Dafoe had asked her to clean and boil all of his instruments, then to place them in ster-ilization jars, and finally to line them up on the shelves along with the bottles of alcohol, jars of cotton balls, towels, diapers, and any other supplies he had managed to lay his hands on. But when Nurses de Kiriline and Leroux arrived, along with a helper, Tante was also ban-ished. The Dionne home was under new management.

Right now, Oliva would have liked to have pursued Dafoe into the back room to express his displeasure, not only with the three intrud-ers, but with all the liberties le docteur had been taking in his home the last few days. But he knew all too well that the room was off-lim-its. This was Dafoe's set-up all the way. No one was allowed in with-out Dafoe's permission – not the relatives; not the children; not him; not even Elzire. "I don't want anyone opening that door and letting flies in," he had proclaimed the day Elzire was moved upstairs. "And that goes for your wife, too," he had stated flatly to Oliva. "If she wants her babies to live, you – and her – are all going to have to follow some new rules around here." Dafoe's look, when he let the three strangers into the summer kitchen a moment ago, had con-veyed the same message.

Oliva watched the closed door to the back room for a resentful moment, then stormed through the summer kitchen and out back.

His father, following close behind, called after him. "Oliva, wait. Everyone is just trying to help."

"Help?" Oliva halted his defiant walk just before he reached the barn. His eyes searched suspiciously for reporters. He relished the thought of finding one, if only for the opportunity to blast him. "How are they helping? By attacking my property? By making me send my kids away? That's how they're helping, by sending in the police?"

"Police?" asked Olivier, puzzled.

"Yes, Ontario Provincial Police," raged Oliva, irritated by the very thought of uniformed men making his home look like the museum he and Elzire had visited in Ottawa on their honeymoon.

"Why police?"

"To guard the house and keep things under control." Oliva folded his arms and leaned back against the barn door, waiting for his father to defend that action too.

Olivier didn't say a word. Although he had felt that, on the whole, everything being done was for the best, he accepted the possibility that things *were* getting a little out of hand.

"And it's going to get worse," Oliva speculated, spotting some cameras being set up to the side of the front porch. "You know, Papa, I wish it had never happened."

"Don't talk like that when your babies are fighting for their lives." Olivier realized that it had been a trying time for all of them, but le docteur was only doing his job, and a good one at that. He was keeping the babies alive, and that was all that counted. Olivier didn't particularly like the way Léon and Marie had been sent away from the house where their entrance had, in the past, always provoked smiles; but even then, he presumed that le docteur had his reasons. And those reasons were more important than family visits or, for that matter, letting Oliva be the master of his own house, at least for the time being.

"Just be patient. Everyone's trying to help in their own way."

It was true. Everyone *was* trying to help, in one way or another. The reporters may have disrupted the peace of the once-quiet community, but not one came empty-handed. And the Government had quickly pitched in, extending emergency health care measures to allow the family to obtain free medical supplies. A false rumour confusing this assistance with relief may have been going around, but the help was nonetheless genuine.

Neighbours were doing their part too, bringing pots of gruel and potato stew, pies, and loaves of bread to save Elzire from cooking, although the ones who benefitted mostly from these kind donations were Dafoe and his nursing staff. Even the curious from Callander, North Bay, and as far away as Bonfield and Mattawa, were sending their wishes for the babies' survival and bringing generous gifts despite their own poverty – a quilt, some diapers, a hand-made card, some wool.

"Those people who just came in," Olivier continued, "I know you don't like them just walking in, but they're following orders. And the orders come from people who care. Even the reporters bring gifts."

"Yes, but you don't think they bring them for nothing!" Oliva declared. "They want a story." As much as he resented Dafoe turning his home into a command centre, he was outraged by the reporters' transformation of his front yard into a gathering place like outside the relief office in North Bay.

"Come on, Oliva. The babies wouldn't have made it this far without everyone's help. You should be grateful. You've just had five children at once. Do you expect people to ignore it?"

Oliva wasn't sure what to expect any more. But it was pointless to continue arguing. He was glad when Ernest, Rose, and Thérèse came bounding out the back door, ending the conversation that was getting nowhere.

"Ready?" Oliva called out to them. As the children skipped down the steps, Oliva heard someone in the kitchen slam the door shut.

"Papa," Rose whined. "Do I have to go? I want to stay with Maman."

"Yes, you do." Oliva's words were firm, his tone less so. He was trying hard to hide his true sentiments. He knew that both Ernest and Rose wanted to stay, though for different reasons. Ernest loved the excitement out front. In fact, he had been more fascinated by the arrival of the press than by the arrival of his five identical baby sisters. If it were left up to him, Ernest would be in the front yard right now, asking questions of everyone. As for Rose, she had no interest in the visitors, but was itching to help her mother with the tiny new babies. She had no way of knowing that, even if she stayed, her help would not likely be needed for a long while. Fortunately, Thérèse was indifferent to staying or going. She just did whatever Ernest did. Her big brother was her protector, and she could trail aimlessly after him for hours without question. As for Daniel and Pauline, now with Tante, they were too young to have choices, or theirs too probably would have been denied.

"It's just for a few days," Oliva promised.

"I want to ride Lagrise, Pépère," said Ernest, thinking of an activity that would replace the excitement he was leaving.

"Me too," Thérèse piped up.

"As long as you promise not to pick on your sisters," Pépère warned Ernest. "No pulling hair, understand?"

57

Ernest hid a smirk by somersaulting on the ground.

Thérèse piled on top of him.

"Why do we have to go?" Rose complained.

Oliva couldn't hold back. He turned to his father. "See what I mean?"

"Don't worry, honey." Pépère leaned over to look Rose in the eye. "You'll have plenty of time to help Maman with the babies." He took her by the hand, and with the other hand, lifted Thérèse off of Ernest. "Let's go. You'll come over later, Oliva? Tante Alma will be coming to cook dinner."

"If I get permission from le docteur," he said sarcastically.

"Stop it!" Olivier momentarily forgot that the children were there, and all ears. "Le docteur is doing his job; you just let him do it. All he cares about is keeping the babies alive, and that's good enough for me. It should be for you, too."

Oliva looked away sheepishly.

"Take care of your wife. She's been through a lot." He turned to the children again. "Come. Let's go."

Ernest pinched Rose and ran ahead. Thérèse followed him, while Rose kicked at thin air and grabbed Pépère's hand.

"You remember what I said, Oliva. Just take care of Elzire. The babies are in good hands."

Olivier led Rose around the side of the house. He picked up speed along the way, determined to stop Ernest from talking to the reporters. When he reached the front, he spotted Ernest and Thérèse about to penetrate a group of five reporters who were huddled together in one corner of the yard. He pulled them away and, amidst stares and pointed fingers, led all three children down the road in the direction of Corbeil.

All the way home, Pépère sang folk-songs, keeping one eye on the road ahead, the other on the children's errant feet. He noticed how the three of them looked back every few yards, appearing as confused as their father about what was happening to their home. Once, he looked back himself, and noticed that the crowd he had left only minutes before had already grown larger. He faced forward again as he heard the sound of a motor, just in time to see a shiny black Ford whiz by at a high speed. He cushioned Thérèse's face from the dust that the car stirred up.

Soon, they were over the hill and on the small side road that led to his home. The cars and the crowd could no longer be seen, the sound of motors and voices no longer heard. But the thoughts that had filled Olivier's head as he left his son's home lingered like a nagging headache. He felt he had given the right advice when he suggested that Oliva worry about Elzire – not the babies. And he also believed he was right in what he had said about le docteur. But his mind would not rest. Despite the excellent care the babies were receiving, and even assuming that all the kindness being extended by everyone was genuine, he still had difficulty in reconciling himself to some of the nonsense that was going on.

It had been a long and tiring trip – by plane, train, and car – but the sight of a crowd in front of the Dionne farmhouse instantly rejuvenated Spear. His excitement almost as instantly evaporated, though, when he considered the awful possibility that someone else might have gotten to Dionne first. He cast a worried eye over the crowd in the Dionnes' front yard as he and Raymond got out of the taxi that had brought them from North Bay.

Raymond made a full three hundred and sixty degree turn, grimacing at the bleak surroundings. He wondered how anyone could actually live here. His eyes settled on the crowd of city people standing in front of what he considered a shanty in the woods. The contrast startled him.

"What a crowd," exclaimed Spear, counting heads. "There's at least fifty, anyway."

Raymond was watching the listless movement of the crowd. "Looks like they've been here awhile," he said, noting the passive faces.

Spear was also checking faces, but he didn't spot any other promoters; just some big-name reporters shuffling about and asking each other impatiently when *he* was coming out. The father, Spear assumed. He approached two young reporters, who were talking and, at the same time, taking turns at keeping an eye on the front porch.

"Excuse me," Spear interrupted. "Are you waiting for Oliva Dionne?"

"You kidding?" came the reply. "Who cares about..." he cut himself off at the sound of the front door creaking open, "... hey!" He turned to his colleague in excitement. "I think he's coming."

Before Spear could ask who their *he* was, the whole crowd surged forward, drawing Spear and Raymond with them. Everyone started to yell different questions at once as a short, stout man wearing eyeglasses and dressed in a wrinkled brown woollen suit – despite the hot weather – emerged.

The reporters anxiously vied for a view, pencils poised, cameras ready, voices raised in an effort to be the first to get the little country doctor's attention.

At first, Dafoe stood nervously, eyeing the group, and not knowing what to do. In a hesitant effort to do something with the loud, expectant throng before him, he tentatively raised his hand. But the silence that fell as the talking subsided unnerved him even more than the barrage of shouted questions. Although he had been coming out at regular intervals since yesterday to give the growing number of reporters the latest scraps of news, he wasn't used to being at the head of the class.

"Please," he called out weakly. "There's little change in their condition since I last spoke to you."

A few reporters at the back of the crowd yelled for him to speak up.

"Their breathing has improved slightly," he spoke up with effort, "but they're not out of the woods yet. This is only the fourth day, remember."

The cacophony of questions began again.

Dafoe panicked. He searched the crowd for a familiar face, not an easy task. The invasion of Corbeil had brought more strangers into his circle than there had been since medical school. He finally recognized a face near the back and pointed.

The young reporter he singled out shifted from one leg to the other. He would have preferred quiet anonymity. Content to listen to the questions of the others, he could still hardly believe this was the same place he had cycled up to a couple of days before.

They had sent their page one story out over the wire as a matter of course. Soon after, the phone had started ringing in the *Nugget* office, with reporters from all over Canada and the United States wanting more information about the farm wife who had given birth to five babies. Then came the telegram from London demanding more information. The *Nugget* had never been the recipient of a telegram before. Not from anywhere – let alone London, England. That's when Fellman had told Knight that something big was happening.

Before the *Nugget* could do another story, reporters from Toronto had started to arrive, some of them eagerly trying to sign deals for exclusives with anyone who knew the Dionnes even remotely. The story had quickly ceased to be a local one. And now, here Fellman was, being forced to sound intelligent in front of people he had heard of and long admired, but whom he would never have met had he ignored Léon Dionne's call about free birth announcement gifts.

"Is, uh, the incubator helping much?" Fellman blurted out.

"Helping? It's keeping them alive!" Dafoe was grateful both for the easy question and for the crude, kerosene-burning incubator his brother had sent. With some confidence gained from that smooth exchange, he switched his gaze back to the entire group. "And please, all of you, thank your papers for their donations."

Oliva was working out back when he heard the latest hubbub. He ventured over to the Corbeil side of the house, and began to watch the proceedings. Uncomfortable, and for the most part unnoticed, he wondered why Dafoe bothered giving these updates. It only encouraged the reporters to stay – and others to keep coming.

The reporter to whom Spear had spoken earlier now spotted Oliva. "That's the father," he said, nudging Spear, and pointing through the crowd to the only man standing off to the side of the house.

Spear signalled to Raymond, then looked Oliva up and down. Pretty regular-looking guy, Spear thought. Not the cross between a peasant and a prize stud that he had somehow expected.

The reporters' questions continued. "How's the mother?" yelled one of the new arrivals, a slick, well-dressed young man sporting a panama hat.

"Better. She should be up in a day or two." He took advantage of the opportunity to say more. "As I said earlier, we've moved her upstairs and turned the back room into a temporary nursery."

"Why aren't they in a hospital?" another voice piped up.

Dafoe couldn't see who had asked the question, so he addressed his answer to the group at large. "They couldn't be moved at first, but...."

A seductive female voice from not too far away diverted his attention. "Do you think the Dionnes plan to have any more children?"

Dafoe tracked the voice until he spotted the attractive woman in the front row. "These people?" he shrugged. "When the neighbour lady has eighteen of her own, don't expect the Dionnes to stop at ten." Most of the reporters missed the chuckle that followed his words. They were too intent on their notepads to see it as a joke. The woman who had asked the question just smiled, forcing Dafoe to look shyly away from her.

Oliva, unnoticed by Dafoe and his army of reporters, felt ridiculed. He glared at le docteur, and clenched his jaw to stop the insults he wanted to hurl in return. Instead, he vented his frustration by ferociously kicking the ground every few steps as he made his way to the back of the house.

"Stay here," Spear instructed Raymond, then added in a whisper, "pick up what you can." Spear wound his way out of the crowd, then ran to catch up with Oliva. "Mr. Dionne," he called out when he was still a few yards away.

Oliva turned around.

"I'm Ivan Spear," the strange man facing Oliva said, extending his hand as he approached.

Oliva looked down but didn't offer his own hand. He turned to continue his interrupted progress toward the barn.

"Mr. Dionne, can we talk, please?"

Oliva stopped once more and turned around. "Look, why can't you people just leave us alone?"

The pitch had already gelled in Spear's mind. "I'm not a reporter, Mr. Dionne...."

Oliva walked on.

"... and if you'll just give me a minute of your time," he added confidently, "I think you'll be interested in what I have to say."

Dafoe was warming up by the minute to his new-found celebrity.

"Is it difficult to treat the babies in this environment?" someone shouted out.

"I'm doing the best I can," answered Dafoe, "but I'll tell you this. There's a lot of people in there." He gestured behind with his thumb. "And germs floating around left and right." He paused for effect, then fixed the whole crowd with a concerned gaze and made the point he had wanted to make earlier, before the handsome woman had distracted him. "Those babies should be in a hospital, not a farmhouse." He watched the reporters' pencils scribbling busily over their pads and thought it might be a good time to end the interview. "Well, gentlemen," he said smiling, "and lady," he added, looking at the front row, "back to work." He turned and went inside.

The reporters dispersed quickly. Some went straight to their cars and headed for Callander to telephone their papers. A few drove up the road to Voyer's to get something to eat. Others stopped to talk about what a great story this was becoming, possibly the biggest human interest story of the year. Still others remained, waiting in the hot sun for the next update.

One man, dressed more formally than all the others, remained firm in front of the porch, staring at the door through which Dafoe had just disappeared.

He had been standing at the front of the crowd all morning, carefully observing Dafoe through each of the press updates. He had studied the doctor's reactions to the crowd, watched how he carried himself, listened to the way he handled the questions, and tried to sense his feelings toward the Dionnes. But he wasn't a reporter. No, this man's notepad had different, more profound, information than those of the reporters who stood around him this morning. It was his job to pick up on such critical details. That's what Hepburn paid him for.

Oliva's head was swimming with what he had just been told. He even forgot the rules of the house and absently opened the door to the back room. Dafoe was bent over the incubator with Nurse Leroux when he entered. Nurse de Kiriline was preparing the bath in the opposite corner.

"Close that door," sounded Dafoe, as a father might chastise his disobedient child. "How many times do I have to tell you?"

"I have to talk to you."

"In a minute. Wait out there."

"And close the door," Nurse de Kiriline added authoritatively.

Oliva obeyed. He secured the door tightly, then walked slowly back and forth in the kitchen, thinking so deeply about what Spear had told him that he was oblivious to the nurse's helper, who was sterilizing bottles on the stove just a few feet away from where he was pacing. He walked into the summer kitchen and peeked out the window. Spear was still there, talking now to another man by the barn.

What was he going to do? A half-hour ago, he had never heard of Ivan Spear, and was barely aware of what a world's fair was. Then Spear appeared, making all kinds of offers that he didn't fully understand and throwing about figures that seemed too grand to be believed. As much as he hated to ask, maybe le docteur could explain it to him. He was always reading those books and magazines.

"What is it, Oliva?" asked Dafoe, briskly opening and closing the door to his nursery. "I really don't have time right now."

"They're offering me money, Docteur," Oliva explained, trouble in his voice.

"Who's offering you money?"

"This man from Chicago. He wants to show the babies at the World's Fair down there. He'll pay us a hundred dollars a week and we can all go – you, me, Elzire. And we can cancel if the babies aren't well enough to go."

"They can't be serious." Dafoe was suddenly distracted by the nurse's helper, who had lowered a dirty spoon into the pot of boiling water that was doing duty as a sterilizer on the stove. "Don't do that," he scolded. "Go outside and wash it first." He waited for her to exit out the back door before turning back to Oliva.

"That's what he said," Oliva continued. "I don't know what to do."

"Close that door," Dafoe bellowed, as Elzire's good friend, Gaëtane, stole in the front door with a pot of baked beans. "Leave it there." He pointed to a table in the corner of the sitting area.

Gaëtane, immediately obedient, was startled by this new way le docteur was acting. She hastily put the pot down and rushed out.

Dafoe turned back to Oliva. "Look, Oliva, I'm pretty busy. Do what you want. You can always use the extra cash."

Before Oliva could ask him if he was sure, Dafoe had returned to the back room, shaking his head as he closed the door after him. "Now they want to show the babies at the World's Fair," he told Nurse de Kiriline, scoffing at the idea. "What foolishness. I'll be happy if the babies live to see tomorrow, let alone the World's Fair."

Elzire tried to sit up in bed but couldn't. No sooner did she prop herself up on her elbows and bend her knees to turn, when a sharp pain in her abdomen caused her to sink back down.

Tante Alma sat in the embroidered chair at the foot of the bed. Each time Elzire tried to get up, she would shake her head over and over. "Elzire, you don't listen to no one."

"I'm tired of being in bed. I've got a family to take care of. Pépère with three of them. Ma tante with the others. It's been a long time since she's had a one-year-old at home with her, you know!"

"Adouilda is fine. You're the one that needs to rest. You know what le docteur said."

"Ah, le docteur." Elzire waved the comment away like an annoying fly. "He won't even let me see my own babies. Every time he comes up, it's the same old thing." She was fed up with Dafoe telling her that there were germs all over her house and that she was too weak to hold the babies, who together weighed little more than any one of her previous five. "You saw the first day when ma tante put the five of them in bed with me. They were fine, thank God."

"I know," was all Tante Alma could say.

"It's almost a week now," Elzire complained. She tried to prop herself up again, but the sharp pain crippled her. "Where's Papa?" Elzire had not seen her father, nor her brothers, since yesterday.

Tante Alma looked away. How could she tell Elzire why her family had not shown up today? For one thing, Dafoe had told hard-working Papa Moise that he should clean up before coming into the house. As for her brothers, three of them were outside right now trying to restore order in their own way: by threatening the reporters with pitchforks if they didn't get off the property.

"They'll be over later, I'm sure," Tante Alma finally said, happy that she had thought of something that skirted the truth. She got up to rearrange the sheet that had slipped off when Elzire had tried to get up. Then she fluffed up the two pillows, and passed Elzire the cup of hot tea that was on the night table. "Here, drink some."

"You just want to put me to sleep," Elzire joked, sniffing the whisky that had been added to the cup. She took a sip and wrinkled her face.

Tante Alma got up and walked over to the window. "It's hot in here."

"No, Tante. Please." Elzire wrinkled her face. "All the noise."

"I know, but you need some air." She opened the window to a little breeze, which brought with it the hum of voices and car engines. She immediately lowered the sash a little to cut some of the offensive sounds that rose from below.

A panicked look covered Elzire's face. "I want to see my babies," she appealed to Tante Alma. "And I want the rest of the children back home with me. Rose and Daniel are very lonely without maman."

Tante Alma stayed looking out the window, but only to avoid seeing the frightened and helpless look on Elzire's face. She knew that neither of Elzire's simple requests could be granted. Not now. How could she tell Elzire that the frustration she was feeling now was infinitely better than the abuse she would likely receive once she was able to get out of bed? How could she even hint at the fact that maman's pantry was now off-limits? That the kitchen was being run by Louise de Kiriline and two others? That le docteur had become a dictator?

On one hand, Tante Alma hoped for a quick recovery, but on the other, she felt that by remaining upstairs, Elzire was being spared a much greater anguish – that of being shut out of her own home. Up here, she was still the tough Legros girl who had married a proud Dionne. The family that lived downstairs now was distinctly *Dafoe*.

Elzire was about to doze off when Oliva entered the room. He looked worried, and tired in a way that should have resulted from a hard day in the fields and hauling his truckload of gravel to where they were building the new road in North Bay. But it wasn't noon yet, and if today was anything like yesterday, he hadn't been able to get any work done either.

"Oliva, what's wrong?" Elzire cried, alarmed by his appearance. "The babies!"

"The babies are fine," Oliva assured her.

"Thank God," sighed Tante Alma, sharing Elzire's relief.

"They're fighters," he went on. "Just like their maman."

The sound of another car pulling up outside cut through the reporters' muffled voices. "I wish all that noise would stop," Elzire said.

Oliva went over to the window and lowered it shut. He drew the pink curtains over the glass, then sat on the edge of the bed. "Elzire." He took her hand. "A man from Chicago came to talk to me."

"Chicago?" Tante Alma asked. A picture of Al Capone came immediately to mind.

"He wants to pay us a lot of money. More than we've ever seen."

"For what?"

"To let people down there see the babies at the World's Fair."

The words meant less to Elzire than they had to Oliva. "I don't understand."

"It's never happened before, Elzire. Five babies at once. People are interested. He's interested."

"I just want them to live. I don't care about anything else."

"Me too, but le docteur said it's okay. He wouldn't say that unless they were going to make it."

"Oliva," Tante Alma piped in. "Speak to your father about it."

He nodded.

"Le docteur said they're going to be all right?" Elzire asked hopefully.

He nodded again. "We can both go, and le docteur too. They'll pay for all of us to go. And there'll be others there to help with the babies."

Elzire had heard only one thing. "They're going to be all right." She exhaled deeply and shut her eyes for a moment. "Thank God." She made the sign of the cross, then tried to get up again.

Oliva held her by the shoulders. "What are you doing?"

"If they're well enough to go away, they're well enough for me to see them," she reasoned.

"Not yet, Elzire." He pushed her back down. "Le docteur still won't let us see them."

"But he'll let them go to Chicago?" It made no sense to Tante Alma either.

Oliva looked at Tante Alma, then at Elzire. "I don't understand this any more than you do. But I wouldn't do it unless I thought it was right."

"I know that, Oliva, but...."

"We need the money," he interjected, a little embarrassed by his own words. Like his father, he had never owed a cent in his life. Even now, with everyone out of work, he was scraping up just enough to get by without going on relief. "I'm worried about how I can feed all of you."

Elzire looked up at him. She was still puzzled about the Chicago story, but squeezed his hand tightly. "Do what le docteur says," she suggested, "but ask Père Routhier first. The babies are in God's hands. If he lets them live, maybe they're meant to go."

* * *

Roy Tarnovski stood up from where he had been leaning against a big oak tree, and stretched. He looked at his watch, struggling to read the numbers in the light that filtered through the curtains of the Dionne home. He squinted. A little after midnight. He had already been waiting three hours. A few other reporters were there too, all as impatient as he was, all with the same idea of staying late to catch the doctor on his way out.

Dafoe finally stepped out of the Dionne house, carrying his bag in one hand and rubbing his eyes with the other. It had been another long day that had run far into the night. He stopped before descending the steps, put his eyeglasses back on, and lit up his pipe.

Tarnovski jumped ahead of the rest of the group just as the doctor started down the steps. "Doctor," he called.

Two policemen, new on duty, kept him and the other reporters from getting too close.

Tarnovski got louder. "Roy Tarnovski, *Chicago Tribune*."

At the mention of Chicago, Dafoe stiffened. He could just barely remember the conversation with Oliva. And now, what a mess. The headlines were in every paper: *Father sells Quints to sideshow*. The words immediately spelled trouble to Dafoe. He knew right away that he would need to establish as much distance as possible between himself and the babies' father. This was Oliva's problem, not his. He stretched his usually short footsteps to make it to the roadside as quickly as he could.

Tarnovski was goading Dafoe from behind the policemen. "I was just wondering if you'll be going to the fair with the babies?"

The words stopped Dafoe for a moment, but he decided he had better ignore the comment. He continued walking.

Tarnovski observed the effect of his words, and made a quick move to slip past the policemen. He succeeded, reaching the doctor's side in seconds. The policemen ran over, ready to grab Tarnovski, but Dafoe raised his hand to stop them.

"Look here, young man," Dafoe stammered, nervously waving his finger in Tarnovski's face, "the only place I'm going is to bed, and that's as soon as you stop bothering me." He climbed into his two-door Dodge, proud of his courage in standing up to the emissary of a powerful city newspaper.

"Are you saying you won't let the babies go?" asked Tarnovski, holding onto the car door.

Dafoe spoke more smoothly this time, and for all to hear. "I've just spent another long day with those babies and I can tell you they're lucky to be alive." He started the car. "They're in no shape even to be out of their incubator. How can they go to Chicago? Lands!" He pulled the door from Tarnovski's grasp and closed it.

"What does Dionne have to say about this?" Tarnovski asked through the open window. "I mean, he signed the contract."

Dafoe looked Tarnovski straight in the eye. "I don't care what Dionne signed," he stated candidly. "He can go to Chicago if he wants. The babies aren't going anywhere. Not while I'm the boss."

With that, Dafoe put the car into gear and pulled away, breathing a sigh of relief. He felt that he had made his position quite clear.

5

Guardians

M itchell Hepburn liked things done his way, and his new office showed it. He had been elected Premier of Ontario only a week ago, and already he had ordered the traditional appointments stripped, and supervised a complete refurbishing to suit his own grand and progressive tastes. A new atmosphere for a new Government was his justification for the public expense.

Hepburn believed in doing everything in a big way. But then, he was a big man, with even bigger plans for the bankrupt province with whose future and fortunes he was now charged. He knew that many would oppose his decisions and actions, but he wasn't worried. Not in the least. He had spent half of his thirty-seven years convincing others that he was right, and a cabinet of parliamentarians was no different than an association of farmers. People needed a leader.

Hepburn had first heard the news while campaigning in North Bay the day after the births, and had right away dispatched his assistant, Richard Slocum, to find out what he could. Although they were still in the last weeks of the election campaign, it had been a certainty that Hepburn would be elected. It had also been a certainty that, if elected, the first issue on the new Government's agenda would be the

Dionne Quintuplets. George Henry's Conservative Government had started the ball rolling by providing some medical relief, extending a temporary electric power cable from Callander to the tiny farm-house, and installing two provincial policemen to keep the curious in line. Hepburn knew that it would be the Liberals' obligation to do even more.

Across the desk from Hepburn sat Slocum, reporting on his most recent trip to Corbeil. As he spoke, he flipped one newspaper over the other, stopping when he reached the *New York Times*. He turned the paper around so that the premier could see the spread. "The Americans are still calling it the biggest human interest story of the decade," he reported excitedly. "I'm surprised it hasn't died down yet. It's been a month already."

Hepburn barely glanced at the newspaper. "I'm not surprised at all. After all, the odds are pretty incredible. Fifty-seven million to one, aren't they?"

"Yeah, something like that." Slocum thought for a moment, then let out a little chuckle. "But you know, what really gets me is Dafoe. You'd think that with all the attention he's been getting, the old guy would be overwhelmed."

"And he isn't?"

"He was nervous the first time I was up. But now he's handling them pretty well."

"Did you get to speak with him this time?"

"Very briefly. Just had a chance to tell him what we're planning to do before this old bag of a housekeeper called him to the phone."

"And?"

"Well, it's what he wants, but..." Slocum chuckled again, "...he said he'll believe it when he sees it."

Hepburn raised an eyebrow. "Pretty cocky sort of guy. We should have him in our cabinet."

"That's not all." Slocum smiled, recalling the abbreviated discussion with Dafoe at his house in Callander yesterday. "He said he doesn't trust you."

"What?" Hepburn bolted upright in his seat. "I'm surprised he even knows who I am."

"Oh, that he does. Everyone knows you, Mr. Premier."

"So, why doesn't he trust me?"

"He says he doesn't trust anyone born and bred south of Ottawa. He compares Southern Ontarians to Americans."

"You're kidding!" Hepburn was now as astounded as he was interested.

"*Capitalists* was the word he used."

"Pretty profound," quipped Hepburn.

"Yeah. Especially for someone who doesn't even recognize some of the biggest reporters in the country when they're right in front of him. Gordon Sinclair introduced himself right at the beginning, and Dafoe thought he was the messenger from the Red Cross."

Hepburn snickered. "It's about time someone put Gord in his place."

"We've got to give him credit, though," Slocum admitted. "Know them or not, he's got them eating out of his hands."

"I've known his brother for years, you know."

"Really?"

"William Dafoe, Toronto General. I never even knew Will had a brother till all of this happened."

"No?" Slocum asked, though not surprised to hear that at all. As he had begun to realize the past few weeks, Allan Roy Dafoe was not the best-known person in the country.

During his recent visits to Callander and Corbeil, Slocum had asked neighbours what they knew of Dafoe. Not much, as it turned out. Although virtually everyone had spoken highly of him professionally, they could shed little light on his personal life. His background was an enigma. Everyone knew that he had come from a small town near Peterborough about twenty-five years ago. They also knew that he had married a local nurse and that she had died about eight years ago. Apparently devastated by his wife's death, Dafoe had since spent most of his private time alone, spending long hours listening to foreign broadcasts on his short wave.

Slocum had spoken to Mrs. Henderson briefly, just after she had called Dafoe to the phone yesterday, but the loyal housekeeper had been of little help. She appeared to be very protective of Dafoe, almost as if he were a favourite son, and the abrupt conversation ended quickly with the door being slammed in his face. All he had found out from her was that Dafoe had a son, Bill, away in boarding-school right now. Did Dafoe visit him much? No. It seemed that his work was his life.

"So you think he'll be happy with our plan?"

"If anything's for sure," Slocum stressed, "he wants what's best for those babies. And to him that means getting them out of that house."

"Good." Hepburn got up. "There shouldn't be any problem then."
He buttoned his suit jacket, which fell elegantly around his tall frame,
and ran a hand through his hair. Then out of his office and down the
stately corridors of the Legislature he marched, swinging his arms
and taking big strides ahead of Slocum, who always had to quicken
his pace just to keep in step. They turned the corner to face a pair of
oak doors marked *Conference Room*. Slocum ran ahead and pushed
the door open. Hepburn slid past him and into the room.

Inside the large room, the smell of polished wood filled the air.
Nearly everything was wood. The walls. The ceiling. The heavy table
that occupied most of the room. The chairs. The only thing that
wasn't wood was the rug that covered most of the floor. And it gave
off the faint smell of stale tobacco smoke. Years of smoke that had
risen and fallen from the cigarettes, cigars, and pipes of the powerful
men that had sat around this very table making important decisions,
themselves often far removed from the consequences.

Around the heavy oak table today sat the province's newest cadre
of decision-makers. Would their smoke also rest heavy in this room
for years to come? Only Hepburn, their charismatic leader, could
have any idea. For these were his carefully selected cabinet ministers, each a powerful political figure in his own right, but collectively
the body that would carry out his whims and wishes, whatever they
were to be.

As Hepburn walked toward the head of the table, everyone got up.
"Gentlemen," he nodded, flashing a big smile at a couple of the men
as he passed. He sat, surveying the group as they all followed suit,
then clasped his hands on the polished surface of the table.

Slocum noticed the hands and smiled to himself. It wasn't the first
time he had seen the gesture. He knew that it meant Hepburn had the
meeting all wrapped up before it had even started. He cast a quick
glance toward the far end of the table to see if Clayton had noticed.
He was the only other person in the room who knew Hepburn well
enough to be able to interpret such gestures. But Clayton had been
busy speaking with the minister next to him and didn't notice.

Hepburn cleared his throat. "Gentlemen. As you know, the purpose
of this meeting is to decide whether this Government should grant
Allan Dafoe's request for a private hospital. Now, I'm sure all of you
have been made aware of the events going on outside North Bay
these past weeks."

An older politician, Bernard Stokes, spoke up first. "If you want my opinion," he said aggressively, puffing on his pipe, "I think the whole thing is a lot of ballyhoo for nothing." He leaned back in his chair. "The Conservatives couldn't set up enough work camps for all the miners out of a job in Sudbury. We're expected to do *better*."

A few motionless heads kept extra-still, in silent agreement with what they considered to be a rational public-minded view.

"As far as I'm concerned," Stokes continued, "we're wasting our time talking about five creatures the size of rats. I don't see the point."

Hepburn hadn't expected that Stokes would. He had been put in the cabinet to keep the party's old guard happy, but that didn't mean anyone had to put up with him. "Thank you, Mr. Stokes," he said, dismissing both the man and his opinions, "but that's not the issue right now. *Creatures* or not, the babies are alive. And the eyes of the world are focussed on them, not on the miners in Sudbury." He fixed his own eyes on Stokes.

Slocum watched his boss with admiration. He knew how those deep and penetrating eyes could be as disconcerting as they were appealing. Hepburn used his stare as a tool. It could silence anyone, even Stokes, who was right now looking down and tapping his pipe rigorously on an ashtray.

"Now," said Hepburn, switching his mesmerizing gaze to a few selected men, "we have to decide, and quickly I might add, exactly what this Government is going to do. And I don't have to remind you that we can't afford to make a mistake. We're too new."

The premier's words of warning were made not just in the interest of his new Government, but to remind everyone of whose reputation was at stake. The Liberal Party that had swept into power a week ago had done so largely on the strength of its leader's personal charm. Five years into the Depression, Canadian voters had lost hope in their existing leaders. Hepburn, whose dynamic speaking style, sprinkled with words of sympathy for the little fellow, repeated calls for reform, and promises of more jobs, had gripped people in all parts of Ontario. He had sailed in, becoming the province's youngest premier ever, with political observers the world over predicting that the former farm association organizer would one day be Prime Minister.

Rudy Walters, one of the ministers whom Hepburn had been eyeing, started to raise his hand.

"Yes, Rudy?"

"I agree, Sir."

Hepburn had known that he would.

"We should definitely move quickly," Walters continued. "I'm sure Dick has already told you what a mess it is up in Corbeil. I stopped on my way up to visit my parents in Sturgeon Falls last weekend and I couldn't believe it. The press. The newsreels. Promoters from all over. That one from Chicago was just the start. I even heard there's an offer pending from the circus."

"Thank you, Rudy," said Hepburn gratefully. The point was well made.

Slocum leaned over and gave the premier his next line.

"You should also know," Hepburn announced, "that that hustler Spear is getting ready to sue Dionne for breach of contract. If we don't get control of the situation, he could win." He looked around to see whose faces expressed the most concern. "We have to let the Americans know who's in charge around here."

Walters nodded in agreement. "If we don't build Dafoe his hospital, someone else will; that's for sure."

A few others also nodded.

But Stokes didn't. He could see that the premier's burst of patriotism was only an attempt to mask his desire for control. "I still think...."

"Mr. Stokes, I don't think you understand," Hepburn charged. "The people of this province are looking to us to protect the quintuplets." He paused to let the thought sink into the other men's heads and to convince Stokes that he had already lost his argument. "They *want* us to get involved."

That was true enough. If Hepburn was gauging public opinion correctly – and his instincts were rarely wrong – opposition to his plan would be minimal; on the contrary, people would applaud. It seemed as if the whole North American public had become foster parents to the quintuplets, determined to protect them from their backward mother and greedy father, and to provide them with the best possible care. Whether it was genuine concern for the babies' well-being, or, as Hepburn liked to think, an element of hope to hang onto in these hopeless times, it was a powerful force. It was like an invisible foundation to the hospital Dafoe wanted, before the decision to build had even been taken.

"The Dionnes don't know how to do a damned thing except milk cows and have babies," Hepburn exaggerated. "And Dafoe isn't equipped to handle something this big on his own. The Americans would be in there tomorrow."

"I have to agree," said another minister, Bill Linton. He turned and nodded to Clayton, who sat next to him at the far end of the table. "We have to do whatever we can to help those babies. It's not just our duty as a government," he said passionately, "but our moral obligation."

"My sentiments exactly," concurred Hepburn, pleased with Linton's timely comment. "I move that we build Dafoe his hospital immediately."

Most of the cabinet members nodded their agreement. A few murmured their assent. Still others remained silent, keeping their objections to themselves. They knew that to disagree now would deprive them of the support they would need on matters of greater importance to their respective portfolios. These men all looked to the quiet minister seated at the end of the table opposite Hepburn. After all, the issues being discussed were part of his Social Services portfolio.

Hepburn now addressed that loyal minister. "Nick," he said, his smile reaching the full length of the table, "we'll need a few things put in order before we can go full steam on the hospital."

Nick Clayton looked up.

"I'd like a board of guardians set up, Nick."

The room grew suddenly quiet.

Clayton looked at Hepburn; their eyes met briefly, then Clayton's slid down, deep into his empty coffee cup. He didn't like what he was hearing, but he didn't know why. The idea of the hospital had bothered him a little, but it seemed reasonable given the type of care the babies needed. Even the concept of a board of guardians made sense, considering the attention the babies were getting. The likelihood of another Spear incident occurring was small, but he felt that the Dionnes could use, and might even need, some advice in handling such situations. No, it wasn't the words Hepburn had just spoken that had jarred him. It was more the relish with which they had poured out of the premier's mouth that unnerved, perhaps even frightened, him. He raised his head and looked at his old friend and new leader once again.

"Yes, Sir," was Clayton's dutiful reply. "Who would you like on it? I mean, besides the parents?"

"Dafoe will be in charge." Hepburn announced the appointment as if he were naming himself to the board.

"Dafoe?" someone croaked through the start of a dry, hacking cough.

"Of course," Rudy Walters jumped in, grabbing the opportunity to state the obvious again. "He's the one who's kept them alive."

"He's also the one people like," added Hepburn, getting more to the point. "But I want some of our people on it, too."

"With all due respect, Mr. Premier, I don't think that's a good idea." Clayton felt comfortable in expressing sentiments the other ministers dared not. Even in the caucus, Hepburn had always respected how Clayton spoke his mind, though the yet-to-be premier was always able to change it later. "I mean, we all want action, but these people are French Canadian. And Catholic, to boot. Do you really think Dionne is going to accept our doing this? I'm sure you know that he and Dafoe aren't the best of friends any more."

"After the stunt Dionne pulled with Spear," stressed Hepburn, "he won't have a choice. We won't put him on the board."

There were more murmurs in the room, this time disapproving ones. One minister angrily butted the cigarette he had just lit.

"Not for now, anyway," continued Hepburn. "Not until we have everything under control."

"That's a pretty extreme step, Mitchell," said Stokes, eyebrows raised. "The man's their father, for Christ's sake."

Hepburn's dark eyes flashed. "Yes, he is. And he was also ready to ship his own babies, barely alive, off to Chicago for a few bucks."

Stokes had lost again. If he had been twenty years younger, he would have put the young buck of a premier back in his place in a minute. Instead, he remained silent and puffed erratically on his long pipe.

"I don't think we have to worry about public reaction," Hepburn reiterated, confident now that Stokes would not object again. "We could make the babies wards of the Crown, and people wouldn't say a word."

"The Church will raise bloody hell," assured Clayton.

Slocum whispered another handy reminder to Hepburn.

"The Church?" Hepburn almost spat out the words. "That old priest up there... what's his name?"

"Routhier," offered Slocum.

"That's it, Routhier." He pronounced the name slowly, with contempt. "He was going to take a seven per cent cut from the deal with Spear. Can you believe it? He wanted to be Dionne's manager."

Some of the men snickered, but the rest of them remained tight-lipped. The mood in the room had changed. Though they had all felt that something unsettling was being planned when their attendance at this meeting about the Dionne babies had been ordered, they had had no idea of the break-neck speed at which these issues, affecting so many human lives, would be decided. Those with nicotine habits puffed away apprehensively, the smoke forming a sombre cloud over the table.

"No, I'm not worried about the Church at all," the premier declared. "Now, are we agreed on setting up a board of guardians?" he asked. "Or not?" he warned.

A couple of the men said *aye*; the rest just nodded, refusing to jeopardize their new careers by responding negatively.

"Good." He turned to Clayton. "Nick, let's get a release out from your department this morning."

Clayton nodded reluctantly.

Hepburn stood up. "Thank you, gentlemen. That will be all."

One by one, the men in the room rose to leave, all of them careful, and wise, not to discuss their private opinions with one another until they were out of Hepburn's hearing range.

Clayton approached the premier before leaving. "I'll get my people working on a statement right away."

"Nick, I'd like you to stay behind for a moment."

Slocum watched the last of the men file out, then closed the door. He turned to sit in a chair by the door.

"That's okay, Dick," said Hepburn. "You go ahead. I'll just be a few minutes."

Slocum hesitated. "Of course, Sir. I'll be in my office if you need me." He looked over his shoulder all the way out, wishing he could stay.

"Sit down, Nick," Hepburn invited. He himself sat once the door had closed after Slocum.

"Quite a discussion," Clayton remarked, more concerned about the imminent one.

"Yes, it was," Hepburn agreed. He waited a few seconds before laying the goods on the table. "Nick, how do you feel about what we're planning to do?" Clayton's opinion would have no bearing on his decision, but he trusted him to at least be honest about its implications.

"Well, the hospital won't be much of a problem. Like Stokes said, some people might object to our spending money on a building for

77

five patients. On the other hand, most of the country is caught up in the story. People will support it."

"What about the board?"

"It depends who's on it. Dafoe, sure, but keeping Dionne off? I'm not sure the Chicago deal is sufficient justification."

"Hmm," mused Hepburn, his mind active. "You think we may have a problem, then?"

Clayton shrugged. "We'll have to have a good defence ready."

But Hepburn knew that a defence might lead to more opposition. "You know, Nick, maybe a board of guardians isn't enough."

"What do you mean?"

"We need to take complete charge. We've got to make the babies wards of the Crown. Then no one can interfere."

"You're not serious?" Clayton had thought Hepburn's previous comment merely wishful thinking: one of those statements in which his dreams far outreached the reality of what he could actually do.

"We've got to get them away from their parents before it's too late," Hepburn asserted.

"Too late for what?" Clayton couldn't understand the premier's fixation with the quintuplets. After all, once they were safe in a hospital, who cared about anything else? Wouldn't the Government have done its duty? Couldn't they then get on with other pressing matters, such as rampant unemployment? "Mitch, setting up a board is one thing. But taking the babies away from perfectly able parents... when there's no reason?"

"No reason?" Hepburn stared hard at Clayton, his own defence ready. "I'll give you a reason. Without us, the babies will die, plain and simple. We're saving lives, Nick. Those babies need this Government. Can you imagine the furor if they died now? What would that do to us?"

Clayton said nothing. He didn't see the relationship between saving the babies' lives and breaking up a family.

"After all the attention that's been lavished on them by the press? How would we look if they died and we hadn't taken the proper precautions? We'd be finished."

Clayton lit a cigarette.

"Nick, I'd like you to go up to Corbeil and meet Dionne. Talk to him. Show him our concern."

"What will I tell him?" asked Clayton, baffled about how to tell a father that he was going to lose half of his ten children.

"Just tell him we're building a hospital for the babies, like I said, to help keep them alive. And tell him about the board. That it's there to assist him… and… uh… Eliza, to make the right decisions."

Clayton's look was questioning. He wondered if the premier really believed what he was saying.

"They can't do it on their own, Nick. Trust me. They'll be grateful to us one day; you just wait and see." Hepburn blinked once, then nodded, as if he could foresee the future.

"Whatever you say."

"But nothing about them not being on the board," Hepburn went on. "We'll break that to them once they've accepted this first bit of news. Just make Dionne realize our only concern is what's best for the whole family."

"When do you want me to go?"

"Well, we should get this done as soon as possible."

"Is tomorrow all right?"

"That will be perfect. And one other thing," he added casually, making it seem like an afterthought, "we should get a good business manager on board."

"For what?" Clayton asked, ready to hear almost anything.

"For the family's own good. That way, any offers will come through us. We're obviously better equipped to deal with the likes of Spear than they are. We don't want another mistake like Chicago."

Clayton nodded. The justification was as good as any of the others he had heard so far that day.

* * *

Elzire looked nervously out the front window as a big, shiny black car rolled up in front of the house. Not more reporters looking to crucify Oliva for the mistake he had made with Spear, she prayed. She had been ready to crucify him herself.

Since the story had broken, the barrage hadn't stopped. The reporters harassed them both in print and in person. Each day, more of them came, ready to pounce on Oliva or on any other member of the family who dared venture out front. She and Oliva had warned the children not to leave the house by the front door any more, afraid they would hear some of the vile insults being hurled by the crowds at the gate. Or pick up a newspaper that someone had maliciously thrown onto the porch. It seemed that every day new articles appeared, more hateful than the ones before. Even worse, threatening letters had started to arrive from total strangers, calling her and Oliva all sorts of terrible names. It made no sense to her that millions of people were discussing them so freely, when less than a hundred people in the whole world actually knew them.

Elzire watched as three men, all dressed seriously in dark suits with wide lapels, got out of the car and started walking toward the house. The police will stop them, Elzire decided. Then the coldness of this thought brought her up short. Not so many weeks ago, she would have rushed out to warmly greet these same people, whoever they were. Now, she looked upon any stranger's arrival, even that of someone bringing gifts for her new babies, as an invasion of her privacy. For someone so naturally welcoming, it was a difficult change to accept. But then, so was everything else.

The last month had marked the worst crisis in Elzire's life since her mother's death eighteen years ago. With the exception of her faith in God, almost everything that had guided her life until this May – a strong sense of independence despite hardship, unquestioning faith in the community, implicit trust in human nature, a clear balance between sharing with neighbours and privacy of the home – had been threatened. It was as if she had died giving birth and had found herself not among billowing clouds and angelic choirs, but in a strangely twisted world, not physically unlike the one she had always known, but filled with coldness and distrust.

What made the situation most unbearable was that neither she nor Oliva was in control of their own home any more. Dafoe had turned it into a miniature version of the starched, white hospital in North Bay where she had visited Tante after an operation last year. The doctor himself may have been spending less and less time in their house each day, but he had trained his nursing staff well.

Each of the three women that made up Dafoe's staff knew her place in the Dionne home. Yvonne Leroux tended to the babies; the nurse's helper assisted in preparing formula and cleaning up; and Head Nurse Louise de Kiriline ran the household with an iron hand. The three of them worked beautifully; a real team in every respect, especially when it came to criticizing Elzire. And even though Elzire had sometimes heard them chatting over tea about how hard they had been on her during a particular day, they continued to pick on her, finding fault in everything she did. She's too rough with them, Nurse Leroux would report to Nurse de Kiriline on the few occasions when Elzire was allowed to hold one of her tiny babies. She gets in the way, was the nurse's helper's chief complaint about the woman whose kitchen she had all but taken over. And the one that Nurse de Kiriline never failed to complain about, and report back to Dafoe: She's bringing the other children into the nursery. That was a crime that could not be forgiven.

Dafoe had cornered Elzire one morning and bluntly told her that if she wanted him to remain the babies' doctor, she would have to smarten up. No germs were to get into the nursery, and that meant no opening the door for quick peeks inside, no letting inquisitive Ernest pop his head in to see what was going on, and no bringing Thérèse in to touch her new sisters. And that wasn't the end of the rules: no noise that might wake the babies, no guests for the hasty christening that took place virtually unnoticed, no interfering with his nurses' work, no washing diapers with the other children's clothes.... The list of no's was endless, making Elzire feel out of place no matter where she moved in her own home. Everything she did was questioned. Everything she did was wrong. When to her, everything *except* what she did was wrong.

Elzire looked hopefully to the policemen as they approached the three strangers. But after a short discussion, they let them pass. That was strange. They had been given strict orders not to let anyone near the house, except people delivering medical supplies. And with the exception of one of the three, who had a bag slung over his shoulder, these men were empty-handed. Elzire dropped the curtain and rushed through the house to the back door.

"There's someone here," Elzire announced, a worried look covering her face as she rushed past the nurse's helper, who was sitting at the table in the summer kitchen eating oatmeal with Rose and Thérèse.

The helper was absorbed in the *Eaton's Catalogue* that she had brought from home to pass the time. "Hmm?" she breathed, stuffing another spoonful of oatmeal into her mouth without looking up from her magazine.

Elzire threw the back door open to see Daniel sitting in front of her on the steps. He was separating the reds and blacks from a deck of playing cards. The dog lay next to him, half-asleep. Elzire's eyes searched the yard for Oliva, finally spotting him coming out of the barn with a heaping bucket of grain. Ernest had a grip on the handle, trying to help.

"Oliva," Elzire cried.

He looked up.

"Come. Quick."

Ernest let go of the bucket and ran full-tilt toward the side of the house. The dog at Elzire's feet pricked up its ears and began to rise.

"Ernest!" Oliva shouted.

The dog dashed out to meet the running boy.

"Hurry," Elzire urged. "The police let three men through."

The door to the nursery opened, and Nurse Leroux poked her head into the summer kitchen. "Mrs. Dionne, shh," she demanded. "The babies."

Elzire looked at her resentfully.

"Please," the nurse insisted, promptly closing the door.

"Who are they, Maman?" asked Rose from the kitchen table.

"I don't know."

The nurse's helper finally looked up. "Probably just some more reporters," she shrugged, turning a page in her catalogue.

Pauline, who had been playing with some wooden spoons on the floor by the stairwell, started to cry.

Elzire hated to ask for anyone's help but she was still too weak to lift any of the children. "Could you pick her up?" she asked the helper, pointing to Pauline as she hurried back into the main part of the house and over to the front window. Rose followed, huddling with her mother in the big chair under the window, waiting for Oliva to come around and make the men leave.

Despite the panic in Elzire's voice, Oliva didn't hurry. What good would it do? Whoever these men were, surely they couldn't be worse than the others that had been bombarding his home lately with careless feet, prying eyes, and loose tongues. He actually found it ironic that those who blamed him for his one impulsive act were guilty of as much, and more. The only criticism made of him that held even a modicum of truth was that he was a simple, backwoods farmer. Well, he was proud of that. And now that the whole world knew it, why didn't they let him farm in peace, and live with his family in contentment in their little backwoods home? But they couldn't. Or, rather, they wouldn't. It was as if his five identical babies were too special to share the kind of life that he had been brought up to regard as decent and honourable.

When he finally came around the corner of the house, he spotted Ernest looking through the window of a gleaming new Cadillac, the dog at his side barking frantically. A few other children, those who appeared daily in the yard that was their new playground, had joined him. Then, Oliva noticed the three men that Elzire was so upset about. They had finished having a few words with one of the reporters and were walking up the path, approaching the front steps. Near the gate, several reporters who had also recognized them were trying to persuade the guards to let them through.

Curious neighbours and others who had driven up to see the now-famous house were also watching, and now exchanging apprehensive looks. They sensed trouble, especially when they noticed Oliva walking over to intercept the three men who were about to mount his porch.

Oliva walked right up to them, but it was Clayton who spoke first.

"Mr. Dionne?"

Oliva noticed that Ernest was circling the big car, conversing about it with the other children. "Ernest," he shouted, "get in the house."

Ernest came running, with the dog following at his heels. "Papa," he said, excited, "I want to get in the car." He had seen the likes of it only in pictures at Voyer's and at school.

"Go right ahead, young man," smiled Clayton, turning back to Oliva. "He asked, and I said it was all right."

Ernest turned to head back toward the car, but Oliva grabbed him. "In the house!"

Ernest hesitated.

"Now!"

Ernest reluctantly climbed the steps and slipped inside, where he joined the rest of his family in the window. The dog stayed right behind him, but stopped outside the door to lay down on the mat.

"I really don't mind, you know," said Clayton ingratiatingly.

Oliva didn't like or trust the overly friendly voice. "I do," he stated. He moved up onto the first step where he could simultaneously block their way and gain the advantage of height. "If you're looking for Dr. Dafoe, he's not here."

"Actually, we're here to see you."

Oliva was nervous, but not intimidated. "Whatever you're selling, I'm not interested."

"I'm not selling anything, Mr. Dionne." But in fact, he was. And it looked like it was going to take an even bigger selling job than the one Hepburn had done on him. "May I call you Oliva?"

Silence.

"My name is Nick Clayton," he said, extending his hand. "I'm the Minister of Social Services for the province."

Oliva was unimpressed, and didn't offer his hand in return.

Clayton was embarrassed at being shown up. He looked over his shoulder to see if anyone had noticed, then dropped his hand and gestured toward the house. "Do you mind if we talk inside?" Not only did he not want the conversation overheard by any of the reporters before the Government was ready to make an official announcement, he also didn't feel morally right about delivering the news with which he had been charged in front of a huge, gaping crowd.

"Out here will do," Oliva said. "What do you want?"

"Fine," Clayton said, a little perturbed at being addressed so rudely. Wasn't his job hard enough in the first place? He continued the introductions. "This is Jack Sharkey," he said, pointing to the taller of the two men, "and that's Fred Davis." He nodded to the other, who had a large camera bag hanging over his shoulder.

"Pleased to meet you," offered Sharkey.

"Mr. Dionne," nodded Davis.

Clayton hadn't had much time to fill either one of them in. But Hepburn had wanted them to accompany him anyway. To meet the man with whom they would surely have encounters in the future.

"Okay," said Oliva, suspiciously eyeing each one of them in turn. "Now that I know who all of you are, do you care to tell me what it is that you want?"

Clayton was worried about how to phrase his message. Oliva was not likely to be too receptive. Not with that scowl on his face, that anger in his eyes, and those bitter words coming out of his mouth. "We've come to share some good news with you," he said. "Is Mrs. Dionne home?"

"I don't think I want to hear your good news." Oliva turned to check on Elzire, who was looking out the window with an alarmed expression on her face.

Clayton understood the move as a gesture to follow, and began to move forward, laying one foot on the bottom step.

Oliva turned sharply. "Hey, where do you think you're going?"

The dog raised itself to its feet and growled.

"I just want to...."

"I don't care what *you* want. I want you to get off my property. I told you we don't want to hear anything you have to say."

"Mr. Dionne, we're not here to bother you." Clayton tried to lay on his own brand of Hepburn's persuasive charm. "We want to put an end to all of that."

"Yeah, how?"

"You must know about the hospital Dr. Dafoe has asked us to build for your babies."

How could Oliva *not* have known? Dafoe had been asking every reporter he could find to write about it. What could the babies get in a hospital, he wanted to know, that they couldn't get right here at home? Especially since Dafoe had turned the back room into a hospital in all but name already. And if that wasn't enough, Oliva had offered to build an addition to the house. Anything to keep the family together.

"We don't need a hospital," he asserted. "We don't want anything from anyone."

"If you would just let me explain."

"Please leave," Oliva forced himself to ask politely. "You're scaring my wife, coming here with that big car of yours. Look at what we already have to deal with," he said, gesturing to the rapt, news-hungry onlookers, and becoming more agitated as he spoke. "Isn't that enough? I can't farm in peace any more. I can't get my truck out onto the road without being stopped. No one rents my hay press any more; they're afraid to come around. What are you trying to do, ruin me?"

Clayton turned to look at the group of people watching them. He wished again he was inside the house, this time not just so the people couldn't hear him, but so they couldn't hear Oliva talking to him this way. Hepburn would never stand for this type of treatment, not publicly anyway.

He turned back to face Oliva and, for the first time, noticed Elzire and three young faces huddled together in the front window, watching his every move. He was surrounded by eyes, and it made him uneasy. "I understand how your wife must feel," he said sympathetically, "but your babies need proper care."

"That's the first thing you've got right so far, Mr. Clayton," Oliva railed, his temper showing clearly now. "*Our* babies. Not yours. Not Dafoe's. *Ours*. And we can take care of them without your help." He turned to face the house again, and this time started up the steps.

"Let's get out of here," muttered Sharkey into the silence.

Clayton gathered some courage. Hepburn's type of courage. "I'm sorry, Mr. Dionne, but I don't think you realize just how important your babies are. Do you really think you can provide everything they need?" He pointed to the modest log farmhouse and the infertile land, feeling for the first time since yesterday, when Hepburn had lectured him, that maybe the premier was right. "On your own?" he asked, echoing the premier's words and sounding more condescending than concerned.

"Yes, I can," Oliva yelled from the porch. "If everyone would just leave us alone. Now, I told you to leave once. Do I have to tell you again?"

Clayton was losing the battle to keep his composure. Even Hepburn wouldn't have been able to get through this farmer's thick skull. "I'm sorry, Mr. Dionne," he apologized, although the sympathy had deserted his tone. "I really wanted to talk this over with you quietly, but I can see that's impossible. We'll leave, but you have to understand that a hospital is going to be built for your babies."

"Get out of here!" Oliva shouted with contempt, the veins in his neck starting to bulge. "Get off my property!"

Clayton turned and took a step toward his car. He noticed the reporters busily jotting notes in their pads, the other onlookers watching attentively, the two policemen not knowing what to do. His face turned red. He had tried to be understanding, but no one should have to take the kind of abuse he had just received. Especially with people watching. Hepburn had often preached to him about how to deal with the little man. Try to help, he would say, but if they won't listen to reason, show them who's in charge.

He stopped and turned to Oliva, his nostrils flaring. "By the way, Mr. Dionne," he said, his voice as clear and sharp as acid, "we'll also be setting up a board of guardians to ensure that the right decisions are made for your babies. And you're not..." his anger almost made him indiscreet, "... uh, Mr. Sharkey will be handling business affairs," he continued, "and Mr. Davis, here, is from the *Star*. He will be the official photographer. I imagine you'll be seeing a lot of both of them from now on."

"Wh... what are you talking about?" Oliva's voice began to shake as he tried to make some sense out of what he was hearing.

"It's obvious you aren't interested in doing the right thing for your babies. The Government *is*." He turned spitefully and started walking toward his car.

Oliva rushed down the steps. "Just who the hell do you think you are?"

Clayton could hear the weight of angry feet thumping down the steps. He tried to speed up his pace, but before he could react, Oliva had already shoved him.

"Get out of here!"

There was pounding on the window behind them. Then the growl of the dog again, who was now up on all fours, ready to leap from the edge of the porch.

The policemen rushed forward as Clayton stumbled a few steps off of the path. The reporters and the other onlookers crowded in too, but retreated again from the force of Oliva's fiery glare and threatening posture.

"Get out of here! All of you!"

At first, one by one, then by two's or more, the curious onlookers reluctantly backed away. Even the police backed up, at this point unsure of who their boss was – the Government that paid them, or the man whose property they had been sent to guard.

"Come on, Nick." It was Sharkey who grabbed Clayton's arm. "Let's go. The guy's crazy."

"Okay, okay." Clayton shook his arm loose from Sharkey's grip.

Elzire kept beating on the window, but Oliva didn't look up. He just watched as the three men finally walked through the gate, then kicked the bottom step of the porch and stomped all the way around the corner of the house.

The reporters shouted at Clayton as he stepped onto the road. At first, he tried to ignore everyone in his path, but the clamour got worse. He raised both his arms for silence, then pushed past even those reporters he knew, and looked straight ahead as he stalked off to his car. "He hasn't heard the end of this," he seethed, furious at the assault, but fully aware of the powers at his disposal with which he could retaliate.

6

The Country Doctor

H e was standing centre-stage before a large crowd at Carnegie Hall. The spotlight was on him and the crowd was cheering loudly. It was everything he had imagined it to be.

He was about to thank everyone for coming, when Mrs. Henderson appeared in the doorway to the bedroom. Dafoe jumped back, embarrassed at being caught in his private world.

Flustered, he turned from the full-length mirror that stood in the corner of the room. "Have you seen my good shoes?" he asked, acting as if that was what he had been looking in the mirror for. He padded over to the chest of drawers.

Mrs. Henderson stood motionless, looking straight ahead at the reflection of his silly expression in the smaller mirror that hung directly opposite her, on the wall above the mahogany chest of drawers. Her eyes travelled down to where a pair of shiny silver cuff links lay on the surface of the chest. Over to the right, she noticed the doctor's tweed jacket hanging from one of the bedposts, and the bedspread almost concealed by an assortment of shirts, ties, and trousers. She also noticed that the doors of the wardrobe were wide open, half of the wooden hangers dangling with nothing on them. She had never seen the room in such a mess. Not since she had lived there, anyway.

She moved closer and sniffed the air. "Are you sure you got the mothballs out of those pockets?"

"Very funny."

She came even closer, this time to get a better look at his tweed suit trousers. He hadn't worn them in ages. She instinctively stepped back, this time waving her hand in front of her nose. "What's that you've got on? You smell like an apothecary!"

"It's not that bad."

"No. Of course not. Put a little more on." She bent to look for his shoes under the foot of the bed. "It'll get rid of the smell of the moth-balls, anyway."

On any other day, her barbed tongue would have brought submission. But this wasn't just any day. "Well, don't you think the ground-breaking for your very own hospital is worth getting fixed up for?" he asked pompously.

The faint smile on her face disappeared as she looked up. "You don't want to know what I think." She was saddened that he didn't share her concern over what was going on. She moved past him and started rooting for his shoes in the wardrobe. On her knees, she stopped for a moment to look up at him again. He was adjusting his tie. "I think the whole thing is a crying shame."

"You're right." He continued to pull at the tie, all the while looking straight into the mirror. "I don't want to know." Right now, his chief concern was making his tie. He never could get the damned things to come out right. Out of the corner of his eye he noticed her still looking around aimlessly for the shoes. "They might be under the bed."

"They're not." She got up, more important things on her mind than a dusty old pair of shoes. "Can't you see what all of this is doing to the Dionnes? They're nice people. They don't deserve this."

She knew she was wasting her breath. During the past few weeks, with those creepy Government people coming around every day, briefing Dr. Dafoe on the ceremony, he had been lost somewhere on a cloud. The ground-breaking was all he could talk about. Not once did he mention the effect it might have on the Dionnes. But then, it seemed like everyone around Callander had forgotten the Dionnes, as well as the simplicity of their own lives. *Our Mitch* was coming to little old Corbeil, and that was all anyone could talk about. That was all that mattered.

"Breaking up the family like that," she moralized, wondering if everyone had lost their minds. "It's terrible."

"No one's trying to hurt the Dionnes." The simple GP who had slogged through mud to reach some of his patients poked the softly burnished pieces of silver through the holes in his cuffs. "But can you imagine them trying to take care of those babies without our help?"

"Then *help* them." She checked under the overstuffed easy chair near the window for his shoes. "You don't have to take their children away from them. They're not two months old yet, for crying out loud. They need their mother."

"What are you so upset about?" Dafoe asked. "We're not taking them to China. They're going to be right across the road."

She was aware of that. But she was even more aware of what that signified for the events this afternoon. Removing the babies from their parents' home was bad enough, but making a ceremony of it right across the road? Celebrating? And her Dr. Dafoe at the centre of it all, appearing not to understand what the problem was. If he really didn't understand, it scared her. If he was just pretending, it scared her even more.

"Poor Elzire," she said, finally spotting the shoes under the nightstand beside the bed. "There isn't a nicer woman walking the face of this earth." She reached for the shoes and stood up. "How can you let this happen?"

He finally finished his tie. "Stop turning it into some big tragedy. Elzire can see the babies whenever she wants." He turned away from his reflection, carefully patting his collar down and tugging at his shirt cuffs. "How do I look?" He noticed the shoes in her hand, but ignored her angry stare. "You found them. Good."

"Oh... who cares?" She let the shoes fall to the floor.

"What's the matter with you?"

"Next time," she said, bolting out of the room, "find your own shoes."

Dafoe watched the empty doorway for a second, then shrugged his shoulders and chuckled. He had gotten used to these little outbursts after eight years.

He picked up the shoes, vigorously ran a flannel cloth over them until they gleamed jet black, and laced them on. Then he picked up his suit jacket from the bedpost, and as he slipped on the jacket, returned to the chest of drawers to grab a silk handkerchief out of the top drawer. He tried out a few different expressions in the small mirror, aiming to look less excited and a tad more dignified. Then, as he turned to leave, he looked over his shoulder to catch his profile in the other mirror in the corner.

His eyes sparkled. He was back at Carnegie Hall.

Government officials had been preparing for the ceremony all morning, deciding on the best spot for the podium, figuring out where the press and the visitors would stand, and wondering who might show up. A quick decision regarding VIPs was made, and some paint on the back of a Canada Dry sign announced the area directly in front of the podium as suitable for them. The general public would have to stand behind the roped-off section.

The rehearsal went smoothly, except for a brief moment of panic when Slocum noticed that the podium tipped slightly into the soft ground. Hepburn would be furious, he told the other Government officials, and ordered two of them to get down on their knees and shore up the weak side. That did the trick. Slocum's only real worry now remained the grey skies. He hoped that the rain forecast for today, the first in weeks, would hold off at least until after the ceremony.

The first invited guest to arrive was Mort Fellman. Knight, his editor, had insisted he go early and get lots of shots to illustrate the big front page spread they were planning. This wasn't like most regular local events, where he could turn up late, or sometimes not even show up at all. Knight wanted him there for the whole thing.

Fellman stood in the July heat, watching with amusement as the Government officials rushed about, taking care of last-minute problems, real and imagined. He tried to talk to a couple of them, hoping to get some information on who was coming. But all they could say was later, later, too busy now. So he took pictures of them instead.

He eventually wandered over to where some of the uninvited guests were now standing. Several had gotten there even earlier than Fellman had, hoping for a good view of the podium. There were the locals of course, but also people from further away, from places like Mattawa and Sturgeon Falls. Some had even ventured down from Sudbury, and up from Ottawa, for the occasion. He took more pictures, and asked a few of the people why they had come. Most said, just to see Mitch Hepburn and Doc Dafoe in person. One person that

Fellman spoke to referred to Dafoe as *le docteur*. That was a kindly old woman from Corbeil, who had come by to see if Dafoe could look in on her ailing husband. But he hadn't arrived yet.

Other reporters started to arrive, including some of the *originals*. That was the name Fellman used for anyone who had been around since those first days outside the Dionne farmhouse. People like, in addition to himself, Gordon Sinclair, Charlie Blake, and some of the New York press. And the people from Pathé, who were at this moment setting up their newsreel cameras in a prime spot before the show started.

When the invited guests started to pull up by the side of the road, Fellman's camera went into action. The mayor of North Bay noted the sign, and led the reeves representing Callander and Corbeil into the VIP section. Click. Nick Clayton proceeded behind the lectern to one of three waiting chairs. Click. Michael Peters, the local member of parliament, plunged into the gathering crowd, mingling with any-one who resembled a farmer. Click. Dafoe, looking nervous without Mrs. Henderson, appeared totally unsure of where to go or what to do. Click, click. Hepburn, who arrived with all the confidence the country doctor lacked, eventually pointed Dafoe to where Clayton was sitting. Click.

The reeve for Corbeil stepped up to the podium to address the hundred or so people gathered in the field. "Ladies and gentlemen, we are very honoured to have with us today: the Premier of Ontario, the Honourable Mitchell Hepburn."

Behind the lectern, Hepburn, who was sitting between Dafoe and Clayton, stood up. He looked resplendent in his light morning suit, and strutted forward like a peacock to the hearty applause. Dozens of flashbulbs popped as he gave the crowd of reporters a satisfied smile and the newsreel crew a hypnotic stare to capture on film.

Dafoe watched him closely, on one hand admiring the premier's poise, on the other nervous about his own turn, soon to come. He knew that these same people would soon be applauding him, and he wished that he could be as calm as Hepburn was right now. Having to deal with reporters these past weeks had given him some practice, but this was different. These people weren't here to ask questions about the babies. They were here to celebrate with him. To watch him break ground for his very own hospital. He thought of how com-posed he had been in his vision of Carnegie Hall. Here, his pulse was racing and his throat was dry.

"Thank you." Hepburn's voice was loud and clear. "Thank you for coming here today. For me, this is a very special occasion." He addressed his audience with great confidence. "It's an honour for the Government to help make sure the Dionne Quintuplets have the best possible care anywhere."

The words came easily, chiefly because there was no resistance at all to the hospital. Not on this side of the road, anyway. Everyone listened intently as Hepburn romanticized about the quintuplets' valiant struggle to survive, and proclaimed the Government's sacred duty to do everything in its power to make sure the babies lived and flourished. He spoke with great intensity, each dramatic pause immediately filled with applause. By the time the speech came to a close, a few people in the audience were actually in tears.

"So without further ado, I ask Dr. Allan Dafoe to break ground for the new Dafoe Hospital."

Dafoe froze in his place. He couldn't possibly face the crowd. But Hepburn had spoken, and the people were waiting. The applause cushioned him, but in moments it would stop.

He thought of his father, who would surely have been amazed to see all these people clapping for the boy that was never supposed to amount to anything. For the son that finished near the bottom of his class in medical school. For the older brother that lived in the younger one's shadow. For the black sheep that refused to enter the family practice in Madoc. He wondered if the old man, wherever he was, would at last be proud of him.

The thoughts of his father seemed to last for hours, although it was only seconds before he was up on his feet moving across the podium. The applause was still alive. He tried to smile, but was not sure he could. Two little steps away from the lectern, he noticed that Hepburn's smile was big enough for both of them.

Slocum passed a spade to his beaming premier, who, in turn, handed it to Dafoe.

The able doctor's hands were shaking as he took the tool, but Hepburn gave him an encouraging look and a warm pat on the back as they stepped down off of the podium. Somehow, Dafoe gained the courage and started to dig. Hepburn slapped him on the back again. This time he dug deeper. Then deeper still – deeper than he needed to dig in the first place, as the crowd watched attentively and shouted their approval of the loner child from Madoc.

Across the road, Oliva heard the grate of steel biting into pebble-choked soil, but he didn't bother to look. He was too busy position-ing a wooden sign against the large oak tree in his front yard. For now, the babies were still under his roof and, until the hospital was built, that's where they would stay.

The policemen kept watch as Oliva pulled out a hammer from his overalls. They had been instructed not to let him out of their sight. Slocum had personally informed them that Hepburn wouldn't stand for any trouble today, especially after what had happened with Clayton last month.

Looking straight ahead with as much dignity as he could muster, Oliva nailed his freshly painted sign to the tree. *NO ADMITTANCE* it read.

The signs that faced each other across the road that day might have been harbingers of the future. For on one side of the road, Dafoe and Hepburn were indeed becoming VIPs, both to themselves and to the world at large. And on the other side, the Dionnes would soon have all the solitude they would ever want.

*   *   *

Fellman sat at his desk holding the February issue of *Trend* maga-zine. The cover contained a flattering portrait of Dafoe, his features gentle, his eyes compassionate. Underneath were the words *MIRACLE DOCTOR*. The magazine opened easily to the page that everyone else in the newsroom had already read.

"With the quints ensconced in the Dafoe Hospital and under the protective wing of Doc Dafoe," *Trend* announced, "we can all feel confident that the five tiny Dionne Quintuplets will pull through their ordeal. Dafoe's indomitable spirit, unprecedented medical skills, and kindly manner serve as an inspiration to us all."

Fellman thought he was going to be sick. He closed the magazine and walked over to Knight's desk.

"Have you seen this?" he asked, tossing the magazine, cover up, in front of him.

"Not bad, eh?"

"I don't believe it. A fifty-year-old GP from Callander. *Miracle Doctor*," he scoffed. "He fixed my sister's broken ankle a few months back, and she's still limping. He didn't work any miracles on her."

"You think he was just lucky with those kids?"

"Well, come on. It's getting a bit out of hand, don't you think? First the Nobel Prize nomination, now this. What are they going to do next, make him a saint?"

Knight chuckled. "He should be hitting New York around now."

"I know. The big tour," Fellman growled. "But explain one thing to me. The guy claims he doesn't want attention; he's just doing his job, no raises in pay, nothing. So what's he doing running off to New York? It's the middle of winter and half his patients have got colds."

"I don't know about that," Knight shrugged, "but he's supposed to get quite a welcome. Why don't you check the wire to see if anything has come in yet?"

Fellman walked over to the teletype. He was still trying to understand Dafoe, but it wasn't easy. Although he had talked to the doctor on numerous occasions – usually on the telephone when he was seeking updates on the babies' health, and a few times over tea at Dafoe's house when he was doing feature stories – he had not learned much about him. Occasionally he prodded gently, but Dafoe remained secretive about all personal matters.

He had finally managed to track down one of Dafoe's classmates from medical school, someone who was able to shed a little light on the doctor's past. The conversation had been brief, but it led Fellman to believe that Dafoe had spent his twenty-five years in Callander escaping from something in his past. His refusal to join a family practice in Madoc had apparently led to a terrible fight. It was the first time that young Allan had spoken out against his father, and the rift that developed between the two men became irreparable. Dafoe had left Madoc shortly afterwards, eventually drifting north.

The classmate had lost touch with Dafoe at that point, but Fellman had been filled in by a few of Dafoe's old acquaintances, people who had known him when he had first arrived in Callander.

When he came to Callander, Dafoe had met the local doctor, who was retiring and looking to sell his practice. Dafoe had jumped at the chance, buying the practice for a hundred dollars, putting a down payment on the house, and settling down for life. Apparently, he had never returned to Madoc, even though it was only two hundred miles away, and had communicated with his family all these years only by mail. He had seemed, until now, content with a quiet life in the shadows, where he received the appreciation and respect he had never gotten at home.

Fellman watched the copy roll out of the teletype. There was nothing on the New York trip yet. Just a cheery Government release on the *quints* being nine months old, and the usual dreary bulletins about failed work camps and reform programs. A little good news, and a lot of bad. It was no wonder everyone was getting so caught up with the Dionnes' adorable quintuplets. In the eyes of the world, the babies were much more than oddities of the human species. They were symbols of hope and survival at the bleakest time in everyone's lives. If the babies could beat the odds and make it, so could the rest of the world. Without the flicker of hope that grew each day the babies lived, people had little to hope for. As for Dafoe, he was the one who was keeping that hope alive. To the public, he was more than a saint. He was a saviour.

Fellman waited for more than an hour for something from New York, but nothing came. It was after five o'clock and everyone was gone. His duffle coat was the only one hanging at the row of hooks by the door. He went over and slipped his boots on, then bundled up against the February cold. Before leaving, he returned to Knight's desk to retrieve the copy of *Trend* for his wife, Doris, to read after dinner.

The magazine was open at the impressive spread on the story that just wouldn't die. There was Dafoe, in one photo standing nervously next to Hepburn at the ground-breaking ceremony. What a pair, Fellman thought; the obscure country doctor who had become the toast of the world, looking shy and out-of-place in almost every picture, and the larger-than-life premier who, without accolades and fanfare, looked in this photograph like he had the most to be pleased about.

Dafoe was transfixed by the sights of New York City from the moment the train pulled into Grand Central Station. The station platform, filled with hundreds of cheering and waving spectators, was the first. Signs of welcome were held high above the multitude of heads. It was all New York's finest could do to keep the crowd back until Dafoe was met by his tour organizer, a man named Applebaum, and escorted into a long black limousine.

"You know," Dafoe said to Applebaum in the back of the car, "at night, if the weather is clear, I can sometimes pick up one of your radio stations on my short wave." The folks back home were always impressed when Dafoe told them of the places he had picked up the night before. Until now, the distant voices had been his only friends.

Applebaum nodded politely. Just like a lot of stars, he thought. Nothing much to say.

The two motorcycle escorts circled to a stop in front of the Waldorf-Astoria, Manhattan's elegant new hotel. Once again, a crowd was waiting, this time in the circular drive that led to the hotel's grand entrance. It seemed as if all of New York had turned out for Dafoe's arrival. But then, an itinerary for the tour had been published in all the papers, giving his fans notice of where they could see him every hour of the day.

Many in the throng at the hotel had been waiting for hours, shivering in the cold. But the wait was forgotten, and the chill defrosted, the minute Dafoe's limousine pulled up. The entire crowd immediately burst into applause, and surged as close to the car as the police officers would allow.

When a few of the officers had managed to clear a safe passage to the doorway, Applebaum stepped out of the car and signalled Dafoe to follow. There were shouts for Dafoe's autograph, pleas for him to turn around for pictures, and simple screams of excitement.

Dafoe's head turned from this direction to that every time his name was called. These were the cheers normally reserved for athletes and movie stars, not doctors. It puzzled but, at the same time, warmed him. It meant they approved.

With Applebaum leading, the two of them made their way through the lobby, where more people gawked and cheered, and up the elevator to the hotel meeting room that had been specially set up for his press conference.

When the door opened and Dafoe entered, the sixty odd reporters and more than a dozen photographers all buzzed at once. Most of them had already been up to Corbeil; a few were seeing Dafoe for the first time. Nevertheless, he was familiar to them all. And so he should have been, for he was their creation. Their articles, their radio reports, and their newsreels had in nine short months made Dafoe the most famous doctor on earth. The fact that he was a simple GP, a dedicated country doctor who knew little of the world of big city hospitals and expensive research institutes, didn't hurt his image in the least. On the contrary; it gave the press their angle.

Dafoe, tracked by over seventy pairs of eyes, took his seat at a table lined with microphones. He looked at the group unassumingly.

They returned their own look of reverence. To them, he appeared every bit the character they had created.

"Gentlemen," shouted Applebaum over the din, "and ladies, thank you for coming." The buzz settled down to a quiet hum. "As usual, we don't have enough time; so please, keep your questions short. I'm sure Dr. Dafoe would like to answer as many of you as possible."

The reporters all yelled at once; some jumping up, others raising their hands. The organizer pointed to a handsome reporter from the *New York Times*.

"Dr. Dafoe?" asked the *Times* reporter, "what is the latest word on the babies?"

Dafoe leaned into the bank of microphones, remembering how he had handled the ground-breaking ceremony. A year ago, this type of equipment would have been foreign to him. Today, he knew to get just close enough so that his small voice would reach all corners of the room. "I'm pleased to say they're beginning to look like normal, healthy babies. They're not in the pink yet, but they're all gaining weight and coming along just fine."

"Who's taking care of them while you're here?" asked an older man from the *Mirror*.

"I've got a good staff of nurses in the hospital, and they'll be giving me daily reports by phone. If anything goes wrong, I can be back within a day."

A few photographers crawled out in front of the first row of chairs and took some shots. The flashes of light made Dafoe blink.

Applebaum noticed. "Uh, gentlemen," he pointed out politely, "could you please wait until afterwards to take your pictures. Thank you." He looked to his guest for approval, but Dafoe, who hadn't really minded the pictures being taken, didn't acknowledge the concern.

"Doctor," shouted an aggressive correspondent for *NBC*. "Would you say that the quints are over the danger period yet?"

"It's hard to say. As you know, this is the first time quintuplets have lived past a few days. With no medical history to tell us, we don't know what to expect. There's always a chance some new problem will crop up, so we just have to take things one day at a time. At least until they've made it past their first year."

The reporters scribbled down the generalities as if they constituted some enlightening medical sermon.

"Were you surprised to hear about your Nobel Prize nomination?" asked the editor of the *World*.

An *aw shucks* expression, perfectly suited to Dafoe's press image, crossed his face.

"It's an honour, of course, but I haven't made any discoveries or anything. All I've done is deliver some babies."

Everyone loved it, and wrote more furiously than ever.

Dafoe just smiled, knowing that it was his naivety they liked best. "They weren't the first," he added, "and if I know my French patients, they won't be the last."

The reporters tittered. Some even applauded the slur.

"While you're here, do you plan to consult with any hospitals about your techniques in keeping the quints alive?" It was the big voice of the *Herald-American* this time.

"Techniques?" These city folks always thought things had to be so complicated. "The only technique I've ever used is common sense. I kind of doubt that your doctors here could learn anything from me."

He was being honest, though some of the reporters laughed. For them, it was just the right touch.

"What are your plans for your first night in New York?" asked the *Daily News*.

"Well," he said shyly, "I hear you have some good shows playing. Wouldn't mind seeing one." He glanced sideways to Applebaum. "Never been to one."

That was all Applebaum needed to hear. "Yes," he said, as on the spot, he changed the evening's itinerary from a violin recital at Steinway Hall to Ethel Merman on Broadway. "We'll be going to one tonight."

"I hear you've been invited to our boss's Valentine's Day party," the female reporter from Hearst's *Journal* announced.

"Oh, yes," gushed Dafoe, having no idea of what a newspaperman's party would be like. "I guess I'll see all of you there."

Everyone took his last comment as a joke and started to laugh. But when they saw the puzzled look on Dafoe's face, some of them wondered if he was serious. Could he really be that naive? They looked to each other for the answer, and failing to find it, started to laugh again.

The doctor, at a loss, joined in.

Dafoe had never seen as lavish a house as the New York estate that belonged to William Randolph Hearst. The circular foyer was three times as big as the church hall back home. Crystal chandeliers hung from high ceilings. Broad French doors opened into massive rooms with white marble floors. Everywhere he looked, he spotted something that he had only imagined could be real. Even the pictures of royal palaces and Hollywood mansions that filled the pages of *Mayfair* gave no hint that homes like the one he was in now actually existed.

The ballroom in which the party was centred was filled with noise and colour. Beneath a flood of red balloons and cut-out hearts, sleek black tuxedoes paired off on the dance floor with gold and silver sequined gowns. Two grand pianos at opposite ends of the room, their pianists decked from head to toe in red silk, played endless choruses of *Anything Goes*. Many of the guests sang along. Some just ate and drank. Others played with the red doilies and napkins that lined the tables and looked about to see who was there. Still others chatted with old friends, all the while waiting, and hoping, for a chance to meet the guest of honour.

Hearst led Dafoe around the room like a prize pony, showing him off to selected friends. They passed by many of the less important guests, the *friends of the stars* that came to all of Hearst's parties. These people just smiled as Dafoe passed. They knew they were there to create noise, act outrageous, get drinks, and make some of the other guests feel more important than they actually were. Regretfully, they knew they were not there to actually meet the guest of honour, who was now headed in different directions and to greater heights than theirs.

Hearst and Dafoe approached a distinguished man of Dafoe's age.

"Doctor, I'd like you to meet William Astor."

"Very pleased to meet you, Doctor," said Astor, shaking Dafoe's hand rapidly. "You should be very proud of the job you've done." He took a sip from a glass of red wine.

"Thank you," Dafoe answered humbly.

"Mr. Astor is the owner of the hotel you're staying in, Doctor."

"Oh, really?"

"I hope you're enjoying your stay," smiled Astor.

"It's a lovely hotel."

"Why, thank you. We like to think so, but it's always nice to hear it from our most important guests."

Hearst spotted some eager faces across the room. He signalled to one, then another: promises that they would get their chance soon.

"I wish my wife were here." Astor's eyes searched the room. "She's flitted off somewhere, as usual. I know she'd love to meet you."

Hearst was already leading Dafoe away. "I'll do the honours if we bump into her." He waved above a group of heads. "Jeff, how are you?"

They walked over to join a man holding a cocktail in one hand and a heart-shaped cracker in the other. Next to him stood a tall attractive woman with a glorious tan and an emphatically red dress.

"I thought you'd never come over," Jeff told Hearst.

"Everybody wants to meet our man here," Hearst grinned. "Doctor, I'd like you to meet Jeff Casey."

Casey gulped down his cracker and extended his free hand. "Pleased to meet you."

"And his wife, Jane."

"A real pleasure." Mrs. Casey shook Dafoe's hand. "We're all just rooting for those girls of yours."

"Thank you, ma'am."

"We sure are," someone from behind shouted out. "But those awful parents!"

"We're all so lucky the quints are with someone as caring as you," Mrs. Casey continued.

Dafoe just smiled.

Hearst drew Dafoe's attention away from Mrs. Casey. "Jeff here is president of Colgate."

"Oh," said Dafoe, nodding to the first familiar name mentioned all day. "I use your dental cream all the time."

"Good. Glad to hear you say that."

"Those babies are just the cutest little things," gushed Mrs. Casey. "We watch them every month, getting older in those newsreels. It's like watching our own babies grow up."

"Funny you should mention that," bantered Dafoe. "I was just telling the people from Pathé yesterday that people aren't interested in seeing every little thing about them."

"Oh, but we are," Mrs. Casey insisted. "All my friends are."

"Perhaps we can meet a little later," suggested Jeff. "There's something I wouldn't mind discussing with you."

"Sure, why not?" Dafoe was agreeable to discussing anything with anyone.

Hearst was already heading toward another part of the room. "Doctor," he beckoned.

As they crossed the room, a sultry female voice spoke up from behind them.

"Mr. Hearst."

They both turned. Dafoe thought he recognized the pretty face, but couldn't quite place it.

"Aren't you going to introduce me?" the woman asked Hearst.

"Of course," said Hearst unceremoniously. "Doctor, this is Sally Rand."

"That's it! I knew I'd seen you before. I didn't recognize you at first without your...."

"I know," Sally smiled warmly. "Well, it's a real thrill to meet you."

"Why thank you, Miss Rand." He surveyed her long legs and firm body, hoping she didn't notice.

"I see Mr. Hearst is giving you the VIP treatment."

"Yes," Hearst replied on Dafoe's behalf. "And the doctor still has a lot of people to meet. If you'll excuse us."

Although a little hurt, Sally understood Hearst's impatience. Last year, she had been the star of this same party, and he had dragged her around to meet all of his fancy guests then, too. This year, it was Dafoe's star that was rising. "Good luck," she said, wrinkling her nose at Dafoe.

"Thank you." He watched her turn and leave, then nudged Hearst. "Not bad," he whispered, winking at Sally as she blended into the crowd.

The waving arm of Al Smith, the former New York governor, caught Hearst's eye.

"Here he is, Al. Dr. Dafoe."

"Doctor." Smith grabbed Dafoe's hand and shook it hard. "We've all been following your quints quite closely. It's a pleasure to meet the man who saved them."

"Just doing my job, Mr. Smith."

"You hear that, Bill?" chuckled Smith. "Just doing his job."

"You're a modest man, Doctor," said Hearst.

"I understand you'll be meeting one of my former opponents in a few days," remarked Smith.

Dafoe looked at him, confused.

"Roosevelt."

Dafoe didn't understand the connection and didn't try to. "Oh yes. And I'm looking forward to it." He still couldn't believe that he was going to meet the President of the United States.

"You give him my best," Smith laughed. "I hope, though, you'll have a little extra time before you run off to Washington to let me take you up to the top of the Empire State Building."

"Why not?" shrugged Dafoe, whose desire to see and do everything was as intense as that of a child who had stumbled into a magical castle.

"Why not?" chuckled Smith, walking away.

Hearst turned to Dafoe. "Are you enjoying yourself?"

"Yes," said Dafoe exuberantly. "Your friends are very nice."

"Not really," Hearst said with amusement, and headed straight for another group of eager eyes.

They continued their progress through the crowd, meeting politicians; sports figures; movie stars; a few business tycoons with their inevitably younger, diamond-studded wives; some ambassadors from foreign countries that Dafoe had reached on his short wave; a few models; a host of other pretty faces on the party circuit.

He loved it all. The colour. The frivolity. The people. The way they walked. The things they said. And mostly, the attention they heaped upon him. This may have been Hearst's annual Valentine's Day party, but for Dafoe, it was a coming-out of sorts. And although his debut was into a world that was quite new and different to him, it was one with which he was quickly becoming enchanted.

*   *   *

Every time Elzire wanted to see her babies, she had to leave the house, cross the road, go up the path to the Dafoe Hospital, knock on the door, wait for the nurse to answer, and ask if she could come in. It was a procedure she had followed every day, without exception, for the past six months. It was also a procedure she resented.

She hated everything about the hospital: the antiseptic smell; the sterile atmosphere; the prim, English-speaking nurses who always accompanied her into the nursery and made sure she didn't stay too long; the rules that governed virtually everything except the babies messing their diapers; and, most of all, her children being there in the first place. The fact that her babies lived in a hospital, not a real home.

Today, Elzire stood on the front porch of the hospital, waiting in the cutting wind for her hard knock to be answered. It was bitterly cold, and even though she had only to walk across the road, she had bundled up tightly.

It had snowed heavily the night before, and Oliva had cleared a path for her from their doorway to the road. From there, it was no problem, since the Government made sure that the road was regularly plowed all winter long. Quick and easy access for the trucks that were constantly making deliveries to the hospital was a Government priority.

When the door opened, Elzire found herself facing one of the new nurses – one that she had met only a couple of times before. *Harper* her name tag read.

"Hello, Mrs. Dionne."

"Hello. Are my babies awake yet?"

"Oh yes, they certainly are."

"Good." Elzire started forward, but Nurse Harper raised a hand to hold the door firmly in place.

"Uh, didn't Dr. Dafoe talk to you before he left?"

"About what?" Elzire asked, concerned. "Are the babies all right?" Why would he leave if they weren't?

"You know," the nurse implied, shifting from one foot to another. "Daniel's cold."

"What?"

"You know how the doctor is about germs," she said, trying to divert Elzire's anger. "He told us before he left not to let you or Mr. Dionne in. Not until he got back and checked everyone."

Right now, Elzire was too cold to be angry at the nonsense she was hearing. "It's freezing out here. Let me inside."

"I'm sorry, Mrs. Dionne."

"But *I* don't have a cold," Elzire said, frustrated. "And if you'll remember," she grumbled, "my children aren't allowed in here anyway."

"Please, Mrs. Dionne. If Dr. Dafoe were here now, maybe he'd say yes, but his instructions were very specific. You'll have to wait until he returns." She started to close the door – slowly, to avoid being rude.

"This is ridiculous." Elzire forced the door back open, and started to walk in once more. "Let me in."

The nurse blocked her path.

Elzire tried to slip by.

"Mrs. Dionne, please." The nurse was embarrassed, but continued to hold the door as firmly as she could.

"Will you excuse me?" Elzire tried one last time to remain calm.

"Please, Mrs. Dionne. I don't want to get into trouble. I'm just following Dr. Dafoe's orders."

"Well, I'm not," Elzire said firmly. "Now get out of my way." She pushed the nurse aside and quickly swept by her, marching past the staff room on the left, down the wide hallway that faced into the kitchen, turning right at the corner, and right again into her daughters' nursery.

Nurse Harper followed Elzire around the corner, but could only watch in amazement as Elzire closed the door to the nursery behind her. At the far end of the T-shaped hallway, she heard the sound of another door, and looked up to see Nurse Leroux coming out of the children's playroom. Nurse Harper stared at her colleague, speechless, not knowing whether she should admit her delinquency. She looked back to the closed door and shuddered. Dr. Dafoe would not like this at all.

7

Happy Birthday

R iding back into Callander, Dafoe was struck by how foreign familiar sights now appeared. The cold, frozen lake he had passed on the way in. The small station the train pulled into. The field next to the station, where his car sat alone, covered with snow. The fifty, not five hundred, people gathered there to greet him. The lonely turn-off to Callander. His house at the end of a long ride – not Hearst's mansion.

He dragged himself out of the car in front of the small red brick structure that was his home. As he stood up, the cold snatched at his breath and he noticed how the snow was piled into high banks on either side of the walk. More snow and colder than in New York, he thought, desperately trying to stretch the final moments of his journey.

His mind was still enveloped in memories of huge crowds, sustained applause, luxurious rooms, and fawning celebrities, when Mrs. Henderson rushed out to greet him, a big racoon coat wrapped around her.

"Doctor," she exclaimed with a big smile, genuinely glad to see him. "Welcome home."

"Mrs. Henderson, how are you?" he asked dryly, more out of politeness than of pleasure in her welcome. "It's good to be back."

"Now, don't keep any secrets from us. I've been hearing all about you on the radio." She reached into the back seat of the car to drag out the big black suitcase he had bought especially for the trip.

"It was just wonderful," he said dreamily. "I can't even describe it. You know where I was just two days ago? Sitting and having coffee with President Franklin D. Roosevelt himself." He paused, letting the impressive fact sink in. "Right in the Oval Office. You know, the round one."

"What was he like?" she babbled.

"Decent sort of man, you know. Just like you or me."

His matter-of-fact tone suggested a familiarity she knew did not exist, but she smiled anyway.

"We talked for fifteen minutes," he added proudly.

"You can tell me all about it. I've got a nice dinner on. I want to hear all about New York, too."

How could he explain, or she possibly understand? The trip was more a feeling than a series of events, momentous as those events had been. He could describe the sights he had seen, and tell her of the people he had met, and the things he had done, but that wouldn't convey how important he had been made to feel, nor the sheer excitement that all the recognition had caused.

"I'll tell you everything later."

"What do you have in here?" she asked, straining with the unexpected weight of the suitcase.

He reached to help her. "Never you mind," he said, thinking of the baby blue chenille housecoat he had brought back for her.

The woman's eyes lit up.

"You'll find out soon enough. Right now, I want to take a quick run over to the hospital."

He started lugging the suitcase up the walk toward the house, but Mrs. Henderson grabbed his arm. She hadn't wanted to tell him right away, and spoil the returning hero's welcome, but now she would have to. "Doctor?" Hesitation crept into her voice. "Before you go in, you should know, Oliva Dionne is waiting inside. He's been here almost an hour."

"Oh." The mention of Oliva's name pricked his balloon. He stalled half-way up the walk, the suitcase thudding to the icy ground. "What does *he* want?" he asked petulantly, knowing that it could be any one of a hundred different things he didn't want to deal with right now.

"He wouldn't say. But he's pretty upset, I'll tell you that."

"Great," Dafoe sighed. "I knew I should have stayed in New York. At least I was treated with respect there."

"Now don't you start getting highfalutin with me. I told him I wasn't sure if you were still coming back today." She didn't lie for just anyone.

"Obviously it didn't work," Dafoe answered.

"Just put yourself in his place," she implored. "Think how he must feel."

Dafoe started back up the walk, irritated by the thought of the discussion ahead. "He brings it on himself. Before, it was not being on the board. Now he's on the board – and getting a tidy salary, I might add – and he won't come to any of the meetings. Whose fault is that? Mine?"

"But you're the one in charge," she pointed out.

"Not as much as you think," he replied casually, wondering if the remark held more truth than he liked to think. "I guess the trip is really over now," he muttered on his way into the house.

"You be civil with him, now," she ordered, knowing that even that might be asking too much.

She had watched the relationship between the two men deteriorate steadily over the past nine months. Every conversation they had ended in an argument. Oliva would complain about something the nurses did; Dafoe would tell him to worry about farming and leave medicine to him. Oliva would say that his other children should be allowed to visit freely with their sisters; Dafoe would repeat his concerns about the amount of germs that children carry around with them. Oliva would point out that Elzire's motherly concern and perfectly natural way of handling the babies was being discouraged by everyone in the hospital; Dafoe would joke about how "you Catholics" have great imaginations. They couldn't agree on a single point.

Dafoe took a deep breath as Mrs. Henderson opened the door for him.

There, in the small waiting room to the right, off the hallway, waited Oliva. He sat upright in the hard wooden chair that stood alone in the corner of the room, by the window that looked out into the front yard. It was obvious to Dafoe that Oliva had chosen that chair so that he could watch for his arrival. Otherwise, he would have done what all the other visitors to that room normally did: sit in the big, comfortable, brown sofa along the far wall, and while away the time with the array of fascinating magazines spread across the sofa table. They were what enlivened everyone's visit to the doctor. Most of his magazines, like *Harper's*, the *Saturday Evening Post*, *Mayfair*, and *The Ladies' Home Journal*, were not otherwise available in that neck of the woods.

Oliva sprang out of his chair, leaving Mrs. Henderson standing between the two men like a referee at a boxing match. For a moment, that's how the doctor and the father acted. They were sizing each other up, looks of distrust passing back and forth between them, both of them reluctant to make the first move.

"Oliva." Dafoe forced a smile. "I hope you haven't been waiting long." He was determined to be pleasant, though he doubted that Oliva knew how.

"Well, well," Oliva jeered. "The Miracle Doctor, is it? I hear that... 'Manhattan took you to its hard-boiled heart'." Oliva's sarcasm about Dafoe's wildly successful trip was partly the result of unpleasant memories from his own brief trip to Chicago the previous month. Friends had suggested the idea as good public relations, an attempt to change the popular image of the family after the horrible Spear incident. Both he and Elzire had gone. But the plan had backfired. They had been left looking even more ridiculous than before, an outcome that only proved, as far as Oliva was concerned, that the Dionne story had already been scripted, the roles of hero and villain assigned.

"Must have been nice," Oliva said to the hero.

Dafoe's effort to be nice abruptly ended. The curved lips of his forced smile straightened and slipped downward. "What can I do for you, Oliva?" The tone was suddenly cold and businesslike.

"Why did you tell your nurse to keep my wife out of the hospital?" Oliva demanded.

"What?"

"Don't play innocent with me," Oliva warned. There was a dangerous light in his dark eyes, and his arms and neck were stiff with tension.

Retiring from the centre of the fray, Mrs. Henderson shook her head. "Here we go," she mumbled, wishing that Dafoe would, for once, take the time to listen to what Oliva was saying. More often than not, she agreed with Oliva, and told the doctor so. But he didn't listen to her any more than he listened to anyone else he considered beneath him.

"Look, Oliva," Dafoe wearily sighed, as he stripped off his fox-collared coat. "I've had a long trip. Can't we talk about this another time?"

"I don't care about your trip. I want to talk now."

"Mrs. Henderson," Dafoe said, still looking at Oliva, "would you take care of my unpacking, please? And call the hospital and tell them I'm on my way over."

"Yes, Doctor," she said, taking the suitcase with both hands and easing out of the room. She looked over her shoulder all the way out, then hefted the bag up the long, straight staircase, one step at a time.

Dafoe waited until he felt Mrs. Henderson was too far away to hear. "Now, what's this nonsense about my nurse?" To avoid direct eye contact with Oliva, he fumbled with the coat that was flung over his arm.

"She tried to keep Elzire out because of Daniel's cold."

Dafoe said nothing. He turned and hung his coat on the stand that was located near the doorway. It kept him from having to face the angry man.

"She said you left instructions."

"Oh, that," Dafoe remembered, finally facing Oliva.

The sound of quick footsteps.

"Doctor, how could you let that happen?" Mrs. Henderson had rushed down the steps and was back in the room on a wave of sympathy. "Poor Elzire."

Dafoe decided he could do without this conspiracy. "Mrs. Henderson," he warned, "please get out of here!"

"Well, I think that's the worst...."

"I don't give a damn what you think," bellowed Dafoe. "I asked you to take care of my unpacking."

"Okay, okay. You don't have to shout." She disappeared from the room as quickly as she had come in.

Dafoe sighed as she left, knowing he was going to get a full dose of her opinions later. He was tired of listening to them, as he was tired of repeating the same points to Oliva. "I've told you a hundred times what germs can do to the babies." He felt that he could explain it another hundred times, and Oliva still wouldn't understand.

"I'm sick and tired of hearing about germs," Oliva said through clenched teeth. "If my other children get sick, I don't keep them locked away from everybody else."

"That's just the point," lectured Dafoe. "The quintuplets aren't like your other children. They're not like any other children in the whole world. We can't take the chance of exposing them to any kind of germs, not even the common cold."

"Why don't you let me worry about that?" Oliva resented the implication that he couldn't take care of the quintuplets as he had his other five children. "What do you think I'm going to do to them?"

"You're not a doctor." Dafoe sidled over to his desk in the adjacent examining room. "They need medical protection, don't you understand that?" he asked. He was positive that he had always made the right medical decisions for the babies.

"What you really mean is protection from us." He glared at Dafoe, who didn't respond. "Elzire got in, you know. Nothing happened."

"She did?" He recalled the explicit instructions he had left for the nurses. He'd deal with *that* later. Right now, maybe he could end this ridiculous meeting. "What are you complaining about, then?"

"Why don't you admit that you love having all of us under your thumb?"

"It's not what you think. Not at all." Dafoe shuffled some papers on his desk. "Look at all this correspondence from the Government. Can't you see that the quintuplets belong to the world now?" His mind began to wander back to New York, to the memory of interested, approving faces.

Oliva was mystified. "What are you talking about?"

"Even *Time* wants them for its cover," Dafoe said dreamily. It was true. At Hearst's party, he had met Henry R. Luce himself. Luce had deferred to Dafoe as he would to a visiting head of state, whose loyal subjects the quints were. "*Time* magazine," Dafoe emphasized. "What do you think of that?" In his trance, he expected the news to have as much of an impact on Oliva as it had on him.

Oliva gawked at the absent creature before him and said nothing.

"And the newsreels," Dafoe added rapturously. "They're coming up in a few weeks to do something for the girls' first birthday."

"Their birthday isn't for almost three months." Oliva was still baffled, but less surprised at what Dafoe was saying. He could see that *le docteur* was slipping away.

"I know, but they have to film early to get the newsreels into the theatres in time for their real birthday. We've just moved the party up a bit." Dafoe talked as if it should make perfect sense to anyone. It had to him, when the people from Pathé had approached him in New York. He wouldn't have to agree to it if he didn't want to, but then, why wouldn't he? The attention of the world was focussed on the quints. How could he pass up the golden opportunity to share the spotlight?

"And all of that is more important than letting Elzire see the babies?" Oliva asked. "Her own children?"

"Times have changed, Oliva. Why don't you just enjoy what's happening?"

"Enjoy?" came the astonished reply. "You're out of your mind!"

In a manner of speaking, Dafoe *was*, and enjoying every minute of it.

Mrs. Henderson, still within earshot, couldn't restrain herself any longer. "Why don't you listen to him?" she called down from the top of the stairs, interrupting his daydream for the second time since he'd arrived. "He's making the only sense I've heard around here in a long time."

Dafoe was suddenly back in Callander. "Look, there's no point in discussing this any further. You obviously don't appreciate what's being done for your daughters."

"I don't believe this." Oliva's face stung with the heat of exasperation. "You haven't heard a word I've said." He turned and stormed out of the room.

Mrs. Henderson was on her way downstairs. "He's right, you know," she called out to Dafoe, who was still in his examining room. "You haven't heard a word anyone has said. I wouldn't blame him if he never spoke to you again."

"That would be fine with me," Dafoe shouted back, furious that a man of his position had to listen to this from her. And from Oliva. Neither of them could see that what was happening was for the best. He appeared in the hallway. "You're being foolish, Oliva," he chided, trailing after him.

But Oliva was already on his way out the front door, where he slammed past Mort Fellman, who was getting ready to knock.

"Hello to you, too." Fellman's head followed Oliva as he swept by without a word.

Dafoe wondered if Fellman had overheard any of the conversation. "Mort. Come in." He closed the door as soon as Fellman was inside. "How are you?"

"I'm fine." Fellman was so preoccupied by what had just happened that he almost forgot his reason for coming over. "I can see Dionne is happy that you're back."

"The things I put up with," Dafoe sighed, turning to see if Mrs. Henderson was still hanging around.

She was, and looked icicles at him.

"Have you finished that unpacking yet?"

"I was just getting to it," she sniffed, making a sour face and heading once more upstairs.

Dafoe led Fellman down the hallway and into the living room at the back of the house. The room was cluttered with dull furniture, remnants from Dafoe's predecessor. The walnut tables were stacked with books and magazines about every imaginable topic. Against one wall was a big RCA radio receiver. Next to it, on a table, his short wave. A brass floor lamp stood over a brown wing chair, whose seat was sunken from constant use. Dafoe collapsed into that; Fellman settled down on the settee directly opposite.

"What was that all about?" asked Fellman, intrigued by Oliva's hasty departure, not to mention Mrs. Henderson's lingering scowl.

"Don't even ask, Mort. You know, the same old thing."

"I can see that." Fellman was well aware of the growing discord between the Dionnes and Dafoe. Although he and Dafoe hadn't become friends, the doctor was beginning to confide in the young reporter. He needed someone in town to talk to, as more and more people in and around the hospital began to disagree with some of the things he was doing. Fellman himself had mixed feelings about the developing battle over the quints. At times, even he felt that Dafoe was overdoing it. If he were Dionne, he'd probably complain too. "He is their father, Doc. You have to expect that he would want his children back."

"Let's not get into it." Dafoe had had enough for one day. "I honestly wish that family would just disappear from my life," he added absently. "It would save a lot of aggravation."

Fellman was less surprised with the bluntness of Dafoe's comment than with the intensity with which it was stated. Dafoe obviously believed that he should be able to guide the Dionnes' destiny according to personal whim. He didn't like what the doctor was saying, not at all, but decided to remain silent. He shrugged instead.

"Anyway," resumed Dafoe, "enough about Oliva Dionne. Aren't you going to ask about my trip?"

"That's what I'm here for," Fellman said cheerfully, though he wished he didn't have to change the subject. "I read the wire reports every day. Sounded pretty exciting."

"It was chaotic." Dafoe rose. "But before we start," he announced coyly, "I'm going to fix you an Alexander. You know what that is, Mort?"

Fellman shrugged as Dafoe vanished into the kitchen.

"Hmm?" Dafoe had returned with a small bottle of cream.

"I bet that's one of those fancy drinks that you had in New York," Fellman replied.

"Walter Winchell – you know, the columnist – taught me how to make them," enthused Dafoe, back turned to Fellman as he measured and mixed at a corner cabinet.

Fellman shrugged again, thinking of more momentous and newsworthy things than a cocktail from New York. He wanted to get back to the revealing topic of Dafoe's feelings toward the Dionnes. But he knew, and had learned very early in his career, when to leave well enough alone. He didn't want Dafoe distrusting him before he was able to find out more.

*   *   *

The room was set up for a party, with decorations in abundance. But all the multi-coloured ribbons and crepe paper in the world couldn't hide the utilitarian nature of the Dafoe Hospital with its snow-white walls, sparkling grey linoleum, and glaring bare bulbs. Surely the roomful of chattering people, some of whom sported enormous smiles, could only be pretending the occasion was a festive one.

Fellman looked around the crowded room curiously. Festive was hardly the word to describe this staged event in honour of the quints' first birthday. How ironic, Fellman thought, that less than a year ago, his editor had considered moving the quints' birth to page two because of last-minute news of a break-in at the mayor's house in North Bay. Today's celebration would easily make the front page of every newspaper in the world.

The idea of moving the birthday up by two months was strange enough, but what puzzled Fellman the most was the absence of the type of guests you'd expect to see at a one-year-old's birthday party. There were no other children, no family, and no friends. Just lots of reporters, a newsreel crew, some Government officials, and the odd chicly dressed man or woman who nobody seemed to know. Like the man carrying the *Twentieth Century-Fox* bag. Everybody thought he was part of the newsreel crew – that's what Dafoe had said, anyway – but Fellman was doubtful. Pathé had the exclusive newsreel contract, not Fox-Movietone. Besides, the man never got around to doing anything.

The party was a rare treat for most of the invited guests. Until today, the public had not been allowed into the hospital. Most of the reporters were about to see the quints in person for the first time. The anxiousness on their faces was obvious.

"Look at how excited everyone is," Dafoe whispered to Fellman. "They're like a bunch of children."

The babble in the room was exhilarating, Fellman had to admit. "There's a bit of the child in all of us," he replied, not knowing if it was the right thing to say. "I'm pretty excited myself," he added.

"Won't be long now, Mort," promised Dafoe. "The newsreel crew is all set up. We're just waiting for Fred Davis to come in. He's doing a few outside shots while there's still some snow on the ground. The Americans love to see their quints pictured against the snow."

"Where are the *Time* photographers?" Fellman enquired, looking around. "I thought this whole thing was arranged for them."

"Well, it's for the newsreels too," Dafoe said. "But you know Davis has exclusive rights to photograph the babies. *Time* has to buy all their photos from him."

"You'd have to be a politician to understand everything that's going on," quipped Fellman.

"It's not that complicated yet." Dafoe looked away and waved at the man with the *Twentieth Century-Fox* bag, who had caught his eye.

"Who's that?" asked Fellman, pointing not to the man with the bag, but to a woman standing near the door.

"Who?" Dafoe followed Fellman's gaze to the shapely woman dressed in a mid-calf-length silk dress with the squarest of shoulders. "Oh, her. She's from Corn Brand, you know, the corn syrup people. Everyone's after us for endorsements these days. They think I'm going to let the babies advertise products they don't even use. What nonsense!"

Just then, Fred Davis walked through the door. He was immediately encircled by a group of men and women. Probably the *Time* writers, Fellman guessed. He observed how all of them were dressed more for work than for a birthday party. How appropriate.

"Excuse me, Mort," said Dafoe. "I've got to get this organized before they mob him." He darted off.

Dafoe had no sooner left his side when Fellman noticed Jack Sharkey, the quints' shrewd business manager, talking to the newsreel director from Pathé. They were standing in the corner of the room, and seemed to be having a heated dispute. He sauntered over, just close enough to listen to the conversation.

The two men were deliberating at great length about the guests at the party. The director felt that the more people there were, the more it would look on film like a real party. Sharkey meanwhile, felt that most of the guests shouldn't have been invited in the first place, let alone be allowed to appear in a movie with the quints.

Fellman wandered away. What did it matter? Whether they got in the film, or whether they didn't, none of the guests at this party belonged here anyway.

Fellman glanced over to Dafoe, who was unsuccessfully trying to disperse the handful of people who were hounding Fred Davis. It seemed that whoever had the goods on the quints was the man of the minute. When the babies were dying, it was Dafoe. Now that they were well and as cute as cute could get, Davis, with his photos, was the one in demand. Tomorrow, the situation would be different, and someone else would get the attention.

Just then, the door glided open. All heads turned as in came five nurses, each carrying one of the quintuplets. The room grew suddenly quiet, until one of the babies' cries initiated a thunderous applause, followed by a stream of excited chatter.

The quints had no sooner made their illustrious entrance when the newsreel director barked his first order. "Put them over there!" He pointed to the five highchairs that had been placed against one wall, where a backdrop resembling flowered wallpaper had been set up.

The guests tentatively shuffled forward, their eyes glued to the strange but wonderful sight in front of them.

Sharkey moved through the crowd, asking people he didn't recognize to stand back.

Dafoe, meanwhile, was fussing over the babies, all the while keeping a watch on Fred Davis' lens.

"Let's shoot before they start crying," the newsreel director announced indifferently to his people.

The lighting crew flicked on their klieg lights and aimed them at the quints, causing all five babies to squint and turn their heads.

"Great," complained the director, turning to Dafoe. "Can you do something about their expression, Doctor?"

Like a stage mother, Dafoe implored the children to look up at him and smile as the cameras rolled. He had a hard time, though, especially with trying at the same time to keep his own face turned to the camera.

"Okay," said the director, not particularly pleased with the highchair segment. "Let's do the presents now."

"How about the cake?" questioned Dafoe. "Shouldn't we do this in sequence? I mean, you always blow out the candles before you open the presents." He smiled, remembering.

"Excuse me, Doctor," the director said politely, as the cameramen and lighting crew moved their equipment to another corner. "We can't have candles. Not with the lighting in this room. And I'd just as soon shoot the presents scene without cake and icing all over the kids' hands. You understand?"

"I suppose so," said Dafoe, pondering for a moment. "That's show biz, I guess," he laughed, but the director, now talking to one of his cameramen a few feet away, hadn't heard. Dafoe looked to some of the reporters to share his thoughts, but they seemed preoccupied as well. A rumour was circulating that Jimmy Stewart was outside, asking to be let in to see the quints. That couldn't be true, Dafoe assured himself, or someone surely would have summoned him.

The camera focussed on a pile of about twenty presents. Dafoe knelt down and began to pick through them at random.

The five nurses marched over and sat the baby girls on the floor next to him. Each nurse moved slowly, with deliberation, as they went out of camera range, posing as they disappeared. How ironic, thought Fellman, that these small-town nurses, destined for jobs in small country hospitals and marriage to farmers or to men from the ranks of the unemployed, would be envied matinee stars in a few weeks' time.

Dafoe sat flat on the floor, legs splayed, with the babies climbing all over him. He opened present after present, showing them to the camera and to the babies. When the segment ended, he looked straight at the *Time* writers and pointed to the opened gifts. "You see, no gift from the Dionnes."

Fellman, ready to leave, turned and stared incredulously at Dafoe. He wondered if the doctor had really expected the Dionnes to send a gift, or if he was simply trying to ingratiate himself with *Time* for the big cover story they had planned.

It was just as well the Dionnes hadn't shown up, Fellman thought as he left the party. It would have been hard to write them into the script.

Elzire arrived on the doorstep of the Dafoe Hospital about eight o'clock that evening. She had waited until the newsreel crew had packed up and left before she started over. It was five hours past her usual afternoon visit, and she was anxious to see her babies.

"Elzire!" It was Dafoe, coat on and ready to leave, who answered the door. "We didn't see you at the party," he remarked, implying that she had actually been missed.

"I'll celebrate my babies' birthday when it comes," she said coldly. "And besides, I don't need to be invited to see my own children." She and Oliva couldn't believe it when they had received the invitation. It was bad enough that it had been sent, but had anyone really expected them to attend?

"Well, it would have been proper for you to be here," Dafoe lectured righteously. "You could have thought of that."

Although he had presented her with an opening, Elzire didn't want to get into an argument. Not now. She just wanted to see her children. "I'd like to see the babies for a little while," she said politely.

"I'd rather we didn't disturb them right now. They were pretty restless after all the excitement. The nurses had a hard time putting them down."

The refusal somehow didn't surprise her. She had watched the changes in le docteur since the birth of the babies. "Why don't you want me to see them?" she asked, struggling to remain calm. "What do you think I'm going to do to them?"

"Why don't you come over tomorrow?"

"I would like to kiss them goodnight, that's all."

Dafoe narrowed his eyes. "Look, Elzire, I'm not one of my nurses. You can't push me around. You had your chance. You could have seen them earlier like everyone else."

"But I want to see them now," she persisted. The frustration of being at someone else's mercy over seeing her own children was tearing her apart.

"I told you, they're sleeping. Now, I can't let you come in and wake them any time you want." He started to close the door.

Elzire was too shocked to resist.

"You really should have come to the party," he repeated as he shut the door.

Elzire's first reaction was to start pounding on the door again, and to keep doing so until it opened. But as she raised her hand, she heard the lock snap inside, followed by the sound of Dafoe's short footsteps fading down the hall – he was probably going to leave another instruction for his nurses before he went home. She stood there, tears welling in her eyes, incapable of comprehending what had just happened. The little control she had felt she still had over her babies was shattered in the futility of the moment. She dropped her hand from the storm door, letting it slam, and cried her way back across the road.

As soon as she walked into the house, Oliva saw that something was terribly wrong.

"What happened?" He was alarmed at how shaken she appeared.

She sagged into a chair and told Oliva about the encounter with Dafoe.

"That bastard thinks he can do whatever he wants to you," Oliva exploded. He prowled the kitchen in a rage, then grabbed his cardigan from the back of one of the kitchen chairs. "Well, not when it comes to me."

"Shh, Oliva, please," Elzire pleaded, thinking of the children asleep in their beds. "Let's not make any trouble. I'll see them tomorrow."

"Who does he think he is?" Oliva raved, not listening to Elzire's call for silence. "Come on!" He headed toward the front door.

"Where?"

"We're going to see the babies," he declared. "No one's going to tell you when you can and can't visit. Not any more."

Elzire remained seated. "No, Oliva. There's just going to be more trouble."

Her trepidation angered Oliva. "Do you want to see your children or not?"

Elzire faced him, afraid to say anything. Especially something like *let's not make things worse.* That would really rile him.

"Then, come on." Oliva marched over to the table, grabbed her by the hand, and led her out the door.

"No, Oliva, please!"

Oliva stalked across the road, the dividing line between home and hospital, towing Elzire in his wake. As they approached the hospital, Elzire tugged on his arm and urged him to turn back, at least until he calmed down.

"What are you so afraid of?" he asked, stopping for a moment.

"I can't take another fight," she said, drained from the recent encounter.

"There isn't going to be any fight." He continued pulling her up the path. "We're going to see them, and that's that."

Oliva rapped hard on the hospital door. The nurse on duty answered, but before she could say anything, Oliva spoke up. "We're here to see our children," he announced.

"They're sleeping." The nurse watched Oliva nervously. He looked as if he'd been prepared to tear the door off its hinges had she not answered promptly. Then, she noticed Elzire hiding behind Oliva. "I thought Dr. Dafoe just told Mrs. Dionne that."

"He did," Oliva answered sharply, determined that this time, there would be no discussion. He flung the door open with a bang and marched past her, leading Elzire down the hall and around the corner toward the nursery.

The flustered nurse trailed behind. "Wait," she shrieked. "You can't go in there."

Oliva stopped outside the door. "No?" he said, as he turned and stared her into retreat. "Stop me."

The nurse could only look helpless, much as Elzire had in the confrontation with Dafoe just minutes before.

Oliva quietly opened the nursery door and prodded Elzire in ahead of him.

The nurse dashed to the telephone on the desk in the front hallway. Her hand shook as she held the receiver, waiting for the operator to answer. Her heart was pounding, but she wasn't sure why. She didn't even know who she was most afraid of: the angry father and desperate mother who had just forced their way in, or the doctor, whose reaction would be outrage when he found out she had let the Dionnes into his hospital.

Mrs. Henderson shook her head as she put the telephone receiver down. She heard a car outside and looked out the window to see

Dafoe pulling up. She ran down the hall, and was standing in the open door as he swung his leg and ducked his head to climb out of the car.

"The hospital just telephoned," she called out nervously. "They want you to go right back."

"What's wrong?" he asked. "The babies?"

"Just get back there right away," she repeated. "I knew this would happen sooner or later."

"What?"

"The Dionnes forced their way in."

Dafoe swung back inside the car and started it again.

"And I don't blame them after the way you've treated them," she continued. "Your little nurse is all panicky. Serves her right for taking a job in that prison of yours. I bet she'll quit like all the others, too."

Dafoe had already pulled away, and was racing down the road when she shouted a final "Be careful" to the little man she had once felt a need to protect, but from whom she now felt the need to protect others.

By the time Dafoe arrived at the hospital, he was fuming. Damn Oliva. Why couldn't he leave well enough alone?

He leapt out of the car, up the steps, through the front door, and past two waiting nurses. "They're still in there?" he asked, running down the hall as fast as his short stride would permit.

The nurses followed him around the corner toward the nursery. "He said Mrs. Dionne is going to stay all night," one of them said. "On the floor if she has to."

"We'll see about that." He was determined to let no one but himself set the rules in his hospital. Least of all, Oliva Dionne.

Dafoe opened the nursery door. The lights, except for one small lamp near the doorway to the private bathroom, were off. He could barely see Elzire, who was beside a crib holding one of the babies. Oliva leaned over another of the cribs. "Oliva," Dafoe hissed, "you can't come barging in here any time you feel like it."

Oliva told Elzire to stay put and walked over to meet Dafoe near the door. "Keep your voice down," he said. "They're sleeping. They've had a busy day, remember?" He eased Dafoe out and followed, closing the door.

The nurses watched fearfully as the two men stood facing each other just outside the nursery.

"What the hell do you think you're doing, breaking in here and intimidating my nurses?"

"Don't lecture me. I've had it with your telling my wife when she can and can't see her own children."

"This is *my* hospital, Oliva, and I set the visiting hours."

"I don't care about your visiting hours any more," Oliva said boldly. "From now on, we're going to come whenever we want, and leave when we're ready to."

"I'll have to tell the board about this," Dafoe threatened.

"Tell your damned board anything you want," Oliva said defiantly, opening the door to go back inside.

"Don't make me call the police," Dafoe cautioned, almost wanting Oliva to push him that far.

"You can call in the army if you want," Oliva brazened through the crack of the closing door. "We're not leaving." The door shut in Dafoe's face.

Dafoe was almost purple with rage. He strode down the hall, past the telephone in the main hallway, past the playroom, and into his office at the far end. He shut the door, and didn't reappear until two police officers arrived a few minutes later.

Dafoe stood smugly behind the two uniformed policemen as they ordered Oliva and Elzire out of the nursery and out of the hospital.

Oliva was just as defiant with them as he had been with Dafoe. "If you want me to leave," he roared, "you're going to have to arrest me and put me in handcuffs." But when they threatened to do exactly that, Elzire begged them not to. And when Oliva wouldn't leave with her, she started to walk out by herself. On top of everything else, she didn't need her husband in jail.

Dafoe stood at the doorway, the policemen by his side, watching Elzire and then Oliva retreat into the cool March night. He felt more relieved than triumphant. For it was clear that he hadn't really beaten them this time. He just had the law on his side.

*   *   *

Hepburn sat contentedly, enjoying his morning coffee in the plant-laden conservatory of his big house. As he skimmed the early edition of the *Toronto Daily Star*, the sun shone through the window and reflected off the brass flower boxes under the windows. He thought of what a beautiful day it was going to be.

It was one minute to the hour, so he switched on the radio and waited for the news, already knowing what the top story would be.

"A rumoured plot to kidnap the Dionne Quintuplets," the newscaster announced, "has prompted the Government to increase security around the Dafoe Hospital. A Government spokesman said steps are being taken to prevent another Lindbergh tragedy, and to ensure that our quints are safe twenty-four hours a day."

When Dafoe had called last night to tell him about the Dionnes' invasion, Hepburn had quickly realized the opportunity that could result from a confrontation. He had heard that the Dionnes were sending letters to everyone – the Prime Minister, the King and Queen, even the Pope – asking for help in getting their babies back. If a supportive reply were to result from any one of these pleas, his Government would have a real problem on its hands. This attempt of the Dionnes to "break into the hospital", as Dafoe has phrased it, couldn't have come at a better time. His advice to Dafoe: be very strict with them.

"The new security measures have been applauded by Dr. Allan Dafoe," the newscaster continued, "who, when contacted about the plans, said that he was all for making sure the quints were safe from all possible intruders."

Hepburn was pleased with himself. He switched off the radio, thinking that by this afternoon, newspapers and radio stations from New York to Tokyo would be headlining the story. And even before that, the workmen would be starting outside the hospital. The barbed-wire fence, the guardhouse, the reinforced gates – all would be installed in record time. The hospital compound would be secure; the grounds, a fortress endorsed by the whole world.

And soon, very soon, his own carefully constructed infant industry could begin.

8

Quintland

T he three of them sat in Hepburn's office with the door tightly closed, conspiring as they had countless times in the last year. Sharkey did most of the talking, reading from an open file, while Hepburn offered the occasional grunt, accompanied by either a mischievous or a worried look. Slocum just sat there, looking mainly at his boss, ready to offer moral support whenever it was needed.

Sharkey pulled a letter from his attaché case and carefully placed it in front of Hepburn, who barely glanced at it.

Slocum leaned forward to read the letterhead upside down. "Palmolive," he remarked, impressed.

"Uh-huh," acknowledged Sharkey, oozing with pride. This wasn't just *any* endorsement. Finally, here was a product that the quints actually used. Even Dafoe couldn't fight this one, though they all would have been surprised if he did. It had become increasingly easy to persuade the doctor to change the hospital's brand of corn syrup or cereal if the price was right.

Slocum and Sharkey both looked to Hepburn for a reaction, but this time the premier had nothing to say. He leaned back in his chair and folded his hands. His eyes wandered.

Sharkey pulled the letter back, and started to leaf through a thick file in his attaché case. "Carnation, Lysol, and Remington Rand are renewing." He readied another pitch. "And I just got word this morning that Quaker Oats is signing for thirty-one thousand."

Still no reaction.

The two men regarded Hepburn curiously, wondering if he had even been listening to Sharkey's phenomenal update.

"Impressive," Hepburn finally obliged, though not sounding impressed at all.

Although Sharkey's eyes remained on the papers in his file as he proceeded, he was happy with the acknowledgement from Hepburn, however small it had been. "Pathé is coming up for renewal too. I think we're looking at an extra five grand per short. And here's my prize." He looked to Slocum, who waited anxiously. "Twentieth Century-Fox wants to sign the quints to a three-picture deal." The man from the studio had told Sharkey that they were impressed with the quints' screen presence in the newsreels. "So far, they're offering a one hundred thousand dollar cash advance against ten per cent of the net."

"So now we're in the movie business," was Hepburn's comment.

"I'm holding out for a bigger percentage of the net, though." Sharkey was thinking that the possibility of a financial windfall might register with Hepburn. "We'll get it, too. They know the quints are big business."

Hepburn knew that too. In fact, he sometimes thought that he was the only one who knew just how big. If Sharkey was willing to settle for penny-ante endorsements and some exposure on the screen, that's all they would ever get out of this. He had bigger plans. His eyes focussed on the two men across his desk.

"How's the trademark registration going?" he asked.

"It's not as easy as we'd hoped," Sharkey replied. "The word *quintuplet* is in the dictionary."

"But they're the only ones!" Hepburn ruled.

"Don't worry, it should go through."

"Good." The premier leaned forward to rest his elbows on the desk. "Things seem to be going well."

"I'll say," commented Slocum, looking over at Sharkey and nodding appreciatively.

"But in all fairness," Hepburn proclaimed, "all we're doing is lining a few pockets."

Slocum looked back to the premier, wondering what he could possibly be thinking.

"And building a tidy little trust fund for those girls," Sharkey added defensively.

Hepburn nodded, well aware of what the quints were getting out of his Government's efforts. But right now, he was more interested in what the Government could get out of the quints. "We should be doing something with this that will help the people of this province," he announced. "Something that will bring some general economic benefit to everyone."

Slocum looked to Sharkey for clarification, but recognized instantly that Sharkey didn't understand any more than he did what Hepburn was talking about. What more could they do to cash in on the babies?

"We've got to let people *see* the quints," Hepburn explained. "Not just in ads or on the screen, but in person."

Sharkey nodded enthusiastically, as if he had known what Hepburn had meant all along. "You won't get any arguments from me."

But Slocum was not as readily agreeable with this manifesto. "You mean put them on display?" he asked, remembering that Hepburn had mused about the possibility before. He should have known that the premier was serious even then. Hepburn rarely joked without purpose.

"Imagine," said Hepburn, who had already done some vivid imagining of his own, "hundreds of thousands of tourists – people who have followed the quints in newspapers, magazines, and newsreels since they were born – all heading up to North Bay, spending money there and back. On food, fuel, lodging – the works."

Slocum looked away. He didn't want to agree with the strange plan too quickly. After all, letting a movie studio come in and film the quints wasn't too different from letting the newsreel companies come in and shoot them. But putting them on display for the public? Like animals in a zoo?

"In theory, it sounds okay," he lied, "but it could look like exploitation."

"Exploitation?" barked Hepburn, making Slocum wish he hadn't said the word. "I'll tell you what exploitation is. The girls are getting..." he turned to Sharkey, "... how much, did you say, from Quaker Oats?"

"Thirty-one thousand."

"Thirty-one thousand dollars." Hepburn let the figure linger. "For eating cereal they would be eating anyway."

Slocum shrugged. Hepburn had a maddening way of making everything seem logical.

"Now, you tell me – who's exploiting whom?" Hepburn asked. "Those girls have a pretty sweet deal as far as I can see. My God, they would have died if it hadn't been for us."

Slocum hadn't thought that the hospital had been built with the idea of making it pay for itself later. "I'm sorry, but I think some people will feel funny about it." Himself included.

"Don't you think it's time we spread the money around a bit?" Hepburn asked, piercing him with those penetrating eyes that had humbled stronger men.

"They're an untapped oil well," Sharkey agreed exuberantly. He was not smart enough to come up with such a plan on his own, but he was quick enough to recognize its benefits. "Their potential economic impact is enormous. They could revitalize the whole province. All we have to do is build a fenced-in playground, or something like that, right outside the hospital. People can watch them play."

"That's what most kids do anyway," Hepburn rationalized. "There's no harm."

"Within six months," Sharkey projected, "we could have one of the top tourist spots in the country."

"Better than that," Hepburn assured them. He noticed Slocum's look of displeasure. "We wouldn't charge admission, Dick, if you're worried about that."

Slocum was surprised at how easily both men defended the idea. They made the concept of showing the quints seem inevitable. Maybe it was, but that didn't make it right. He would have to agree, since it was his job to do so, but he wasn't going to gush over it. "People could very easily take it the wrong way," he stated flatly. "I'm not even sure how I feel about it, and I know your intentions." Or he thought he did.

Hepburn offered his ultimate justification for everything. "But the public wants it."

"It never hurts to give the voters what they want," Sharkey added.

"I guess not," Slocum hedged, still not convinced.

"You know," Sharkey said, "it might be a good idea to get Blatz up there."

Slocum looked at Sharkey blankly. He had heard the name, but couldn't place the context in which he had heard it.

"You know. William Blatz, the child psychologist."

"Oh, yes." He remembered reading about him somewhere. "The one who wants to observe the girls?"

Sharkey's eyes opened wide. "You mean the one who would *kill* to observe the girls. He's been writing to Clayton for months now. I'm sure he'll endorse whatever we're doing if we invite him to study the quints."

"Perfect," said Hepburn. He admired Sharkey's ingenuity. Not a great idea man, but effective when you start the wheels turning for him. He looked at Slocum. "Still worried about public reaction?" He linked his fingers, clasped his hands behind his head, and leaned back. "With Blatz there," he smiled confidently, "we'll have the support of every mother in the country."

*　　*　　*

Tante Legros and Madame Lebel stopped dropping in to see Elzire as frequently as before. They had caught wind of what the Government was planning and, well, everyone needed the money these days.

*　　*　　*

The traffic going south on the Ferguson Highway was backed up all the way to North Bay. Cars of every make and model, with licence plates representing every part of North America, sparkled in the hot July sun as they lined the jet black highway that had been paved to speed visitors to the new attraction. But *speed* was not the word to describe the pace of the traffic today. In fact, the hundreds of people that walked the roadside were often luckiest, reaching their dream sooner than the cars did.

William Blatz was one of the unlucky, still stuck in traffic. He had strictly followed the instructions in the telegram from Clayton, leaving his hotel in North Bay early that morning, before seven o'clock. At first, there had been no traffic at all. In fact, as he breezed along the lakefront in his De Soto, he wondered if he should have left so early. But by the time he reached the highway, he was only one of a steady stream of cars heading south. It got progressively worse as he continued, and by the time he reached the sign that read *Callander 3 Miles, Corbeil 5 Miles*, he was locked in bumper-to-bumper traffic.

Crawling along the smooth highway, Blatz noticed how prosperous this area seemed in comparison to the other communities he had passed on his way from Toronto yesterday. Houses had their shutters intact, fences were freshly painted, road signs stood erect on the shoulder, flowers blossomed everywhere, and *welcome* signs existed in abundance. How nice, he thought, that the quints were bringing such joy and prosperity to the world about them.

The turn-off for the road that led to the Dafoe Hospital appeared in the distance. He could see beyond it to a long line of cars coming from the opposite direction, from Toronto and other points south. They were all stopping at the crossroads where two men carrying red flags were directing traffic. As Blatz watched, one of the cars turned left, to Callander. The rest turned right, alternating one by one with the cars in his lane, which were turning left. Soon, it was his turn. He drove under a red-and-white banner marked *WELCOME TO THE HOME OF THE WORLD-FAMOUS DIONNE QUINTUPLETS*, and passed a gas station with five identical pumps, each named after one of the quints. Further along there were cottages, cabins, guesthouses, and eateries, from whose lots more cars pulled out and joined the procession. His car crept on, through heavy woods, around curves, and up and down the hills that would eventually take him to his magical destination.

He inched along the road, one link in a chain of metal, noise, and fumes that stretched from one horizon to the other. It was past eight-thirty, and he had spent more than half of his time on the road travelling the last ten miles. He wished he could leave the car where it was, and join the excited hundreds that walked quickly along the roadside or in the oncoming lane, which would not be filled with departing cars until the end of the day. He crept up yet another incline, the last, and there it was: a haven in the great Canadian North – *Quintland.*

The sight before him was not what he had expected. Not by any stretch of the imagination. Acres of stony farmland hardly possessed the natural grandeur of Niagara Falls, Quintland's closest rival in 1935 for the distinction of being the continent's top tourist attraction. Just as the handful of red-painted log buildings failed to recall the physical magnificence of the Great Pyramids of Giza, to which some travel brochures had already compared Quintland. In fact, all Quintland seemed to be was a scattering of nondescript cabins, lost for the moment in a massive parking lot. The proportion of the crowd to the immediate geographical area and buildings made no sense. This looked more like a summer camp for twenty normal-school boys, not the mecca that all of North America was pouring in to see.

The structures closest to him were two small log houses. He pulled out the site plan. The red one to the left was the new staff house, the older whitewashed one to the right, the Dionne home. His eyes rested for a moment on the plain-looking farmhouse that had raised such controversy. But his attention was quickly diverted to a second red log building, longer and larger than the staff house and located just past it on the left. The Dafoe Hospital. It was smaller than it appeared in the many photographs Blatz had seen, but was nonetheless imposing behind the barbed-wire fence that surrounded it.

The cars ahead of Blatz passed the guarded entrance to the hospital on the left, and continued for a few hundred feet until they turned into the cleared field that served as a public parking lot. Blatz stuck his arm out the window to signal that he wanted to turn left at the guard gate, but the gesture was not enough, the procedure not so simple. As he paused to start easing out of line, horns blasted from behind. A few heads were thrust out of car windows, yelling: "Come on, mister, get going!" and "What's the hold-up?"

But Blatz couldn't move any faster. The left-hand lane was filled with people, all moving in the same direction as the cars. They were hurrying to join a line-up a little further down the road. No one would let him pass.

He allowed his car to roll forward, ever so slowly, causing the anxious people walking along the road to shout protests. Listening to variations of "Get out of our way!" and "Hey, are you trying to kill us?", Blatz inched his way through the river of pedestrians. He was determined not to let their impatience ruin this special occasion for him. Finally, he was able to complete his turn. He stopped in front of the little guardhouse at the locked gate of the Dafoe Hospital.

One of the two guards in the hut came out and approached him.

Blatz greeted the man cheerfully, relieved to finally be there. "Hello, I'm Dr. Blatz."

"May I see some identification, sir?" the guard asked formally.

From the rustic surroundings, Blatz had expected a camp leader, not an official guard. "Certainly." He flipped through his wallet, enjoying the privilege of being allowed special entry, and flashed his operator's licence.

"Go ahead," the guard commanded, sticking a key into the padlock that secured the gate. "Quickly, please."

Blatz didn't understand the urgency until after the gate opened and he had driven through. Through his rearview mirror, he could see a frantic crowd trying to rush in after him. The guard shut the gate just in time to stop them.

Blatz's heart was pounding heavily as he proceeded up the driveway to the hospital entrance and parked close to the porch steps. He slid out of the car, then stood for a moment, taking in the spectacle.

The cars just kept coming, down the hill, past the hospital, and into the parking lot. He shook his head in awe. There must have been a thousand cars trying to cram into the lot, and it wasn't even nine o'clock.

The crowds emanating from the parking lot turned to the right and joined the stream of humanity that Blatz had been forced to ford in order to reach the hospital. No wonder they were in such a single-minded hurry, Blatz thought. From here, he could see how the queue, obviously for the observation gallery, already stretched out of sight over a small hill in the distance.

Before climbing onto the porch, Blatz decided to walk around to the side of the hospital that faced the road, in order to get a better look at the observation gallery itself. A wall partly obscured it, but he was able to see beyond it a part of the peculiar horseshoe-shaped log structure that filled the remaining grounds inside the fence. Like the other buildings that comprised Quintland, the gallery was smaller than he had expected. In contrast was the swelling mob of people that stood before the gates waiting to get in. There must have been three thousand of them.

Blatz turned to face across the road, and again noticed the little farmhouse on the right. From here, it was only partly concealed by the high wooden wall that completely shielded it from the parking lot and from the view of the tourists in the line-up. A board fence separated the rest of the Dionne property from the outside world. The secluded house didn't seem to suit this busy atmosphere, he thought. Or maybe it was the other way around.

Blatz finally walked back around to the porch, climbed up to the door, and knocked.

The tall nurse who answered the door spoke before Blatz could identify himself. "You must be Dr. Blatz."

"Yes, I am."

"Please come in," she said. "We were expecting you."

Just before stepping into the hospital, he looked back toward the road. The gates to the observation gallery had just swung open. People were pushing and scrambling to be first into the gallery. Like Blatz, they were anxious and, right now, much closer to seeing the objects of their desire.

He looked at his watch. It was nine o'clock on the dot.

Dafoe looked at his guest warily. He had extended the usual pleasantries to Blatz, albeit cautiously. Until now, he had enjoyed complete control over the quints, at least within the hospital compound, and he didn't relish the idea of sharing that with anyone. From the day Clayton had told him that, despite his objections, Blatz would be coming to study the quints, Dafoe had been worried. He had imagined Blatz as a haughty psychologist who would waltz in full of fancy ideas on how to raise the girls. He had decided there would be none of that in the Dafoe Hospital.

When they entered his office, Dafoe had purposely sat at his desk in the far corner of the room, rather than in one of the two comfortable armchairs along the window wall. He wanted to demonstrate his authority over Blatz, and had read somewhere that sitting across the desk from your guest asserted your position.

Blatz sat in the slippery leather chair in front of the desk.

Dafoe tried his best to be welcoming, but his words contained only false warmth. "It's an honour to have you here, Dr. Blatz. I've admired your theories for quite some time. Rather... new, don't you think?"

"You're very kind." The controversial director of the Institute of Child Study at the University of Toronto, a leader in the new field of child guidance, didn't mistake the neutral comment for a compliment. "Most people refer to my work as more daring than new."

"Of course, out here the folks don't have much of a mind for these new ideas on raising kids."

"I guess they figure the old ways have suited them just fine." Blatz smiled. "Some of my colleagues feel the same way."

Dafoe laughed out of politeness, then decided he could not put off the inevitable any longer. "Would you like to see the girls?" he asked, sounding very much like a proud father.

"Yes, very much," Blatz replied eagerly. "If you don't mind, that is?"

"Well, we usually don't interrupt when the nurses are getting them ready for the show, but I think we can make an exception for you,

Doctor." Dafoe's tone suggested that he liked the visitor, but also implied that Blatz should feel indebted for the great privilege of seeing his prized jewels.

"Splendid." Blatz got up, noticing the framed photo of Dafoe and Hepburn on the wall behind the doctor's back.

Dafoe rose and ushered his guest out of the office.

"Would you mind if later on I saw your records on how the girls spend their day?" asked Blatz, as they walked down the hall together.

"Records?" Dafoe didn't like the inquisitiveness behind the question. "What kind of information are you looking for?"

"Oh, anything written down. Routines, procedures, anything. At your convenience, of course."

Dafoe thought for a moment. "I have to tell you, Doctor, we don't run this place like one of your big city hospitals. I'll have a look through the files later, but I can't promise you anything."

"Fine. Also, if you don't mind, I'd like to set up a schedule for the girls from the time they wake up until they go to sleep at night."

"Hmm," Dafoe sighed, beginning to feel like a boy on the beach whose sandcastle is about to be broken.

"Does the family visit often?"

Dafoe hesitated before answering, unsure of what Blatz wanted to hear. "Oh, once in a while," he began, then added for insurance, "pretty regularly I guess. Why?"

"Well, the kind of schedule I have in mind is very tight," Blatz explained. "In order to get the most from my observations, there should be as few deviations as possible. We'll have to arrange for *some* family time, of course, but I wouldn't want it to interfere with our work."

"No, we wouldn't want that," returned Dafoe, his fears allayed for the first time since their conversation had begun. He was even more relieved when they reached their destination, the quints' nursery. His territory. "Here we are."

"So they're getting ready for the show."

"Yes. We have our own routine here. Twice a day. They just play in the little park inside the observation gallery. They don't even know that anyone is there."

"Even if they did, there's no real harm," Blatz assured him. "It's no different than children playing in a schoolyard under the watchful eye of a teacher."

"True, true," Dafoe concurred, blocking from his mind comments he had heard, even from some of the staff, that it was wrong to show the girls publicly.

"How do they...." Blatz stopped, as one of the nurses, holding a small sewing basket, excused herself and hurried past them into the room. As the door swung open, his eyes widened, and he forgot his question. For there, not ten feet away, were the Dionne Quintuplets.

Even after seeing them countless times in newspapers, magazines, and newsreels, he wasn't prepared for this great moment. He shifted his eyes from one quint to the other, trying to discern a difference between them. But he couldn't. It was like watching a puppet show, but with five living, breathing human beings. He watched as the nurses carefully brushed hair, tied ribbons around curls, and straightened bows on five identical dresses.

Blatz was transfixed. He stared, his eyes like saucers, his mouth gaping open. Behind him, Dafoe watched, enjoying the effect his girls were having on the famous psychologist. Then, while Blatz's eyes were still fixed on the quints, Dafoe closed the door, a blatant demonstration of his control over access to them.

"Well," Dafoe asked, "what do you think?"

Blatz tried to hide the thrill under a scientific veneer, but couldn't. "Extraordinary," he said, shaking his head. "Quite extraordinary."

"They're something, aren't they?"

Blatz started to ramble. "Seeing them like this... in such controlled conditions... few outside stimuli...." He shook his head again. "There's so much we can learn. If you don't mind, I'd like to observe them during their free play."

"You don't need my permission, Doctor," said Dafoe. He liked Blatz's term for the show. "Please make yourself at home."

Blatz was escorted by one of the hospital guards to an enviable spot at the front of the line-up that stretched outside the gates, up the road past a clapboard structure called the Midwives' Souvenir Pavilion, and over the hill toward Corbeil. A number of heads poked out of line and shouted: "Hey, no butting in!" and "Wait your turn like everybody else!" When they were told by the guard that this was the quints' doctor, the cries changed to "It's our turn! He can see them any time he wants!" and "That's not Doc Dafoe!" No one deserved the privilege of getting in ahead of those who had waited hours to see their cherished quints. Blatz found the public's fascination with the babies equally fascinating, and made a mental note to later observe the types of people in the line-up.

The double doors of the observation gallery opened onto two long corridors that stretched along either side of the playground, all the way to the wall of the Dafoe Hospital. The walls that separated the visitors from the quints' open-air playground were constructed of glass from waist height up, and from one end of the gallery to the other. On the playground side of the glass was a fine-meshed wire barrier, designed to block the quints' view of the eager thousands that filed through to see them each day.

Blatz was glad he had chosen this vantage point instead of the window in the door through which the quints entered their public playground. From there, all he would have been able to see was a corner of the little stage, the edge of the sandbox, and the broad back of the oversized doll house. From inside the gallery, he could at least stand on his toes and peer over other visitors' heads to get a full view of the girls running in and out of the doll house, dancing with each other, and surging forward to the dividing glass to respond to the constant tapping and hum of voices.

For a moment, Blatz thought that one of the quints was posing for the woman standing next to him. The woman was crying with relief in finally seeing *her* quints. He considered the possibility that the girls could actually see their visitors, but before he could get a good look, the continuous flow of people had pushed him down the corridor and out the exit. He sneaked a quick last look before stepping out into the real world. The posing quint had gone back to playing with her toys and her sisters.

Blatz walked around the grounds later that afternoon, digesting the spectacle that Canadian travel brochures promoted in the United States as *Canada's Coney Island*. Not quite, Blatz thought. No flashing lights, rides, or spin-the-wheel games. But nonetheless colourful, for Quintland had its own rudimentary midway. There was a look-out terrace atop the midwives' pavilion, a bin full of free fertility stones, a caged bear, an Indian in a teepee with whom you could have your photo taken, some hotdog and lemonade concessions, and several knick-knack stands. There were even public toilets.

"Where's the rides?" cried one young boy, straining to loosen his mother's tight grip. He had been expecting the type of country fair that rolled into town once a year.

"Never mind rides," his mother admonished. "You don't need rides."

No, this wasn't a country fair. Not quite Coney Island either, Blatz thought again, but then Coney Island didn't have a sideshow to compete with the Dionne Quintuplets.

He walked past the many people who were lining up for the afternoon show, past the anxious parents and children, businessmen and farmers, rich and poor, old and young. There was such excitement. An incredible contrast to the quiet isolation of the farmhouse across the road.

He walked alongside people who didn't even notice he was watching them, and listened raptly as murmurs of anticipation gradually turned into squeals of delight. He joined the line-up, and walked back into the observation gallery with what was probably the tenth wave since the afternoon showing had begun at two o'clock.

A different crowd every ten minutes, Blatz thought, imagining the millions of people that would come. The only thing that would remain constant would be the show – five identical girls playing for the changing crowds that would come to see them twice a day, week after week, summer after summer, year after....

Part Two

"Dr. Dafoe is the Quins' favorite human, much more liked than Papa or Mama Dionne (who) are still disgruntled that their children have been taken away from them and sometimes complain that the whole Dionne family could get rich together if (they) could exploit their Quins properly...."

— *Life*, May 17, 1937

9

Rights

E very night, late, when the house was still and the last of the cars had driven off toward the cabins and cottages of Lake Nipissing, Oliva would get out of bed and look out over the fortressed grounds of Quintland. He would stand for a long time, sometimes for more than an hour, letting his imagination drift across the road to the Dafoe Hospital. He would imagine that he was in the quintuplets' bedroom, watching them asleep in their beds, kissing their foreheads, putting his ear close to hear their breathing, staring at them longingly.

One of them was crying. He looked around the room to see which one it was, but his five three-year-olds were all sleeping soundly. The crying stopped for a moment, then started up again, this time sounding as if it was coming from another room. That was peculiar. There were no other children in the hospital.

"Oliva," came a hushed voice from a few feet away. "Did you hear that?"

"Yes," he said, still looking about. "But I don't know who it is."

Someone pulled at his arm. "Oliva!"

The person who had hold of him swung him around and away from the window. It was Elzire. He hadn't noticed her come into the girls' room.

"I think it's Thérèse."

"What?" he muttered, as the quintuplets' room vanished. Suddenly, he and Elzire were standing in their own bedroom.

"Shh," she cautioned, nodding to Oliva Jr.'s crib on the other side of the room. "I'll go see. I think it's Thérèse." She pulled her housecoat over her nightie and followed the soft cries across the hall to the bedroom that Thérèse shared with Rose and Pauline. As soon as she opened the door, the crying stopped.

"Thérèse," she whispered.

Not a sound.

"I know you're up." Elzire tiptoed over and sat on the edge of the bed. "Thérèse." She touched her daughter's shoulder.

Thérèse stirred, pretending to have been awakened from a deep sleep. She turned slowly toward her mother. "Maman," she said, rubbing her eyes, not from sleepiness, but to cover them.

Elzire pulled her daughter's hands away from her face. This close, even in the dark, she could see the sparkle of tears in reddened eyes. "What are you crying for? Did you have a bad dream?"

"No." The eight-year-old's voice was barely audible as she gnawed on the collar of her pyjamas.

"Then what's wrong?" Elzire asked, cupping the child's face and lifting her chin. "Come on, tell me."

"You won't let me have curly hair," she wailed, bursting into fresh tears.

"Are you still thinking about that?" She had been listening to Thérèse complain for weeks now about how the quintuplets were allowed to have curly hair and she wasn't. Apparently, one of the girls at school had brought in the issue of *Life* magazine that contained a cover story and photo spread on the quintuplets' third birthday. And there they were, like living dolls, with curls flowing all over the place.

"I've told you, Thérèse, you cannot have curly hair."

"But you let them."

"I don't let anyone," Elzire pointed out. "I've told you before, if it were up to me, their hair would be straight and beautiful, just like yours. Do you think I like the nurses curling it twice a day just so all those people can look at them?"

"Then why don't you stop them?" asked Thérèse, hoping for an answer that would make some sense out of all the rumours she had been hearing in school.

"I wish I had a good answer for you, sweetheart." Elzire wished that someone could explain it all to her too. "That's just the way God intended it to be. When your sisters were born...."

Thérèse cut her off accusingly. "Louise said that Papa doesn't like the shows because he doesn't make any money off of them."

"That's not true!"

"She said that Papa tried to sell them when they were little and that if it weren't for Dr. Dafoe, they would have died."

"Your friend Louise seems to know an awful lot for such a young girl." Elzire hid her outrage by leaning over Thérèse to pull the covers up over Rose's shoulders. At least the eldest daughter was asleep. Though tomorrow night might be her turn for midnight sorrow, depending on what she heard at school that day. Elzire turned her head to look at where Pauline lay still in the small bed across the room. Not quite old enough for school, Pauline had been spared the nightmares that resulted from the type of badgering her brothers and sisters received constantly, both from other children and from the reporters that hung around the schoolyard. But Pauline's turn would come soon enough. As it would for ten-month-old Oliva. That much, Elzire knew for sure.

She studied Thérèse's sullen face. How could she explain to her daughter things that she didn't understand herself? The unkind words Thérèse had heard at school weren't those of nine-year-old Louise. They were repetitions of her parents' conversations. Conversations that, in turn, were based on the lies they eagerly read in the magazines. How could she ever forget the vicious words used to describe her and Oliva in the same issue of *Life* that had made their five identical daughters look so beautiful? Were there no laws against saying such things?

"Listen, Thérèse. I want you to understand." She lifted her daughter to a sitting position. "The fact that your sisters don't live here has nothing – nothing, you understand – to do with your father or me. Now, people aren't going to stop saying bad things about us, so you may as well get used to that. But who are you going to believe, them or us?"

Thérèse looked at her, wanting to believe.

"Do as your brother would," said Elzire with a note of optimism. "He ignores what everyone says, or tells them to mind their own business."

"Ernest did that yesterday and got into a fight," Thérèse reported. Her wide-eyed expression made it clear that she wasn't prepared to go to those lengths herself.

"Well, I don't want that to happen," Elzire admitted, privately amused at how much like his father Ernest was. Always ready to defend himself. "You could try telling your teacher," she suggested, uncertain of where that advice might lead, since the adults were usually far worse than the children. "But I don't want you even looking at those silly magazines. Your sisters are people. You don't need to see them in books."

Yes, she does, thought Oliva, listening from outside the door, where he had been peering in unnoticed in the dark. All that his six children at home would ever know of their quintuplet sisters would be what they saw and read in newspapers and magazines. The rare visits granted to them by Dafoe, and the shortness of those visits, left little more than a casual memory of five beautiful and special girls who were somehow oddly related to them. At least the picture-stories about the quintuplets had the name *Dionne* splashed all over them. It was an immediate connection, as well as a more comfortable, and vastly more regular, relationship than the awkward *"Bonjour, Yvonne"* and *"Hello, Theresa"* exchange that typified the infrequent visits.

When Oliva saw Elzire get up from Thérèse's side, he tiptoed back into their own room and climbed into bed, pretending to be asleep when Elzire came in a few minutes later. For the next half-hour he lay there, eyes fixed blindly on the wall, thinking about his divided family. The same helpless feeling that he had felt every night for the past three years returned. He thought of saying a prayer, but he was tired of praying and hoping for a miraculous change of events. And he no longer had any faith in the promises that were dispensed so freely by everyone – by the Government, by the Church, by reporters, by the dozens of lawyers that dropped their cards on his doorstep, by a few distant and nameless supporters who wrote letters – that one day his daughters would be returned to him. It was time that he stopped deluding himself. Things wouldn't change just because they should.

He finally turned and leaned over Elzire. She was asleep. He got out of bed and went back to staring out the window. Nothing in the scene across the road was different than before. As he drifted back into the quintuplets' bedroom, he saw that nothing had changed there either. He realized that unless he acted soon, nothing would ever change.

*   *   *

Oliva pulled up in front of a small, three-storey clapboard building in North Bay. He looked curiously at the address on the decrepit entrance, and checked it against what he had scribbled on the back of an envelope: *31 Worthington Avenue*. This was the place. It didn't look much like what he expected of a prominent lawyer's office. But then, he had learned, only too painfully over the past three years, not to judge any book by its cover.

Before he stepped out of his '36 Chevrolet, no one passing by on the street recognized him as Oliva Dionne. Why would they? Critics and cartoonists alike had done a fine job of portraying *Papa Dionne* as an imbecilic farmer whose chief form of recreation was driving around town in a sorry heap of rusted metal. Whereas here, sitting behind the wheel of an inconspicuous car, was a neatly groomed man sporting a pressed white shirt and a brown cardigan. It hardly fit his public image.

Once he stepped out onto the curb, however, a pedestrian recognized his face from the newspapers. Then another, who nudged her companion. A few others looked, and soon, a series of double-takes started, quickly turning to curious and fixed stares.

Oliva kept his gaze forward as he walked into the building. He was by now used to the condescending looks from the men and the carnal glances from the women. He was, at once, the father who gave up his children, and the man who had the sexual potency to produce five babies at one time. Both were stigmas that haunted him every time he showed his face in public. Only the children, if unaccompanied by their parents, ignored him.

He climbed two flights of stairs, and walked the full length of a narrow hallway before he reached a door painted with letters that spelled *Martin Poulin, Barrister and Solicitor*. He hesitated before going in, wondering again if he was doing the right thing.

He had been given Poulin's name by the Franco-Ontarian Education Association. They had written to him months ago, expressing concern about the lack of French cultural influences available to the quintuplets in a hospital full of English-speaking nurses and administrators. It was one of the few genuinely sympathetic letters he and Elzire had received. So he wrote back, thanking them for their concern, and asking if they could recommend a good lawyer to help him regain custody of his daughters. He included in his letter the names of all the lawyers that had offered their services to him since the birth. For Oliva, it was a way of telling the Association who he didn't want to deal with. Had he not done this, and were they to recommend one of the thieves he had already encountered, he might have lost even more faith in anyone's ability to help him. He maintained that anyone who would drop by and leave a card with the words *I can help you out, bud, but I only take cash* written on the back, was no more than a panhandler, of which there were already too many these days.

The Association wrote back with its recommendations. Poulin, who had successfully argued a case for them before the Nipissing County Board of Education, was at the top of their list.

Oliva had made up his mind to call Poulin, but had also decided not to tell Elzire. Not until he was sure that the lawyer could help them. He remembered how he had once broached the topic of getting serious legal help, and how she had talked him out of it. Her attitude was that after the law of the country and the power of the press had taken their babies away from them, they could not trust lawyers and reporters. Period. Oliva shared her prejudices, but he also knew they were getting nowhere without help.

On the telephone, Poulin had sounded both enthusiastic and knowledgeable about the case, and was eager to meet. But even as Oliva opened the door to the lawyer's office, he was wary. After all that he and Elzire had been through, he found it hard to trust anyone. Especially anyone who got excited at the sound of the name *Dionne*.

As soon as Poulin's secretary saw Oliva enter, she jumped out of her chair. "Mr. Dionne!"

Like the people on the street, she had instantly recognized him. And though Poulin had told her days before that the famous father was coming, she had acted like a half-wit all day. So many conflicting things had been written and broadcast about him, she had no idea of what to expect. In the photographs, he always looked angry. Now, here he was, the father of the quints, in person. Quite average-looking, she thought, offering to hang his cardigan on the coat stand. But sexy, she imagined, letting her eyes drop below his belt as he unbuttoned his cardigan, which at the last moment he decided to keep with him.

"I have an appointment with Mr. Poulin."

"Yes, he's expecting you," she said nervously. "Right this way." She opened Poulin's door. "Mr. Dionne is here," she announced proudly, then ushered him in.

Poulin got up and walked around a broad wooden desk that nearly filled the small room. "Mr. Dionne," he said warmly, extending his hand. "Pleased to meet you, at last."

They shook hands.

"Mr. Poulin?" From their telephone conversations, Oliva had expected someone older. Poulin looked to be in his early thirties, perhaps a little younger than himself.

"Would you like some tea?" asked the secretary, as the two men stood sizing each other up.

"Please."

"Sure," added Poulin. He waited until she left and closed the door before he continued. "Have a seat, please." He gestured to one of the two chairs in front of his desk.

Oliva looked at Poulin's cluttered desk. The surface was almost obscured by a confusion of bulging files, loose correspondence, and used notepads. "Those aren't all for me?" he asked, looking at the stacks of files that had papers poking out of all three open sides.

"No, no. Of course not," Poulin said, tidying up things a little as he sat down. "Please excuse the mess."

"They could be, you know," Oliva remarked stiffly.

"Yes, I suppose they could," Poulin admitted. He was fully aware of the fascinating complexities this case held.

He had been surprised when Oliva had called, but had jumped at the opportunity to represent him. The Government's tight control over the famous Dionne babies had puzzled and, at the same time, outraged him. Taking on the Government in a case the whole world would be watching – he'd have to be crazy to turn it down.

Outside the door, the secretary ran a hand through her hair, and straightened her blouse. Then she picked up the tray that held the two cups of tea and carried it into the room. She placed a cup in front of each of them, fussing over Oliva's. She took a moment to smile at him, and almost knocked the cup over. Straightening up quickly, she bolted out of the room, her face flushing crimson.

"What's the matter with her?"

Poulin chuckled. "Well, I don't usually deal with such… well-known clients."

"I'm not your client," Oliva reminded him, glad for the opportunity to make that point clear.

"No, of course not." Poulin's tone suddenly became more businesslike than before. "Anyway, Mr. Dionne, since you called I've been looking at a few of your options. Now, I'm confident I can get your daughters back for you, but the question is when."

An irritated look crossed Oliva's face.

"I know you don't want to hear that."

"No, I don't."

"You probably feel that your case hinges on the question of fundamental family rights," Poulin guessed, "but when dealing with the Government, there are a number of other factors to consider."

"Here we go again." Oliva shook his head at the mere hint of problems and started to get up.

"Wait, Mr. Dionne. I know how you feel, but please, hear me out."

Oliva hesitated, then sat back down, resigning himself to hearing more of what he already knew. "All right. Go ahead."

"Okay. Now first, is there any medical reason whatsoever to keep your daughters in a hospital?"

"There never was," he remembered with great regret.

"It's an important point, Mr. Dionne. I have to know."

"As plainly as I can put it: No!"

"You're sure?"

"Look, Mr. Poulin." He moved forward to the edge of his chair. "Dafoe is the one who started all this business about them being sick all the time. He used it to keep everyone else away. He still does. Why doesn't anyone want to believe that?"

Poulin wanted to make it clear that he was on Oliva's side. "Partly because they don't want to. Do you want to admit to your own mistakes? I don't. Seeing Dafoe in any light other than the best would mean accepting that a mistake has been made. Take, for example, the image Hollywood gave him in *The Country Doctor*. A real humanitarian. That's how everyone wants to think of him."

"That doesn't do me a lot of good, does it?"

"No, it doesn't, but I want you to understand that I'm not asking these questions because I doubt your word. It's just that I have to know the whole situation before I can work out a plan."

Oliva settled back in his chair, patient for the moment.

"Now, we could try to challenge the Guardianship Bill on the basis that the girls no longer require special medical attention. If we establish that the bill was passed largely to protect their health, we might stand a chance of having it revoked."

Oliva nodded.

"We can't change the past, but we can at least guide the course of events from now on."

Everything sounded reasonable to Oliva so far. "And how long would that take?"

"Several months at…." Poulin hesitated, remembering that the man before him had heard lies for long enough. He deserved the truth, even if it meant giving him the worst scenario possible. "To be honest, the Government could conceivably delay proceedings for years if they wanted to."

"Years?" asked Oliva, his expression one of shock. "It's already been three years."

"I know."

"We're like two separate families, Mr. Poulin. Can you understand what that's like?"

The lawyer swallowed his automatically sympathetic response.

"My children don't even know their own sisters. All of my children have never been allowed to play together. Not once."

Poulin couldn't hold back any longer. "I understand, but…."

"I don't think you do," Oliva interrupted. "My wife is made to feel like an intruder every time she goes into the hospital. Dafoe and his nurses act like they're doing her a favour by fitting her into their schedule. Did you know about the schedule?"

Poulin nodded ever so slightly.

Oliva was livid now. "Every minute of my daughters' day is planned. Free play, private play, breakfast, dinner, quiet time, prayer time, sleep time… they can't even use the toilet unless it's scheduled. Their own mother has to catch them between Blatz's observations and their shows, just so she can spend five minutes with them. And you're telling me we might have to wait years?"

Poulin didn't know what to say. "I'll do my best, Mr. Dionne," he said, knowing that his best wasn't enough. "That's all I can promise," he added, also realizing that a promise to the robbed father who sat across from him meant nothing. "I could tell you I'd get them back in three months, or six, but that wouldn't mean a hell of a lot."

Oliva was silent. He fixed his eyes on the wall over Poulin's shoulder, embarrassed for having lost his composure in front of a complete stranger.

"I can't give you any guarantees. This isn't Division Court that we're dealing with. We'd be going up against the whole Government." He thought of the upcoming election. "And probably Hepburn's Government for another four years." He saw that Oliva was leaning forward, about to get up again to leave. "Wait. There are things that you can do in the meantime to get some measure of control."

Oliva got out of his seat.

"I understand that you don't attend meetings for the Board of Guardians."

"No," he answered, turning to face the door. "And I don't intend to."

"I would strongly advise you to start."

"No." Oliva was already at the door, reaching for the knob.

"Wait, Mr. Dionne. It could help."

"How?" He had already opened the door when he turned once more to face Poulin. "If I go to their meetings, they'll just say I recognize the board's right to exist. And I don't. I never have, and I never will."

"Please, let me finish," Poulin begged. "You can use those meetings to your advantage. Go to them. Start picking on every little point they raise. Be a nuisance. You're a board member; you have as much say as any of them do. Criticize the nurses, the schedule, their education. Be a complete pain in the ass."

"That's going to get my girls back? You're dreaming."

Poulin was becoming exasperated with Oliva's attitude. "Look, Mr. Dionne, if you want your children back, you're going to have to use every weapon at your disposal. This is not a straightforward matter by any stretch of the imagination."

"To me, it's very straightforward. They're my daughters. I'm their father. My wife is their mother. What could be more straightforward? If you can't see that, I think we're wasting each other's time." He turned toward the reception area and walked out of Poulin's office.

Poulin rose from his chair. He couldn't disagree with Oliva's logic, but he had difficulty dealing with such stubbornness in a case to which logic had never applied. "Go ahead, Mr. Dionne," he called out. "Go on. If you feel that you can get your daughters back on your own, be my guest."

"I can do at least as much as you," Oliva said proudly. He passed the secretary's desk. "Thanks for the tea."

"Fine," Poulin said, coming around his desk. "Go right ahead." Now he was the angry one. "But you know as well as I do that you can't. Not alone."

Oliva stopped, but he didn't turn around.

The secretary didn't look up, but her typing took on the rhythm of the loud voices.

"Oh, you don't need me. Any half-assed lawyer who knows the rules will do, but you're going to have to follow rules. Because what you're trying to do is change the guard. You're going up against the whole goddamned Government on this one." He watched Oliva standing there, ready to exit through the door that he had entered not twenty minutes ago. Poulin knew there were no better solutions waiting outside for him. "You understand that, too," Poulin continued. "If you didn't, you'd just walk into that damned prison and take the girls without worrying about being hauled off by five guards and half a dozen *sons of Mitches*."

Oliva shuddered, remembering the first two provincial policemen that had appeared on his doorstep so long ago with the pretense of protecting his home and family.

"Go ahead."

Silence. Even the secretary had lost her place and stopped typing.

Poulin turned and started back to his desk. Then he heard the door to his office close behind him. As he turned to sit, he saw that Oliva hadn't gone, but was standing inside the door, a desperate expression on his face.

"I just want my children back."

"I appreciate your frustration, Mr. Dionne. At least as much as anyone besides you or your wife can, but it's going to take time. You're just going to have to accept that."

Oliva couldn't. To him, that would be like giving up, which he wasn't ready to do. Not yet. He sat down, though, and remained in Poulin's office for a long time. He told Poulin the things he and Elzire had told each other hundreds of times. Poulin interrupted from time to time with the legalities of the situation. More than once, Oliva rose to leave. This was followed by Poulin telling him to go ahead. Once, Poulin himself, fed up with Oliva's resistance to new ideas, got up to end the interview. It was the father who then asked the lawyer to stay. And though Oliva still resented the realities Poulin spoke of, he was beginning to like the frank lawyer's determination. And despite the fact that he didn't fully trust Poulin, nor his tactics, he was at least willing to listen.

*   *   *

It was past eight o'clock when Oliva drove through Quintland on his way home from Poulin's office. It was early August, the peak of the tourist season, and although the observation gallery had closed hours ago, people were still milling about the grounds on the warm night. Several refreshment and souvenir stands, open late for the extra business, made after-the-show loitering around the acre of otherwise barren farmland all the more acceptable.

Once again, no one looked toward the simple man passing by in the modest Chev. Those who might have looked probably thought him to be just another tourist out to experience Quintland at night. If anyone was trying to catch a glimpse of a Dionne coming home, they were undoubtedly looking for an old wreck of a truck to come thumping over the hill.

Oliva turned into his property and got out of the car. A couple passing by on foot noticed him, and soon a few others started to gather. Then the looks started. The same as on the street in front of Poulin's office earlier this week, but more concentrated somehow, and accompanied by loud whispers, even some shouts.

Oliva resisted the curious and penetrating looks as he quickly closed the gate, jogged up the path, and climbed the porch steps. His eyes drifted to an upstairs window, then darted to the window of the boys' room downstairs. The lights were off. He turned the key in the door and entered the house, not once turning to face the audience he had conjured just by being who he was.

As he entered, he half-expected Elzire to be standing at the stove, threatening for the fourth night in a row not to set out dinner for him. And although he would tell her that he had called, she would remind him that she didn't answer the telephone when he wasn't there. She was always afraid that it might be yet another nosy reporter who had tricked the operator into putting the call through. Electricity and telephone cables had been installed for more than a year now, but Elzire was still not used to having the telephone. In fact, she resented the brown box on the wall that exposed her to such ridicule. Oliva didn't mind the crank calls as much. They gave him an opportunity to vent some of the hostility that was always building up inside him.

Elzire was not in the kitchen. Not in the summer kitchen, either. Perhaps she was upstairs with baby Oliva. "Elzire," he called up softly. Hoping not to wake the other children, he started to climb the stairs.

"I'm outside," came her voice through the screened windows of the summer kitchen.

He turned and followed the voice out the back door and down the steps, where he found Elzire sitting with his father in the dark. At first he could barely make out their forms, but as his eyes adjusted he saw their faces, then their eyes, watching him intently.

"Where have you been?" Elzire wanted to know. "I'm not setting out dinner again."

Oliva ignored Elzire's question. He looked to the other side of the steps to the bench where his father sat. "Bonjour, Papa." He took a deep breath of the clean country air that returned every evening once the parking lot next to their property had emptied of its cars, then leaned over to kiss Elzire.

Elzire pulled away, pretending to be more angry than she actually was. "You can get your own supper," she pouted.

"That's okay," he said, sitting down on a footstool across from Elzire's rocking chair. It almost tipped over as he sat. "Whoops," he gasped, catching his fall. "I've got to fix that one of these days." As he stood up to adjust the wobbly leg, his eyes met Elzire's. She was visibly upset. He looked over to his father for support.

"If you stayed around home, you'd get something done," was his father's only response.

Oliva looked toward the barn, away from both of them.

"You know, Oliva, I don't know where your head is lately. You're away from home for hours, your wife is waiting for you. You can't even call?"

"I called," he said defensively, sitting back down.

Elzire started to rise. "I'll fix your dinner."

"It's all right, Elzire. Later."

"When?" she asked, on her way into the house. "Tomorrow? Speak with your father. Maybe he can talk some sense into you."

The screen door rattled shut behind her.

Oliva looked over to his father, who was observing him suspiciously. "How are you, Papa?" he finally asked.

"Never mind how I am." He moved over to sit in Elzire's chair, which was still rocking from her departure. "Oliva, tell me what's going on. You're driving your wife crazy with all this secrecy. Isn't everything else enough?"

"Papa, we can't just accept things the way they are any more. I can't, anyway."

"What can you do?" Olivier's own frustration over the situation was evident in his voice. "You can't change the world," he added, leaning forward to stop the chair from rocking.

"No, I can't. But I can change this."

"You think so?" Olivier doubted anyone's ability to change the tragedy that was a part of all of their lives. "If you'd just have faith in God, we'd...."

"God. All anybody around here can talk about is God." He sprang up and started pacing. "The Church sure helped us get our children back, didn't they? Where the hell did they send Père Routhier when we needed him? Alaska?"

Elzire came rushing out the door at the sound of his voice. "Oliva, the children are sleeping. And stop all this talk against the Church!"

"It's my fault," Olivier offered gracefully.

"It doesn't matter whose fault it is. I don't like it when Oliva starts talking like that."

"Elzire." Oliva grabbed her hand before she could return to the kitchen. "Come and sit down. I have to tell you something."

The look in his eyes told her that it was something she wouldn't like. "I have to get your dinner," she said, trying to pull away from him.

He held on tightly.

"At least let me take the pot off the stove."

He released her hand and watched her disappear into the house again.

She lifted the pot from the stove and rested it in the warmer above. Then she took off her apron, hung it up neatly, and went back outside. Taking a few deep breaths to summon up her strength, she sat on the bench where Olivier had originally been sitting. It was as far away from Oliva, and his news, as she could get.

"Elzire, I'm going to have to do something you're not going to like."

"Oliva...."

"I should go," Olivier said, starting to get up.

"Please, Papa. Stay. You're going to hear about this eventually. Now is as good a time as any."

"Sounds a little too serious for my liking," Olivier said, sitting back down.

"You're scaring me, Oliva," Elzire appealed. "Do you realize that?"

"You've been out late for four nights," Olivier added. "And now you're telling us you're going to do something we're not going to like. What are you planning to do? Burn down Dr. Dafoe's house?"

"Hmm." He pretended to think about it. "You know, that's not a bad idea." He grew serious again when he noticed his father's stern look: the one that meant Olivier wanted answers from his grown son, not games from his child. "Seriously, Papa, I'm working out a plan to get the girls back. But what I'm going to have to do, you're not going to like. People are going to talk again. Just like Chicago."

"No, Oliva," Elzire pleaded. "Isn't there enough talk already?"

"I don't care," he declared. "We can't keep on the way we've been going. You see the children, the way they're treated at school. And do you really think you can keep going over there, the way they treat you?

"I don't care how they treat me, Oliva."

"Come on!"

"Really. Not as much as you think. As long as I can see the girls, that's all I care about now. I can't stop what's going on any more than you can. But I'm not going to let it stop me from seeing my children."

"No?" He was irritated for the second time that evening by the implication that he couldn't change things. "And what if they change that stupid law and say you can't go over any more?"

"They're not going to do that." She shrugged off the preposterous idea.

"They can, you know," Oliva assured her. "Very easily. All they have to do is make an amendment to their Guardianship Bill, and that's it. No visits from parents." He snapped his fingers. "Just like that."

"Stop it," Olivier ordered. "Enough of this nonsense about not seeing the girls. Goodness, Oliva, is this what you've learned during your late-night wanderings? I knew you were up to no good."

"Papa, I'm just trying to be realistic. I'm not going to wait until the girls are eighteen to get them back. They won't even know us then."

"At least they know you now," said Olivier sadly. "They don't remember their pépère from one visit to the next."

"I just want all of you to be prepared for what's coming."

"So tell us then," Olivier demanded. "What have you got up your sleeve?"

"We're going to need money if we're going to get the girls back."

"Money?" Elzire spat out the word that was once such an insignificant part of her vocabulary.

"Money!" Oliva emphasized the word. "And lots of it."

"I'm sure you have enough between your odd jobs and what you get from the board," his father cut in. "At least to get by."

"Yes, but it's not enough for what I have in mind," Oliva returned. "I haven't told you this before because I knew you wouldn't like it, but I've been meeting with a lawyer named Poulin."

"Poulin." Olivier was impressed. "French?"

"Yes, but he doesn't speak it. He grew up with an English family in…."

"Oliva," Elzire interrupted. "Don't you know by now that we can't trust anyone? Look at all the people who have come here with all kinds of promises to help. They usually turn out to be either reporters looking for stories or crooked lawyers trying to get money from us."

"I know, but this is different."

"You talk about needing money!" Elzire pressed. "That's what's caused all the trouble. What do you think your lawyer is after?"

"I know. But as long as we know that, we're okay."

"I don't like it either," Olivier cautioned.

"You're going to like it a lot less when I tell you what I'm going to have to do."

Elzire looked at him, eyes not asking what, but why.

"We have to, Elzire. Trust me. You're going to see some changes soon. Right over there by…."

"Stop it!" Elzire screamed, then covered her mouth. She looked out across the yard, hoping that she hadn't woken Ernest and Daniel, who were asleep on a pair of gunny sacks by the barn.

Olivier raised himself out of the rocking chair.

Oliva got up and ran over to Elzire. "What's wrong?"

"I don't want to know," she said. "Just do what you have to do and leave me out of it."

"I'm going home before I interfere more than I already have." Olivier started around the corner of the house. "Come on, Oliva."

Oliva glanced over to his father. "I wish you'd both trust me." He looked back to Elzire. "I know what I'm doing. You'll see. We're going to get the girls back home before you know it."

"Don't have your mind too set on it," Olivier warned. "Elzire is right. As long as she can see them, it's better than creating more trouble for all of us. Remember, if you get them home, you've got new problems to deal with. Those girls hardly know your other children."

"That's why I'm not going to wait any longer," he said, looking to Elzire for a sign of support.

"I trust you, Oliva," she assured him. "But don't bring no lawyer around here, or I'll throw him out myself."

Oliva chuckled at the idea. Although he knew Elzire was joking, he also knew that she could carry out her threat. Growing up with six brothers had made Elzire a tomboy from early on. She had played ball with her brothers and scrapped with the best of them. In fact, Elzire's brothers had told Oliva before the wedding how tough she could be, especially if her family was being threatened. It had been a surprise to all of them to find her so outwardly complacent about the separation of her family, and resistant to actions that might change things. Some of the people in Corbeil had spread stories that she didn't care enough about the quintuplets to fight for them. But Oliva knew the truth. There was simply nothing that she could do.

Oliva laughed at his mental picture of Elzire picking up the lawyer that was half her size and tossing him into the manure pile past the barn.

Elzire knew that he had been thinking of something comical. "What is it?"

Oliva's eyes widened. "Please, Elzire. Don't do anything to him. Not until we win our case. I don't want to scare him off before we even get to court."

"Now we're going to court!" Olivier threw his arms up in exasperation. "Take me home, Oliva. It's getting chilly out here."

"It's the middle of summer," Oliva reminded him.

"It's still a little chilly," his father repeated. "If you know what I mean?" He winked at Elzire, who giggled like a child.

Oliva caught on, looked at the two of them, then joined in the laughter. He was relieved that the conversation about Poulin had ended with a joke, especially when he was expecting an argument.

Elzire wasn't as amused by the light end to their discussion. She hadn't heard Oliva use words like *case* and *court* before. And the last *plan* they had participated in had taken them to Chicago, only to be made fools of afterwards. Would this one be any different? Probably not. Without knowing the details, she was already sure that she wasn't going to like it.

After Oliva had left to drive his father home, she wandered over to see the boys. She covered them with the sheets they had thrown off in their tossings and turnings. She touched both of their faces, then went back to sit in her rocking chair. It was so peaceful in the back yard, she thought, even with the faint murmur of noise that fluttered from across the road all night long. If she concentrated hard enough, she could eliminate even those sounds and enjoy the solitude of this, their private yard. It was the only untouched place in the evil world that surrounded them. She didn't know what she would do if she lost that, too.

10

Eye-to-Eye

"**F**ellman!" Bob Knight's voice boomed out the moment he spotted his star reporter entering the newsroom.

Fellman hadn't even had a chance to sit down. "Good morning," he replied, heading straight for Knight's desk without taking off his jacket. He rubbed his hands together. "It's getting cool out there."

"I want you to take a run up to Quintland. Some interesting developments."

"Developments?" It was October, the tail end of the season; the place would be closing for the winter in a few weeks. "What kind of developments?" he asked, thinking that he would have heard if there were any. Quintland was his beat.

"Looks like Dionne's motives aren't as pure as you thought."

"What do you mean?" he asked, worried by the smirk on Knight's face.

For the past couple of months, he had been closely following Oliva Dionne's legal challenges to Dafoe and to the Government. Most of them had been unsuccessful thus far, in particular those that involved stopping the shows and having Dafoe removed from the

157

board, and had been viewed by many, including Knight, as a ploy to gain control of the quints' huge trust fund. But Fellman's feeling from the beginning had been that many of Dionne's arguments had merit. Especially those that were directed at bringing French-speaking staff into the hospital, increasing family visits, and putting an end to peculiar practices such as curling the quints' otherwise straight hair. He had called Oliva for an interview several times, but each time was refused. That had come as no real surprise. He knew how much the Dionnes distrusted all reporters, even Phyllis Griffiths, the *Telegram* reporter who had written a sympathetic article about them last May. But it disturbed him, nonetheless, that he had been covering the quints for almost three and a half years and had never met either of their parents.

"Go see for yourself," suggested Knight. "You're the one who said he's the only one not making money off his kids."

Fellman wanted to ask what Knight was talking about, but the secretive grin on his editor's face told him that he was going to have to find out for himself. He grabbed the car keys, which were dangling from one of Knight's fingers, scooped his notepad from his desk, and headed out the door.

He knew enough not to take the Ferguson Highway. That would mean a good hour of sitting in traffic. He preferred another route, one that took him down the highway that led to Mattawa, then over a bumpy back road. This road eventually took him through Corbeil, allowing him to finally reach Quintland from the direction opposite to that of the rest of the traffic. Although this route meant a greater distance to travel, it got him there more quickly. Few tourists ever came that way.

As he passed Léo Voyer's store, he noticed that an addition was being built. Then up ahead, he spotted the flagpole jutting from the spire of the Midwives' Souvenir Pavilion. That told him he was close. So did the increasing number of cars that were parked at different angles along both sides of the road. He pulled off, deciding it was best not to go any further and risk not getting a parking spot. In order to turn around amidst the confusion of people and cars, he would lose a good half-hour or more.

He got out of the car and walked the last half-mile, soon realizing that he had arrived at a very busy time. The first show of the day was just ending, and people were pouring out of the observation gallery. They ran past the souvenir booths that lined both sides of the road, and headed to cars in the parking lot or further up the road where he had pulled over. He was walking against the flow, and had to stop several times to let people pass. He bumped into his neighbours from North Bay, who had brought relatives visiting from New Jersey to see the quints before another season ended, and he stopped again for a quick hello. A little further on, he stopped once more, this time to look at the sluggish bear on display in its cage near the lemonade stand.

He hadn't seen anything unusual yet, so he continued to walk along the right-hand side of the road, keeping his eyes open. As he passed the midwives' pavilion on the hill, he watched a number of people carrying binoculars descend from the roof-top deck, which overlooked the observation gallery and the hospital grounds. More people were streaming into the sign-covered shop below, where the original basket in which the quints had been put when they were born was on display. He had been inside many times before. It was quite an operation. Madame Lebel and Madame Legros signed autographs, gave interviews, and sold souvenirs and copies of *Administering Angels*, their book about the quintuplets' birth. They also rented binoculars and offered a good exchange on American currency. It seemed as if they had every angle covered.

Fellman crossed over to the other side of the road, where the public toilets, more souvenir booths, and a few food stands hid the parking lot. He pushed through the crowd of people munching on hot dogs and sipping Canada Dry. All had contented looks on their faces, and most carried bags filled with souvenirs of their pilgrimage.

Between them, the stores at Quintland sold a multitude of products emblazoned with the quints' image: postcards for people to send to their envious friends, story books for the children, plates and placemats, blotters, pennants, glasses, paperweights, clocks – the list of items seemed to be endless. Among the more popular items this season were the new quint dolls. As he walked on, he counted at least ten young girls happily carrying the box that held the five smiling dolls.

He was about fifty yards from the Dionne farmhouse when he noticed something else, a new building up ahead. He had seen it under construction during the summer, but hadn't thought it unusual. New stands were going up all the time.

He walked over for a closer look, stopping dead the moment he realized that this was what Knight had been talking about. He couldn't believe the sign above the door. But there it was, in full colour for all to see: *Oliva Dionne's Wool Shop*. He wished he could blink and have it disappear, but when he did blink, he saw a second store and another sign: *Oliva Dionne's Souvenir Shop*.

He stood, staring from one shop to the other, his sympathies for Oliva Dionne evaporating quickly. Out of the corner of his eye, he could still see the midwives' pavilion. Elzire Dionne's own aunt, he remembered, coming to the swift conclusion that every character in the Dionne story, family included, was rotten.

He stuffed his notebook into his back pocket and sauntered into the wool shop, pretending to be a customer. As he wandered up and down the aisles, he toyed with the merchandise on the shelves: blankets, coats, scarves, gloves, hats. When he reached the counter at the back, he spotted Oliva. He was signing a slip of paper for a woman who looked ready to burst with the excitement of the moment.

"Could you sign another one for my aunt?" she enquired apologetically. "She would never forgive me if she knew that I met you and didn't get one for her."

"What's her name?" Oliva asked graciously.

"Alberta."

Fellman watched, disgusted.

"Oh, she's just going to be thrilled," the woman said, as she carefully folded the two scraps of paper and tucked them into her purse. "Thank you." She pulled out two quarters and dropped them onto the counter.

"Thank *you*, ma'am," Oliva smiled. "Have a good day."

As the woman sped out of the store, Oliva noticed Fellman in the near aisle, absently holding a pair of woollen gloves. "Can I help you with anything?"

Fellman put the gloves down. "Thanks. Just looking." He could feel Oliva's eyes on him as he walked up the aisle toward him. "Quite an operation you have here," he remarked, scanning the store to make sure no one else was there.

"Finest woollen goods in the north," said Oliva proudly, coming eye-to-eye with the reporter.

"How's business?"

"So far, steady." He regarded Fellman suspiciously. "Are you looking for anything in particular?"

"No." Fellman turned. "No, thanks." He started to walk down the aisle toward the door, wondering if he should say something. And if so, what?

Oliva took care of that for him. "You're a reporter!"

"What?" He turned to face Oliva, prepared to deny it.

Oliva pointed to the notepad that had crept out of Fellman's pocket as he walked. "Most of my customers don't carry notepads."

Fellman wished that this first meeting hadn't started under such unpleasant circumstances. But it hadn't been his choice. "My name is Mort Fellman. I'm with the *Nugget*."

"Uh-huh. So you're the one that's been calling all the time. Did you think I'd be more likely to talk to you if you showed up in person?"

"I'd certainly like to ask you a few questions."

"Forget it."

"I think our readers would be very interested in your little operation here."

"Do I have to throw you out?"

Fellman retreated a little. "I assume it'll be quite profitable."

A youthful couple, probably on their honeymoon, bounced in.

"I sure hope so," Oliva said, ignoring the happy pair as he came around the corner of the counter. "Now, I asked you to leave."

The prospective customers sensed the tension and decided to follow Oliva's order, regardless of who it had been intended for.

"What are you afraid of?" Fellman asked, backing up a little more. He heard the door shut behind him and stopped. "That people will find out what you're really like? That they'll find out what you're doing?"

Oliva stopped too. "And what's that? Making a few dollars selling woollen blankets?"

"You make it sound very innocent."

"A man's allowed to have a business, isn't he?"

"Sure, but most people's businesses don't involve making money off their children."

Oliva started moving again. "Most people have their children at home with them."

Fellman backed into a display of scarves. He turned to pick up the few that fell.

Oliva shook his head and chuckled. "You reporters make me laugh. You don't say a word about all the other people around here, or about how everyone all over creation is making money off my children. But the minute I open a little shop, all of a sudden it's wrong."

"You're their *father*."

"Oh, of course. Now I understand." Oliva returned to his post behind the counter.

Fellman followed. "Maybe no one else should be doing it either, but you?"

"Because I'm their father."

"Yes. How can you criticize others when you're doing the same thing?"

"I have the right to do it, that's why. They're my daughters, believe it or not."

Fellman couldn't believe that anyone could be this mercenary. "I sure had you figured out wrong."

"Good. Now figure yourself out."

"What?"

"Why are you here? You're scrounging around for another dirty story. Aren't you getting paid for it?"

"That's not the point."

"That's not the point?" mocked Oliva. "You've been living off my daughters for years now, but that doesn't count. Right?"

Fellman had not considered it that way before, and wasn't about to just yet. "I'm doing my job, that's all. And I'm not the quints' father. Do you think your daughters would appreciate what you're doing?"

"I really wouldn't know." Oliva gestured in the direction of the hospital, visible through the window at the front of the store. "Why don't you go on up to the hospital and ask them?"

"I'm asking you."

"No!" Oliva's voice resounded through the store. "Ask *them*. Go on. 'Cause right now, you've got a better chance of getting in to see them than I do."

"You're avoiding the question."

"And you're avoiding the truth." Oliva pointed a finger at him before turning away. "You're not interested in what I have to say. You'll print whatever you want anyway."

"I print the truth," Fellman said, defending his trade with all the conviction he had available at the moment.

"Truth? Ha!" Oliva snickered with contempt. "How can you print the truth when you won't even listen to what it is?"

There was a raw silence.

"Here, you want some of your kind of truth?" Oliva turned back to face the reporter. "I'll help you." He raised his hands and stretched an invisible headline through the air. "*Dionne profits from Quints' misery.*"

Fellman continued to stare, wordless.

"There. Got your story? Now get out of here. I have a business to take care of." He turned his back to Fellman once more.

On his way out of the store, Fellman paused in the doorway to look back. Oliva was again facing the counter, rearranging some woollen mittens that were lying there. He didn't look up, though. Not until a customer rushed in, breezing past Fellman with her young daughter.

"That's him," the woman cried, pulling her daughter along. "That's the quints' father!"

Oliva gave the woman as big a smile as he could.

The reporter walked away, not sure of who troubled him more, Oliva and his immoral operation, or the woman to whom he was about to sell another autograph.

Fellman raised his hand to knock, then stopped himself. Instead, he gazed around yet another time – at the simple pine railing, at the torn screen door that the children had likely poked through, at the half-open window with the lace curtain drawn out by the breeze to press against the screen mesh, at the galoshes on the rope mat by the wood box full of kindling. It was all so homey. And though the door in front of him had once been known to fly open with unquestioning welcome, he couldn't bring himself to rap.

He had been standing on the porch of the Dionne farmhouse for ten minutes now, trying desperately to muster the courage to knock at the now-forbidden door. But each time his knuckles met the door, his mouth lost its rehearsed words, and his hand froze. Then, the slightest noise behind him was enough to put off another attempt for several minutes.

He looked at his watch, then over his shoulder to the observation gallery. It was past eight o'clock. The gallery had closed hours ago, and still people were wandering about. He couldn't understand why they stayed after the show closed, their shrill voices piercing the autumn night. Only when the snow came would they stop coming. In a few short weeks, they would all return to their houses to be with their families – to prepare the Christmas pudding, to make decorations for the tall fir trees they would cut, to bring in the biggest sticks for the fire, and to summon their children from snow fights for the big feast.

Standing at the threshold of what appeared to be one such home, and looking out over the walled-in structure across the road, Fellman speculated about what the tourists thought. Did they think that the quints stayed in the sterile security of the hospital while snow made yet another barrier around it? Or that they went to spend a winter vacation with Dr. Dafoe in his now-favourite New York City? Or perhaps that they went to their parents' home across the street to spend a big French-Canadian family Christmas, for endless days afterwards telling their brothers and sisters about all the funny people that came to see them? Or had the tourists all been like Fellman, and not thought about it at all?

Thoughts such as these didn't help boost his courage. Neither did the curious looks from the people who passed by and saw him standing there. He was sure they imagined him a brave passer-by trying to gain the courage to knock and ask for an autograph. Were they all that wrong, he thought, remembering how many times in the last three years he had knocked on the same door in an attempt to get an exclusive for his paper?

He had often felt uncomfortable about the stories that had given his and so many other newspapers such popularity over the years: that Dionne was an ignorant farmer who would sell his kids for a dime; that Mrs. Dionne was a fat and slovenly peasant who didn't have the right to have such beautiful babies; that the quints' siblings were too dirty to play with their royal sisters. Then today, he had started to believe that it was all true. After all, selling wool was one thing, but souvenirs of his own children? And autographs?

Yet here he was now, wavering, and not sure why. Dionne's outburst in the store hadn't really made that much of an impression. It was something else. It was walking in and seeing an ordinary man, not some kind of ogre, standing behind the counter. Oliva Dionne was not, by appearances, anything like the descriptions that had appeared in his and countless other newspapers and magazines. He was clean cut, well-dressed – certainly better than the reporters at the paper were – and spoke pretty good English. Moreover, his words had made sense. Fellman wondered how he could produce yet another damaging article about the Dionnes without at least trying to resolve right and wrong in the story that had made his career.

He finally found the strength to knock by forcing himself to act the way his job had trained him. As a reporter. He rapped hard on the door.

There was no answer.

He rapped again.

Still no answer.

It didn't really surprise him that no one would come to the door. Would he have answered his door if it opened onto the whole intruding world? As he turned to leave, he heard a soft clicking sound to his left. He looked over in time to see the curtains being drawn in by a thick hand, and the window sash being forced down by a plump woman with a roundish face and short, straight hair. Just before the blind dropped to seal off the outside, he caught the look of alarm on the woman's face.

He had already started down the steps when he heard the sound of a door opening. Looking back, he could just make out, through the screen, a man's face filling the opening between the big inner door and the jamb. It was the same angry face he had seen earlier today. In the wool shop.

Fellman stepped back up toward the door, but on his way, he heard the latch on the screen door lock. Oliva had seen who it was and had started also to close the inner door. "Wait, Mr. Dionne," Fellman blurted out, raising his hand as if to signal some sort of truce. "Please?"

"What do you want?" Oliva held the door open a little. "Don't you have enough for your story? Stop by the store tomorrow and I'll tell you how much I make. That should be pretty good copy." He started to close the door again.

"I just want to talk for a few minutes." This time, Fellman raised both his hands to show that he was empty-handed. "I don't even have my notepad with me."

Oliva gave a mocking laugh. "You reporters have very good memories." His smirk turned to a scowl. "I mean, if I came out there and threw you off my property, I think you'd remember enough to write about it tomorrow, notepad or no notepad. Am I wrong?"

"No, you're not wrong," Fellman conceded, "but I hope you won't do that."

"If you don't leave, I will," Oliva assured him. "There's no doubt in my mind, maybe even in the Government's mind too, that you're now on my property."

"Look, Mr. Dionne, you can call the police or come out here and do whatever you want, but I really would like to understand what's going on."

"So would I. Why don't you go and ask your good friend, the doctor, exactly what he's been doing with my children all these years?"

"I mean about this morning. Maybe I judged too quick, without knowing all the facts."

"Facts!" Oliva opened the door wide and faced the humbled reporter. "Since when did facts matter to you? All the terrible things your paper said about my wife and I. You don't even know us. You've never even met my wife."

"What can I say?" He knew how much truth there was in Oliva's words. His only previous encounters with the man he had written so much about had been either distant views, or seeing at close range an enraged face rushing to an unknown destination. They had never actually spoken with one another until today. "I'm sorry," was all he could finally come up with. "That's like a kick in the ass right now, isn't it?"

Oliva didn't respond. He stared past Fellman to some people on the road who had gathered to watch them, and to try to peer into the house beyond.

Fellman noticed Oliva's preoccupation with the uninvited guests. Where the people were standing had once been considered part of the Dionne land. He looked back at Oliva and noticed, in the background, a gangly adolescent piercing him with a hostile stare. A young girl with a curious look on her face had also moved in to take her father's hand.

Fellman saw an opportunity to prove his sincerity. He turned to the unwelcome group on the road. "What are you looking at?" he shouted, then turned back to Oliva. Behind him he could hear quick footsteps disappearing in different directions.

Only Oliva now remained in the doorway, an amused look on his face.

"I can't apologize for everything the world has done to you," Fellman said earnestly. "I can't even apologize for what *I've* done. But if you're willing to talk, I'm willing to listen. That's all. I can't promise that I'll understand or anything like that, but I will listen; I promise you that."

Oliva's amusement disappeared. His blank expression returned.

Fellman reached out to grab the handle of the screen door. It was still locked. "I really don't blame you for not letting me in," he said. "But, you know, it's easy to lose track of what the truth is. Or at least what we think it is."

They looked at each other for what seemed like hours, Fellman with hope, Oliva with prejudice.

Then, Oliva turned away inside the house, and let the heavy door swing shut.

Fellman shrank back, not only from despair, but with relief. On one hand, he was disappointed that he would not get past the threshold of the house. But on the other, he was grateful for the amount of time he had been given. He buttoned up his jacket and turned to leave.

Just as he was about to take a step down from the porch, he heard the door creak again. He looked over his shoulder to see it open about six inches, just enough to let a hand through. As the hand disappeared, he heard the click of a latch.

He walked back up to the door and gripped the handle tightly. He turned it, slowly. Then, with greater determination than he had ever known, he pulled the door open, and stepped out of the cold and into the Dionne home.

Fellman hesitated before getting into his car. To one side of him was the Dionne house, which rang with laughter, smelled of tourtière, and radiated warmth. To the other was the Dafoe Hospital, which shone with fame, reeked of sterility, and exuded a coldness that even its staff complained about. He remembered Dafoe once rationalizing the separation by saying that the quints were right across the street from their parents. Until tonight, he had never realized how far away that was.

At midnight, there was no traffic along the road that led to Quintland. He could have easily sailed down to meet the Ferguson, and on into North Bay. But instead, he chose to take his accustomed route through Corbeil.

His headlights illuminated the sleepy buildings along the way: Voyer's, the Catholic church, the farmhouses that lay on both sides of the road. These houses belonged to families just like the Dionnes. He wondered how they would feel if the security of their families were threatened, then stripped completely away.

When he reached North Bay and his own little house, the feelings welled up again. What would he and Doris do if the Government were to walk in and snatch their two precious daughters, who were at this moment tucked safely in their beds in the room next to their mother? What could they do if the whole world were against them?

He set the clock for seven, then lay in bed, thinking about all he had learned. He dozed off a few times but mostly stayed awake, tossing about, getting up to go to the bathroom, checking the girls, and making enough noise, surely, to waken Doris so that he could tell her about his visit. But her sleep was sound, her conscience clear. To her, the Dionnes were just a news story that Mort worked on. It was he who had seen things a certain way for so long, but had let others override his own instincts.

How could he have let himself be swayed by the opinions of others for so long? By the world, to whom the girls' birth was not just a wonder, but an oddity? By his editor, who thrived on criticizing Dionne for everything imaginable? By his media friends from Toronto, who like himself, were always peeved that the Dionnes refused all interviews? By the Government, whose greedy motives were accepted as divine intervention by almost everyone? And, at the very beginning, by Dafoe, who had been so successful in keeping the babies alive that his reward became an unheard-of form of human sacrifice?

He had been asleep for only about two hours when the alarm rang. He jumped out of bed, wildly alert, and dressed quickly. He dashed downstairs to the telephone in the hallway, clearing his throat a few times while the operator rang the Dafoe Hospital. When one of the nurses answered, he didn't bother to ask for Dafoe, who wouldn't be in this early anyway. He didn't ask for Dafoe's secretary either, for he might not grant an appointment until three weeks from now, depending on the doctor's busy schedule, which included a CBC radio program, a syndicated column that appeared in over two hundred newspapers, and frequent trips to New York. All he did was ask if the doctor would be in today. When the nurse said yes, and asked if Dafoe could return the call, Fellman recited all in one breath, "Tell him it's Mort Fellman, *North Bay Nugget*. I'll be there around nine," and quickly hung up. A bowl of porridge and a cup of tea later, he was on his way.

For the second day in a row, he had to fight his way through the thick crowds at Quintland. But this time, he could go all the way with the car, for he had an appointment within the gates of the Dafoe Hospital. As he drove past the guard-post and through the gate, he wondered what purpose his visit would serve, especially when he expected no revelations and didn't anticipate hearing anything new. But then, he had thought the same thing yesterday when he charged into Oliva's store, ready to accuse. It wasn't until last night that he had really *heard* anything. He felt that he owed it to all of them, himself included, to listen to the doctor with a new ear, too.

As the nurse led him down the stark corridor to Dafoe's office, he noticed how barren the hospital environment actually was. He had thought about it before, but not in quite the same way as now, after Oliva had described it last night. Everything was white: the walls, the floors, the bed linens, the kitchen dishes, the nurses' crisp uniforms. And that antiseptic smell in the air. He had been inside the hospital many times, but the smell of a good story was the only one he could remember.

When he arrived at Dafoe's office, that same smell greeted him once again.

"Mort," Dafoe called out as he rose from his desk to greet the reporter. "Good to see you."

They shook hands.

"Sit down." Dafoe turned to Nurse Harper. "Give me a ring in ten minutes, Nurse," he instructed, then turned back to Fellman. "It's been a while, Mort. Where have you been?"

Nurse Harper closed the door and left.

"You're looking pretty chipper," Fellman said. The radiant look on the doctor's face went well with his pressed suit, starched shirt, and Indian madras bow-tie. Fellman hadn't seen Dafoe in several months and was surprised at how well he looked. If the doctor was feeling any stress from Oliva's attempts to discredit and even displace him, his appearance didn't show it.

"Thank you for seeing me on such short notice."

"Nonsense, Mort. You know I can always spare a few minutes for you." He sat down again. "Besides, I understand you didn't give my nurse much of a choice when you called." He peered over the rim of his eyeglasses and smiled.

"I hope you don't mind," Fellman said, knowing that the doctor didn't. The Dionnes were right; Dafoe and his girls always had time for reporters. He settled into the worn leather chair across from Dafoe's desk and flipped open the notepad that last night, for the first time in years, he had been without. He found it curious that he had learned so much without writing a single word.

"Let me show you something, Mort." Dafoe proudly held up a large envelope. "I received this just yesterday." Out of the envelope slid a photograph of himself flanked by Clark Gable and Carole Lombard, the three of them standing in front of the hospital, smiling the biggest Hollywood smiles conceivable. "It was taken when they were up. Davis had it blown up for me as a gift. They signed it. See?" He turned it over. "Pretty nice, don't you think?"

"It'll look good up on your wall," Fellman remarked, glancing upwards.

The wall displayed an assortment of framed photos of Dafoe posing with some of his celebrity friends and acquaintances: Premier Hepburn; Amelia Earhart; Sally Rand, with William Randolph Hearst; Jean Hersholt, the actor who had portrayed Dafoe in *The Country Doctor;* Bette Davis; a few others – probably business people – that' Fellman didn't recognize. No pictures of the quints, though. Maybe they were too much like family to be part of the collection that represented the doctor's business circle. He figured that Dafoe's home was probably filled with photos of the smiling five.

Dafoe carefully returned the photograph to its envelope. "So what can I help you with today, Mort?"

"We're putting out a special supplement on the quints this Christmas. I'm doing a feature on what's in store for them."

"What's the rush?" Dafoe asked, puzzled. "Christmas is two months away."

"Yes, but uh… Doris and I are taking the girls to Niagara Falls next week and…."

"Pretty cold to go down there now," Dafoe cut in.

Fellman just smiled.

"I thought you'd be editor of that paper by now," Dafoe said out of the blue.

"I'm working on it."

"Well, you deserve it."

The false charm made Fellman's stomach churn. He could see that Dafoe was almost as good as Premier Hepburn in buttering up the press. Maybe that's what kept everyone interested. After all, he had to drum up something to replace the incredible naivety that had once attracted the reporters' attention and that had since worn away.

"Mort, I hope you don't mind if we get down to business right away. I have a meeting with the Board of Health in fifteen minutes."

"No, of course not," Fellman said, the reporter in him itching to get past the small talk. "I'll try to keep it short. I just want to get an idea of what you see for the future."

Dafoe leaned back in his chair. "Well, as I've told you before, I think that all we can do is make sure the quintuplets are prepared."

"For leaving the hospital?"

"For everything," Dafoe generalized. "How to deal with people, how to live in the public eye. You know the attention they get. It's going to get worse as they get older."

"In what way?"

"Well, right now, people come to see them, but the girls aren't really aware."

Fellman searched the doctor's face as unobtrusively as he could. Did Dafoe really believe that? Had he not been in the observation gallery? Had he not seen how the girls pressed their noses against the wire-mesh barrier, listening intently to the excited voices and the persistent tapping on the glass, posing for those visitors who squealed the loudest? "Do you mean that the girls think of the observation gallery area as a playground?" he asked.

"Yes, I guess so," hedged Dafoe, unsure if that was what he had meant. "I guess what I mean to say is that they have no complaints. They're waited on hand and foot. They play all day. They get everything they want. They're having the time of their lives."

Fellman scribbled enthusiastically. "A bit of a fairy tale, isn't it?"

"That's a fair statement," Dafoe agreed, "and all the more reason we have to prepare them for being adults."

"What do you think they'll be doing when they get older?" Fellman tried to picture the polished princesses scrubbing floors, milking cows, baking for a dozen people, and changing diapers for as many – the lot of most women in small farming communities such as this one.

"Well, I feel that as they get older, people will stop looking *at* them and start looking *to* them." The doctor's eyes brightened with images of the glorious path ahead – world tours, meetings with kings and presidents, appearances at prestigious dinners and ship launchings, royal treatment at every turn. "They may go on tours together, give

171

lectures, become goodwill ambassadors… whatever, but they'll have to set an example as responsible Canadians. Model citizens. They'll have to be leaders," he emphasized. He looked to make sure that Fellman was getting everything down. "You know what I mean."

"Yes, I do," agreed Fellman, knowing exactly what the doctor had meant. A certain type of life would be theirs for the asking. "So, you don't really feel they'll want to lead ordinary lives?"

"How can they?" Dafoe asked, discounting the possibility. "They're not ordinary girls. They're *the quints*. That will never change."

Dafoe had it all planned, Fellman thought. Nobody else would have a say. Not the Dionnes. Not even the girls themselves. Only Dafoe and the powers that be.

"What about their immediate futures, then?"

"Well," he said a little anxiously, "the Guardianship Bill goes on until they're eighteen, so we don't have to worry about that for now."

Oliva's comment last night that Dafoe would never give up the girls voluntarily was still fresh in Fellman's mind. "Will they stay in the hospital until then?" he pressed.

"It's still too early to tell. We haven't discussed a timetable yet." He looked to Fellman expectantly, hoping for another, different, question.

But Fellman remained silent, forcing Dafoe to continue.

"I'd say until they're… I don't know… at least eleven or twelve. It's hard to say right now."

"That long?"

"Oh, yes. At least. They're not ready for the outside world."

"Aren't you concerned about Dionne's legal challenges to get them back?"

"Not really," Dafoe answered smugly. "Not as long as I've got the Government on my side. But wait till you hear what his latest complaint is…." He looked at his watch as he heard steps outside the door. By the way, did you see the premier on the cover of *Time*?"

"Yes. The man's really going places."

Just then the door opened and a pretty young nurse poked her head in. "Doctor, the people from McCormick's called from the gas station. They're going to be a little late. They're caught up in a traffic jam at the turn."

Dafoe was enraged. "I'm in a meeting," he scolded the nurse, getting up to wave her out of the room. "Can't you wait until I'm finished?"

"I'm sorry." She quickly closed the door.

"Rude," Dafoe remarked. He sat back down only after the sound of the nurse's footsteps had faded down the hall. "Now, where were we?"

"McCormick's?"

"Yes, yes," he said, still rattled. "They want to do a presentation during our Board of Health meeting this morning. Of all things."

"I see." Fellman made another note. "What kind of presentation?" He couldn't see what biscuits had to do with a Board of Health meeting. But then, he had never understood what Remington Rand typewriters had to do with quintuplets, either.

"Mort, I think we'd better stick to the topic," Dafoe said, wishing the reporter would stop writing. "I've got a lot of other work to do too, you know."

"Sorry." Fellman looked up from his pad to see Dafoe worrying at the corners of the pages in his day-book. "You were telling me about Oliva Dionne's latest...."

"Yes, well, that's not important. Do you have any more questions?"

"Just a few," Fellman said in an attempt to pacify the doctor. "I was wondering if the Dionnes will have a say in how the girls are raised as they get older?"

"We consider what they have to say," Dafoe answered, sounding as noncommittal as always. It was a sign that he had regained his composure.

Fellman wondered how he and the rest of the press had let Dafoe get away with such empty statements these past three years. "Yes, but how do you fit them into the decision-making process?"

"Mort, you have a lot on your mind today. Why don't you ask Dionne these questions?"

Realizing that his sympathies might be showing, Fellman quickly covered up. "You know I don't talk to the man. You know what he's like." He dug up a roguish smile from somewhere in his past.

Dafoe grinned back, some of the old trust between them returning. "Well, Dionne is on the Board of Guardians," he said, giving his stock answer. "He has as much right as anyone to raise an issue."

"So he has an equal say to you?"

"Absolutely."

"I understand he's complaining all the time that none of his suggestions are considered. The idea of bringing in French-speaking staff. Changing the head nurse. Bringing the family closer together. Getting

Blatz's nurses out. Isn't all that beginning to interfere with your plans to do the right thing?"

"It certainly is!" Dafoe's tone didn't hide his irritation over how Oliva had become a royal pain in the ass. "I'm just glad *I* have the final say. I have to consider what's best for those girls."

Fellman couldn't let that opening go by. "Don't you think their father has their best interests in mind?"

"In his own simplistic way, I guess," Dafoe conceded. "But it's hard for the Dionnes to understand what we're trying to do. They look upon the quintuplets as they do their other children."

"Is there anything wrong with that?"

"Of course there is. The quints won't live the lives of ordinary people, so why give them an ordinary upbringing? Even they know they're different. The Dionnes are the only ones who forget."

"For argument's sake, what do you think would happen if the girls went to live with their parents?"

Dafoe shook his head rapidly. He didn't even want to think about the possibility of his precious girls living in that barn. "First off, they're not ready. And even if they were, their parents aren't." He opened his top drawer and pulled out an envelope. He started to open it. "They can't give the girls what they need. They're not fit to do that kind of job. We'd only be hurting the girls by letting them go back to that old farmhouse." Out of the envelope he pulled a white card embossed with gold. "Look at this," he said, offering the card. "It's a request from the King to meet the girls during the Royal Tour in '39."

Fellman just stared. If Oliva wasn't good enough to hold the invitation, neither was he. "Advance notice, eh?" he finally chuckled.

"What would happen if the girls were living across the street in that pigsty when the King and Queen came? I'll tell you. Your friend Dionne would expect them to go there. Can you imagine?"

Fellman looked at Dafoe carefully, hoping that the doctor had used the word *friend* loosely. He didn't want the conversation to be cut short. Not yet. "I guess you're right," he obliged.

"This hospital is their home," Dafoe went on. "It always has been. If they were to go to live in that shack across the road, the Dionnes would ruin everything we've tried to do."

Fellman stopped taking notes, afraid that Dafoe would put a quick end to the interview. "Dionne wouldn't agree with you," he said casually. It was becoming hard to keep his composure in the face of the appalling things he was hearing.

"It's not his decision," Dafoe said bluntly, wondering why Fellman was defending the ignorant farmer.

The reporter couldn't hold the human being inside any longer. "But he's their father!"

"In name only," Dafoe said coldly, leaning forward. "You've seen them, Mort; you know how they are with me."

Yes, he did. And that's what bothered him the most.

"Tell the truth," Dafoe prodded. "Who do they look to as their father?"

Fellman didn't answer right away. He looked at Dafoe, feelings of loathing and pity contending with each other. He could see that for the heralded doctor, the estranged parents of the quintuplets no longer existed. Like almost everyone else, Dafoe had conveniently forgotten that the girls had a real father and mother – perfectly fit, loving parents who had been waiting for more than three years now to bring their daughters home.

"Yes, you're right," Fellman admitted, though he didn't want to.

"Actually, I like to think of them as belonging to the world."

"You've always said that, haven't you?" He remembered that all of Dafoe's interviews ended with those words. He dropped the other questions he had wanted to ask.

Dafoe glanced at the clock on the wall. "Mort," he said, getting up, "I'm going to have to cut this short now." He was smiling as he stood up, but appeared uneasy nonetheless. "I hope I've been of some help," he commented, unsure of what good his remarks had been. It wasn't the first time they had talked about these things.

"It was good of you to spend this much time with me."

"Always time for you, Mort. We go back a long way."

"Yes, we do."

"You were the first," Dafoe reminded him. "The girls owe you a lot."

"I was afraid you'd say that." The innocent remark was a crude reminder to Fellman that he, too, had played a role in destroying people's lives.

"What?"

"Oh, nothing." He turned to leave. "Thanks again, Doctor."

As Fellman walked toward the door, Dafoe started to follow. But Fellman stopped him with a brief shake of the hand. "I know my way out. Thanks."

He didn't stop to close doors as he made his escape from the hospital. He didn't feel he could breathe again until he got out-of-doors. He felt feverish, his stomach upset. When he reached his car, he took a few deep breaths, then got in and drove off. As he waited for the gate to be opened, he glanced back at the Dafoe Hospital, promising himself he would never return – unless to help destroy it.

Dafoe remained standing for a long while after Fellman had gone. He replayed their conversation in his head, but couldn't figure out where Fellman was going to find a feature in the empty exchange they had just had. He couldn't recall saying anything he hadn't said many times before.

Part Three

"...But the Quints will go on smiling."

– *Maclean's*, July 15, 1941

11

Changing the Guard

They all agreed it was best to downplay the news of the libel suit. If they had learned anything from Hepburn these past seven years, it was to avoid showing panic when you'd made a mistake – and to be damned sure you didn't make the same mistake twice.

Slocum, Sharkey, and Clayton sat around a reading table in the musty, cluttered archive room of the Justice Library, where against the four walls, stacks of law books and transcripts towered high to the ceiling, seemingly ready to topple at any minute. The three of them had sat for a long time without speaking, preparing for another one of Hepburn's fiery monologues.

Hepburn had called the meeting as soon as word had come out that Oliva Dionne was suing Dafoe for libel. Over the telephone with Slocum, the premier hadn't elaborated about what the problem was. He had just made some remark about Dafoe's having made a public fool of himself at a private function in New York. But whatever Hepburn had concealed, the press didn't. The morning papers had done a fine job of describing the embarrassing and potentially damaging incident that one reporter called "a mockery of everything the doctor stands for".

"Dionne is blowing the whole thing out of proportion," remarked Clayton, breaking the silence and pointing to the headline that shrieked from the front page of the morning's *Globe*. "He'll never win a suit like that. My God, if it wasn't for Dafoe, there'd be no quints to fight about in the first place."

"I hope you're right." Sharkey was concerned about the possibility of lost accounts, not any gratitude due to Dafoe. "We don't want any bad publicity. Especially after all that business in court between Corn Brand and Beehive. I can name ten companies that won't touch us if there's anything fishy going on. And Colgate won't sign if Dafoe's not part of the deal." He turned to Slocum, who was sitting closest to the door. "Have you had any calls yet, Dick?"

"Only from reporters. I told them it was news to us, too." He knew that Hepburn would want to keep a tight lid on how concerned they actually were. "I told them that it's between Dionne and Dafoe, that it doesn't concern us." That was partly true. They weren't going to let Dafoe hang, but they weren't about to bring themselves into it.

"Hell, with a war going on, you'd think the paper would have more important things to write about than that farmer making trouble for everyone."

Slocum shot a disapproving look across the table. He knew how much Clayton disliked Dionne – the animosity that had resulted from their run-in at the beginning had festered – but talk against the man who was now fighting with a vengeance for his children was dangerous. Especially considering the way things had been changing in Dionne's favour lately. Four new nurses had come on board in the past year alone, all of them French-speaking, as well as a French teacher. And in that same period of time, Oliva had all but taken control of the Board of Guardians, winning virtually every point he raised, with the exception of the closure of the hospital and the dismissal of its doctor.

The door to the archive room opened wide. Premier Hepburn entered first, followed closely by another man. Dafoe trailed in last, looking sullen.

Once Dafoe was inside the room, Hepburn closed the door, and sat down between Slocum and the stranger. "Gentlemen, I'd like you to meet Dennis Foley from Justice."

They all leaned across the table to shake hands.

"Mr. Foley has been advising Dr. Dafoe on how to handle our little problem."

"Shouldn't Conant be here?" Clayton thought it reasonable that the Attorney General be present when a matter that concerned his portfolio was being discussed.

Hepburn glared at Clayton. "I don't want to waste his valuable time on this matter."

"But, Sir, it only seems...."

"I don't like wasting my own time either," Hepburn added, turning the comment to Dafoe. "The fewer people that are in on this, the better. The *Star* has been calling Conant's office all morning. Having him here would just cause speculation. It's bad enough that we had to smuggle our dear doctor in here this morning."

Dafoe cringed at the sarcasm in the premier's tone.

Clayton's demeanour quickly changed from humility to annoyance. "Aren't we overreacting a bit? I mean, it's obvious that Dionne's only goal is to try to make life difficult for all of us."

"Yes, it is. And he's succeeding." Hepburn's steely look suggested that the current situation was far more than the *little problem* he had referred to when the meeting began. "I think it's time that we all stopped underestimating Oliva Dionne."

Clayton looked pained, as if he were unable to bear the thought of the temperamental farmer being discussed with anything but contempt. "Well then, what's our position on the matter?" he asked brusquely.

"We don't have one," Hepburn announced. "The best way to avoid speculation about our position is not to have one. No comments at all." He thumped the table with his fist to emphasize the gravity of his point. "I want that to be very clear to all of you."

"So what do we tell the reporters?" asked Clayton. "I stalled them this morning, but they'll want a comment eventually."

"Tell them you don't know a thing. Let's not aggravate an already delicate situation. I don't need to remind you of how increasingly sympathetic the press has become to Dionne." He stared one by one at the faces that surrounded him. "Or maybe I do, judging by your lackadaisical attitudes."

Slocum didn't have to be reminded. He knew all too well that Oliva Dionne's libel suit against Dafoe had come at a bad time. Almost every morning this past summer, he had clipped another newspaper or magazine article that questioned the cloistered upbringing of the quints. At first, this renewed interest in the quints had been limited to the French press, which was complaining mostly about the lack of

French education available to the girls in a hospital full of English-speaking staff. Ontario hadn't been too concerned about what Québec thought, but when the English press in their own province had started questioning the Government's involvement in Canada's number one export, and editorializing about the possibility of the quints going to live with their parents, it had started to have an effect on all of them – especially Hepburn.

The last thing the premier wanted was to read articles like the one in *Cosmopolitan*, where psychologist Alfred Adler was quoted as saying: "The Quintuplets live like inmates of a model orphanage." Other damning observations included: "Emotional starvation is inseparable from institutional life," and "Life in a glass house is not conducive to normal human development." Adler concluded his remarks with the foreboding words: *"There is danger ahead."*

"We have to be concerned," Slocum finally said, just as Hepburn's stare had settled on Dafoe. "I understand that some of the new nurses at the hospital are on Dionne's side as well."

The statement drew a cold look from Dafoe.

But before the doctor could deny that he was losing control in his own establishment, Foley cut in. "True, but that's a separate matter. I think we should confine ourselves to the problem at hand."

All eyes turned to Foley for direction.

"Mr. Foley," asked Sharkey, thinking of the contracts he wanted to close, "is there any way of getting Dionne to drop the suit?"

"Yes, I think so. Premier Hepburn and I have discussed some possible concessions, and the most obvious thing is to let the Dionnes have free access to the hospital."

Dafoe was visibly upset by the suggestion, but remained silent. He had received a heated lecture from Hepburn just before the meeting, and didn't want to experience another such dehumanizing episode. Not in front of an audience.

"That should keep them happy for a while," said Slocum.

"I'm glad it will make someone happy," Dafoe muttered, unable to resist the opportunity to make his feelings known.

Hepburn stared Dafoe into another silence. "At least it will keep the pressure off. That's the most important thing right now."

Sharkey shook his head. "I don't know, Mr. Premier." His mind was working harder than ever. "Once the parents get some control, they'll only want more."

"I know that."

"Then you also know how they feel about the endorsements. And the shows. What if they start objecting to those, too? Giving in now sets a bad precedent."

Dafoe looked to Sharkey hopefully.

"The quints aren't always going to be this big." The premier's words came out more as a proclamation than a speculation. "Gentlemen, let's not fool ourselves. They're not adorable little girls any more. They're seven years old. And there's a war going on. People have more important things on their minds than the quints. Right now, it's more important to think about the reputation of the Government than it is to make a few dollars."

"We're not talking about a few dollars," Sharkey reminded everyone, then faced Hepburn. "They're a five hundred million dollar asset to this province."

"*Now*. But not forever."

"It's the principle," argued Clayton. "Why should we let Dionne make us run scared?"

"Because there's a lot at stake," said Hepburn, thinking of the history books. "And I won't stand for anyone's words... or actions," he added, turning to Dafoe, "casting even the slightest doubt on the Government's role in this affair. Do you understand that? We've already got the press breathing down our necks."

"Premier Hepburn is absolutely right," endorsed Foley.

"Now," Hepburn continued, "the parents will be told that they can come into the hospital whenever they want. Dr. Dafoe has already agreed."

"It will be a pleasure." Dafoe tried to be meek, but the words were nevertheless tinged with sarcasm.

Hepburn gave Dafoe another cold look, then addressed the group again. "And let's make sure that we don't do anything, and I mean *anything*, to excite Dionne again. As a government, we can make it appear that we're taking this matter lightly. But I assure you, gentlemen, it would be a mistake for any of you to actually do so."

Hepburn slowly got up, surveying his men. Then he gave one of his *Now let's not make any mistakes* frowns to end the meeting. "That will be all."

Before they could all get up to leave, Hepburn was already ushering Dafoe out of the room and toward a door marked *Exit* at the far end of the library.

Slocum watched the premier walk out, hesitantly preceded by the little doctor they had all watched rise to fame. Not the first man Hepburn had moulded to his liking, then thrown away, Slocum thought. And probably not the last.

No words passed between Hepburn and Dafoe until the door through which they had exited was tightly shut, and they were walking alone down the long narrow corridor that led outside.

"Allan, what in hell could you have been thinking?" Hepburn asked viciously. Although he had not been there to witness it, he could picture Dafoe in the long pink robe, riding the buggy around the stage in front of a hundred of New York's most influential people. The sign on the buggy, clear for all to see: *DOCTOR OF LITTERS*.

"It was a joke," Dafoe said defensively. "At a private party."

"A joke!" thundered the angry premier. "I just hope this plan of Foley's works, or we're all in big trouble. You know that, don't you?"

"I'm sorry," stammered Dafoe, still not fully aware of what he was apologizing for.

Hepburn picked up his step and passed Dafoe. "Look, until I say otherwise, I don't want you talking to any more reporters," he ordered over his shoulder. "I warned you months ago about trusting your friends in the press. Especially that one in North Bay. He's always praising Dionne in spite of us."

Dafoe almost had to run to keep up with the premier. "I get ten calls a day for interviews," he said, panicking. "It's going to make me look guilty if I refuse them."

"More guilty than you look right now?"

Dafoe didn't know what he looked like. But he didn't *feel* that guilty.

"Just tell them that you're busy being a doctor for a change, instead of parading around like some Broadway star."

"It's Fellman, you know," complained Dafoe. "He's the one who started turning everyone against me. How was I supposed to know he had changed sides?"

Hepburn stopped in the middle of the corridor and spun around to face Dafoe, who almost bumped into him. "Whose side he or anyone else is on is not the problem. If you had kept your mouth shut and simply done what you were supposed to do, we'd all be a lot better off than we are right now."

"Okay, okay. But giving the Dionnes free access to my hospital?"

Hepburn finally blew. "We're vulnerable as hell, can't you understand that?" The words bounced against the marble walls and echoed down the hall. He looked from side to side to make sure no one was around. "Don't you realize how bad it could be for all of us if we're examined too closely right now? I won't let the reputation of the Government suffer over some stupid thing you've done without thinking."

Dafoe tried, but couldn't think of an appropriate response. "I'll do my best," was all he could think of.

"Don't do your best," Hepburn instructed. "Just do what you're told and everything will be fine. And don't make the mistake of not taking me seriously." He strode off again toward the door, Dafoe still a step or two behind. "The trip to Toronto next summer for the Victory Bond Rally. Why don't you ask Dionne to escort his daughters?"

"What?" Dafoe stopped.

"Sure," said Hepburn, pleased with the idea. "It might calm him down a little if you show some good faith."

"Good faith!" He was forced to run this time to keep up with Hepburn, who hadn't stopped when he had. "We haven't said a civil word to each other in years. All of a sudden I'm supposed to show good faith?"

"It will do you some good."

The doctor didn't respond.

Hepburn stopped just before the door at the end of the hall. "Okay, let *me* ask him."

"You think he'll listen to you?" Dafoe asked doubtfully.

"He'll go," Hepburn said confidently, opening the door and signalling to the driver of the waiting car. "After all, it's for the war effort. I'm sure the man has some patriotism." He patted Dafoe on the back a couple of times, then pushed him out into the late October wind. "Besides," he added as Dafoe ran clumsily toward the car, the wind almost catching his hat, "it'll be a chance for him to spend some time with his kids."

*   *   *

Every Sunday, the whole family got together. Pépère and Tante Alma usually came straight from church, while various other members of the Dionne and Legros families came and went all day. Whoever arrived early enough enjoyed a big lunch of eggs, bacon, fried potatoes, and toast with butter and strawberry preserves. Those who came in the afternoon usually stayed for the big family supper, when after prayers, they warmed their stomachs with hot soup, and feasted on the biggest bird that they had been able to catch the day before. The ones who dropped by in the evening arrived to the fragrance of the apple pie coming from the oven, and attacked leftovers while they waited for the pie to cool. Then there was more eating until late into the night. It seemed that whatever time of the day it was, there was always a table full of food in the Dionne home.

Oliva looked around the table dreamily. Above the mounds of sweet-smelling chicken with liver stuffing, heaps of mashed turnip, gleaming cranberry sauce, and loaves of fresh bread, he could see his family. All of them. Those at the table and those on the wall. He could easily picture those same five heads that smiled out now from oval cut-outs in a wooden frame, as part of the group – waiting anxiously for pie, fighting with one another, and giggling uncontrollably under cupped palms. But as clearly as he could imagine his five identical daughters, behind them, even more clearly, and towering above them all, he could picture Dafoe, the hospital's white-clad nurses, and Hepburn. It always broke the spell.

"I was talking to Martin Poulin today," Oliva announced through a mouthful of chicken. "He's coming over later," he added, noticing right away how Elzire looked up from her plate.

"Do we have to talk about this at supper?"

"What's he got now?" asked Olivier, who shared his son's enthusiasm for the fight.

Tante Alma gave both of them discouraging looks from across the table. She positioned baby Victor to rest against her arm, and put the bottle back into his mouth.

"He thinks we're pretty close now," Oliva said hopefully. "There's a lot of pressure on the Government over the libel suit."

"Big deal." Ernest broke a silence that had lasted all supper long.

"Ernest," Elzire warned. "Don't talk to your father like that!"

"What do you mean, big deal? You could be a little more excited."

"Oliva." Elzire switched her attention to Oliva, trying to stop the argument before it started.

"What's there to be excited about?"

"Ernest, you don't mean that." Pépère gave him a stern look. "Eat your supper."

"Yes, I do mean it," Ernest said boldly. "If they come to live in our house, people will be coming around here like they do at the hospital. My friends won't be allowed to visit, and there'll be police all over the place."

Oncle Léon was busy refilling his plate. "The boy's got a point. There will have to be police."

"Everything will be exactly as it was before all of this trouble began," Oliva stated.

Oliva's certainty troubled Elzire. "That was a long time ago, Oliva," she reminded him.

Pauline, sitting next to Rose, looked at her father curiously. She was too young to remember a time when there had been no crowds, no cars, no fences. "Papa, what was it like before?"

Elzire didn't want Oliva to answer. She wished they could go just one night without talking about the way things used to be, or the way things were going to be. "More chicken?" she asked no one in particular, in an attempt to enjoy the present.

"Over here, Elzire," said Olivier. "Is there any dark?"

"I'll take that leg," Léon called out over everyone.

Elzire got up and walked around the table, carrying the still-heaping plate of chicken pieces. "Anyone else, while I'm up? Oliva?"

The sound of boots crunching through the snow on the porch made Elzire turn, just in time to see the door fly open and Elzire's brother, Lias, walk in with his wife, Huguette, and their three children.

"Whew," Lias exhaled as he shut the door to the wind.

"Take your boots off," Huguette screeched as her three children shucked off their winter jackets and made a beeline for the table where the other children sat.

The dog heard the commotion from under the table, where he had been lying. He raised himself up on his front legs, stretched, then lay back down again. There were too many comings and goings to go to the door every time.

"Where's Papa?" Elzire asked, noticing that her father was absent from the group.

"He's got a touch of the flu," Lias said. "It's better he stays in. Aurel and them stayed with him."

"Here, Elzire. Take this." Huguette held out a pot of beans. "They'll need warming up. It's cold out there."

At the table, Pauline persisted. "What was it like, Papa?" While her friends' families dreamed of Florida and other far-off places, her family didn't. Their fantasies were all engaged in a place called *the way things used to be.*

"You can take Papa some soup on your way back," Elzire told Huguette as she took the beans from her and put them in the oven. "He can have it tomorrow."

Both Lias and Huguette followed Elzire to the stove. Lias bent down and stuck his hands just inside the oven door to warm them. Huguette followed suit, while the children crammed themselves into the open spaces and free seats at the table.

"Did you listen to the hockey game last night?" Léon asked Lias.

"No. Who won?"

"Les Canadiens."

"Good."

"Papa!" Pauline wanted an answer.

Oliva finally turned to Pauline. "It was wonderful, Pauline. So quiet, you could hear a butterfly land. The birds, the cows in the back, the wind blowing through the corn. It was wonderful," he repeated, his smile gradually switching to a grimace as his thoughts of the past melted into the reality of the present. "Now, you can't even hear yourself think."

"Those were poor days too, Oliva," Olivier remembered. "The Depression was no fun for anyone."

"Do we always have to talk about the past?" Elzire asked.

"Did you have Lagrise then, Pépère?" Pauline asked.

Olivier turned to answer her.

"I'll tell you one thing," Ernest interrupted, fidgeting in his chair. "When the quints come home, they aren't going to get my room."

"Don't call them that," insisted Elzire. "And stop that, Oliva," she added, turning to Oliva Jr., who was dumping spoonfuls of turnip onto his cousin's plate.

"I'll have some turnip," was Marie's attempt to turn the conversation.

"Come on, Elzire," Oliva placated her. Even he had called them *quints* on occasion. "It's hard to go through all the names."

"I don't care. They have names."

"They still can't have my room."

Olivier jumped in. "What's all this about taking Ernest's room?"

"I don't know." Oliva frowned at Ernest. "We haven't even thought about that yet."

"What are you going to do, anyway?" Olivier asked. "Build an addition?"

"You'll have to," added Léon.

"Léon will help," Marie offered. "It won't take no time at all."

Oliva shrugged. "We could do that, you know." He thought for a moment. "Or build another floor. Who knows, we could always move to a new house and get away from that eyesore across the road altogether."

"I bet that's a problem you'll be happy to deal with," Olivier added.

"Sure will."

"I don't want to move," pouted Ernest. "I like this house."

"The house isn't important," Oliva chided his son. "Being together is."

"Ernest," Olivier commented, "you're very disagreeable tonight."

"Don't you start too, Olivier." Tante Alma moved baby Victor to the other arm while she lifted the big plate of chicken and passed it to her brother. As she did so, she noticed Thérèse playing with her food at the far end of the table next to her father. "Thérèse, that's God's food you're playing with."

"Why is it so important to be together all of a sudden?" Thérèse asked.

"We never were before," reminded Ernest.

Oliva looked hurt. "If you're going to talk like that, you can both go to your rooms. And if this is going to be your attitude when your sisters come home, you can get used to eating all your meals there."

"Why?" Ernest got up. "Are they going to get special treatment here like they do at the hospital?"

"Sit down, Ernest!" insisted Elzire. "Now stop it, both of you! Fighting at God's table."

Ernest dropped back down, poking Rose as he sat. "I'm not hungry."

"Eat!" Oliva pointed to the full plate in front of his son.

"Will I be allowed to play with them, Maman?" asked Pauline after a brief silence.

"Who'd want to play with you?" Ernest kicked at her chair under the table.

"He kicked me," complained Pauline.

Rose piped in. "He's always poking me."

"Ernest," scolded Elzire, "go to your room!"

Ernest started to get up again.

"Sit down," Oliva commanded angrily. "And stop all this arguing."

"It wouldn't be Sunday without it," Léon remarked.

Ernest kicked his chair back. "I wish everyone would leave me alone," he grumbled, then ran off.

"Ernest, come back here," Oliva yelled. He rose from the table too, but Ernest had already rushed out of the kitchen and into his room. "I said, get back here!" Oliva shouted, just before he heard the door slam. "What's gotten into him tonight?" he asked as he sat back down, noticing that Oliva Jr. had climbed over Pépère to grab the empty seat and perch himself there as if it were a throne.

"Leave him be." Elzire knew that it wasn't just tonight. Oliva had been so involved with plans, tactics, and strategies that he hadn't even noticed how Ernest was picking fights every time the topic of bringing the girls home came up. It worried her. So did the fact that, although the other children didn't complain, they treated the return of their special sisters more as a visit than a permanent arrangement. Members of their own family were strangers, friends that they could play with, then leave when they were finished. Besides Ernest, only Rose, now fourteen, had any recollection of the quintuplets' birth, and of their presence in the house for the few short months before they were taken away.

"Let him go," Rose added. "He's so stubborn all the time."

"Sorry, Papa," Oliva apologized.

"I can remember you storming out from supper more than once when you were his age," Olivier recalled.

Elzire looked at Oliva with resentment. "If you didn't talk about your lawyer so much, this wouldn't happen."

"I wasn't even talking about him. And you're the one who told Ernest to go to his room. Just because he called them *quints*."

"You know what I mean, Oliva." She sighed. "Every night, it's the same thing."

"Sounds like our house," Michel, one of Léon and Marie's boys, piped up.

"Now..." Marie warned, covering his mouth for a moment.

"Why don't we laugh around here like we used to?" Tante Alma chirped.

"Did we ever?" muttered Thérèse, wiping up some cranberry sauce she had dropped on the oilcloth.

"Come here, you," Oncle Lias winked at four-year-old Oliva, who was still in his chair, sporting a proud smile.

Oliva couldn't let the subject drop. "There's nothing wrong with talking about bringing the girls back." He appealed to the entire table. "Is it a crime to talk about this to my own family?"

"Could I have some stuffing?" asked Tante Alma loudly, trying to detour another argument that she suspected was on its way. "I just love the way you make it, Elzire."

Elzire passed the bowl. "But it's your recipe!"

"I know," Tante Alma said, carefully spooning stuffing onto her plate, "but it's always better when someone else makes it."

Marie noticed Tante Alma trying to manoeuvre the big bowl with Victor on her lap. "Here, let me take him," Marie offered, getting up and coming around the table.

"No, I'm fine. You sit down."

Marie was already standing. "I'll clear some of the dishes, then."

Elzire turned to Oliva and started to get up. "Are you finished?"

"No. I want to make this clear. If I want to talk about the girls at...."

"I meant your supper."

"Oh."

Elzire smiled a little at Oliva's sheepish look. "Now I hope you're good and embarrassed," she said, getting up and helping Marie collect the dishes from the table. "It serves you right for this kind of talk at supper."

Just then, a knock sounded at the front door. Pauline jumped out of her chair and ran across the room to get it.

Elzire, plates piled in her hands, followed, expecting one of her other brothers or one of Oliva's cousins to be there with his family. "Come in," she called, as Pauline opened the door to a stranger.

"Mrs. Dionne?" The man who asked the question was unknown to Elzire, too.

"Close the door," Elzire ordered Pauline. She let all the plates rest on one arm so that she could reach to close the door with her free hand.

"Please?" The man pushed against the door to keep it open. "I'm Martin Poulin, your husband's lawyer."

"Get Papa," she told Pauline tersely, then called out to Oliva before Pauline had even made it across the room. "Oliva, come here."

Poulin stood nervously on the threshold, a cool barrier forming between him and the woman he had heard was once the warmest in Corbeil. "Your husband asked me to stop over and meet the family," he said. "I hope you don't mind."

Elzire backed away from him, opening a view of the visitor to everyone at the table.

Oliva was there in a second. He knew how Elzire felt about strangers, but when he had asked Poulin to drop over, he was extending an invitation to a friend, not an acquaintance.

"Why didn't you tell me?" she gasped.

"I did," he whispered loudly, but she had already disappeared. He turned to Poulin. "Hello, Martin."

"Good evening, Oliva. I seem to have dropped by at a bad time."

"We were just finishing supper. Let's talk outside for a while."

"It's pretty cold out there. If you'd like, we can leave it till another night."

"No, no. Elzire will be fine. She's just shy at first." He slipped on his boots and, at the same time, grabbed his mackinaw from the peg on the wall. He put it on while he pushed Poulin out the door ahead of him.

Elzire heard the door close. She turned to Tante Alma, who was offering the last slices of bread to Léon and Lias. "On a Sunday night, now," she said, upset. "We can't even have one day of peace in our home any more."

"Elzire, don't worry so much." Marie could see that she was almost in tears, and nodded the children out of the room. "Go and play in the boys' room until the pie is on the table."

Rose had an idea. "I've got a bag of honeymoons hidden in the summer kitchen. First one who finds it, gets it."

Daniel darted from the table first.

The rest of the children jumped from their chairs, all trying to beat him, but Daniel was already at the closed door, trying to push it open.

Oliva Jr. dropped from his chair last.

"Wait, Oliva," Elzire beckoned. "I'll get your coat."

But young Oliva had already followed the rest of them into the cold room.

"He'll be all right," Rose assured her mother, smiling as she disappeared into the summer kitchen to control the chaos.

"I hope she's got them in there," Tante Alma remarked. "They won't come out till they find them. They'll freeze to death."

"They'll be fine." It was Marie's assurance this time.

"Marie, I'd like to lie down," Elzire said, untying her apron. "Will you clean up?"

"Are you all right?" Tante Alma asked, lifting Victor into one arm as she stood up.

"I will be." Elzire backed away from the table.

"Go see to your sister," Huguette suggested quietly to Lias.

Alma nudged Olivier as Elzire disappeared upstairs.

Olivier sighed, getting up. "I'll talk to her." He motioned with his hand for Lias to sit down. "It's my son that's upsetting her so much."

Olivier followed Elzire up the stairs, stopping in the doorway to her and Oliva's bedroom.

Elzire was standing by the window, looking out at the snow-covered grounds of Quintland. It was not dark yet, and she could clearly see the lit windows of the hospital. The untracked snow that surrounded the hospital sparkled as if sprinkled with diamonds. Her head was tilted down, enough for her to see Oliva and his Mr. Poulin standing in the shelter of the huge wall that separated their property from another untracked patch of white: the field that would become the public parking lot again next spring. Despite the light flurry of snow that had started, she could see Poulin gesturing toward the hospital, and Oliva shaking his head in exasperation over something that he was being told.

Olivier cleared his throat.

Elzire turned away from the window, but did not face him directly.

"What's the matter, Elzire?"

"I'm okay, Pépère. I just had to get out of there for a minute." She put her head down. "Embarrassing the whole family like that."

Olivier walked over to her. "It was a great supper, Elzire. As usual."

"Thank you."

Olivier paused for a moment, guessing Elzire's thoughts. "He's excited, Elzire, that's all. There's nothing wrong with that. He's not trying to upset you."

A troubled look crossed her face. "I'm worried, Pépère."

"You're going to win this, Elzire."

"I know, but what are we winning? Oliva's so caught up in the law, in *the case*, that he can't think about anything else."

"What else is there for him to think about?"

"He could think about the fact that even if they do come home, it's not going to be easy."

"Not *if* they come home, Elzire. *When*."

Elzire ignored the comment. "You know, Ernest has more sense than his father sometimes. There are going to be police all over the place, whether Oliva wants to believe it or not. There will have to be."

"So? I think we're all pretty used to that by now."

"And I've never liked this lawyer business."

"Until Oliva got the lawyer," Olivier reminded her, "you weren't getting anywhere. Remember that."

"Things would have worked out. Look at how it's been getting better lately. I go over whenever I want."

"Yes," Olivier emphasized, "thanks to Oliva and his lawyer."

Elzire shrugged.

"Don't forget, it's better right now because everything is closed. Remember last winter, it was fine too. But wait until the shows start again in April. Then they won't let you wander in and out whenever you want."

Elzire looked pained. She didn't want to think about that.

"You need that lawyer, Elzire."

"But look at what we have to do," she moaned. "The store, and those souvenirs Oliva sells. It's a disgrace. First, ma tante, and now Oliva. How are we any different from the others?"

"You are different." Olivier was disturbed that she would name Oliva in the same breath with thieves out to make a quick buck.

"How? Tell me."

"I don't know about Adouilda, but Oliva's not doing this to get rich. Don't you think selling that stuff bothers him, too?"

Instead of answering, she looked out the window again. Oliva and Poulin were still at it.

"I tell you, Elzire, I'd do the same thing. And if Maman were still alive, I would have expected her to support me."

"I want to support him, Pépère," she said, facing him again with fear in her eyes. "You saw how I stopped the girls from speaking English during the radio broadcast last Christmas. What good did it do? They *wanted* to speak English."

"That's because they're not used to speaking French yet."

"I know, but I can't help thinking of these things. All the damage that's already been done."

"When you're a family again, everything will be easier to work out."

"I'm scared of when they come back. I'm not sure I'll know how to handle them."

"You'll know. They're your daughters. No one can ever change that."

"I know, but I don't know how they're going to feel. Or how the other children will feel. You heard Ernest."

"Ernest is sixteen years old. All boys are full of independence at his age."

"Don't remind me," Elzire asked. "He's been talking about working in his father's store next summer."

Olivier chuckled. "The girls seem excited."

"The girls don't even know their sisters," Elzire said bitterly. She looked back out the window at Oliva and Poulin, and gestured to Olivier to look too. "Look at them. They look like they're planning to overthrow a country."

Olivier followed her eyes and looked too. "They are," he said, before turning Elzire's head to face him. "You're a good mother, Elzire. And you'll be a good mother to the others, too. You watch; things will be easier to work out when you're all together again."

Elzire looked out the window again, but not to Oliva this time. Instead, she just stared at the frozen landscape on the horizon. She considered what Pépère had said, but found it of no consolation. She didn't need to be reminded that she was a good mother. She knew that. Nor did she need to be told that Oliva's motives were sincere, for she felt that deep inside. What she really needed, she knew she could never have. Reassurances for the future were not enough. There was no way the future could ever give them the past they had lost, and without which their lives would never be the same.

*   *   *

Oliva went to the store early. It was the beginning of another tourist season, the eighth, and he was expecting a shipment of blankets. He knew that the truck drivers liked to come early, before the heavy traffic on the road to Quintland rendered useless their schedule for the rest of the day. This suited Oliva fine, for it gave him a chance to get the shelves stocked before the morning influx of tourists. There was always someone stopping by to pick up something on their way to line up for the observation gallery.

He was standing at the back of the wool shop with Aline, his assistant, when Elzire walked in. They both looked up from the blankets they were taking out of a large box on the counter. As Elzire headed for the counter, Oliva turned to Aline and asked her to run to the other shop to get him a package of gum.

Aline could tell by the looks on both their faces that they wanted to be alone. "Bonjour, Madame," she greeted Elzire warmly. She squeezed Elzire's wrist as she passed her.

"Bonjour, Aline. Ça va?"

Oliva heard the uncertainty in Elzire's *bonjour* to Aline. He also noticed the tenseness in her walk as she made her way up the aisle. When she finally got close to him, he could also see the apprehension in her eyes.

Elzire walked right up to him and penetrated his questioning look with one of her own.

"You're going over now?" he asked cautiously, not wanting her to think that he was pushing too hard.

"Yes," she said glumly.

He walked around the counter, and put his arm around her. "Now, don't let them tell you anything. Stay as long as you want."

"I think the whole idea of going over now is silly," Elzire pointed out. "I'll be getting there just as the show is about to start."

"Fine. A visit from maman is more important than any show."

"I don't see why I can't go later, at my regular time. Then, if something happens, well...."

"Elzire, nothing is going to happen unless we make it happen. We went through that last night."

"Yes, we did," she agreed. "But I still don't know what good will come of it."

"You're beginning to sound like Ernest." He led her up the aisle to the door.

"Leave Ernest alone." Elzire wished she could find the right words to express what she felt was an understandable indifference in all of her children toward a reunion. But as she pulled away from him, she simply said, "He's got a lot of sense in his head."

"How come I'm the only one that wants the girls to come home?"

"You're not!" She grabbed both of his hands to assure him that although she sometimes seemed to be against him, she was always with him. "I'm just not sure what's best for the girls themselves. They've never been with us."

"They will be soon."

She let go of him. "Yes, and what good will it do?"

"Don't talk that way."

"Why not? You're so busy fighting this war of yours that you don't even see what's happening over there. Those five girls aren't like our other children. They don't want to come to our home. They're home already."

"You're just worried about going over."

"Shouldn't I be? Do you think they want me to go over and delay the show?"

"I don't care what Dafoe and his nurses want."

"I mean the girls. Our daughters. They like the shows."

"Come on, Elzire." Oliva shrugged off the possibility.

"It's true. They do. Can't you see, they've grown up a certain way. They're used to a certain life, and they like it just as much as our other children like theirs."

"They'll get used to another," he declared.

Elzire turned her head slightly. "Don't be so sure about that. I've talked to them. When I mention coming home, they just look at each other and giggle."

"All girls giggle."

"No, not like that." She stood by the door, her hands working as she spoke. "They're like strangers to me. I talk to them about coming home; they laugh. I speak in French to them; they answer to be polite, then go back to speaking English before I'm even out the door. I kiss them, and they look to the nurses to see if they should kiss me back. How can you say that everything will be just wonderful?"

Oliva was becoming frustrated by her negative attitude. "Okay, if you don't want to go, then don't."

"No, I'll go. It's too late for any good to come out of this either way. But I want you to realize that everything isn't going to be the way you think it will be."

"I know that," he said softly. "But what do you want me to do? Leave them locked up in there until they're eighteen?"

She had no answer for that. "I also want you to know that I don't like doing this. I don't like creating more trouble than there already is."

"I know you don't. But they play dirty, Elzire. Remember that. We're only doing what we have to do." He wrapped his arms around her, at the same time glancing out the window. The line-up for the morning show had already extended down the road past Tante's shop. "Okay," he said, pulling away from her. "Now go. Before the girls are already out. And don't let anyone stop you."

She mustered up as determined a look as she could. "I just hope something happens soon," she wished aloud, "because I can't go through much more of this."

"Sure you can." He squeezed her arm. "You're stronger than I am. And you know that, too."

She walked out the door.

"Don't be afraid," he whispered, but she didn't hear him.

From the doorway, Oliva observed her stiff walk as she crossed the road. So unlike the usual sway that had once characterized her relaxed attitude to simple things like a walk down the road to visit her old friend Gaëtane.

A few people outside the shop recognized Elzire and stared. Others passed by without noticing her. To most of them, she was simply another tourist among the thousands they would encounter on the road today. Only if she were to force her way into the line-up would anyone actually talk to her, and then only to tell her to wait her turn. How could she tell them she had waited long enough?

When Oliva saw her reach the other side of the road, he ran out of the store. He waved to Aline, who was on her way back with the gum, then ran along the fence toward his property, where he whipped through the gate, leapt up the porch steps, and raced into the house.

"It's Dionne." He was at the telephone in the kitchen, breathing hard as he leaned forward to peer out the front window. "Get me the hospital." He could see that Elzire had reached the guard-post and that one of the guards was opening the gate for her. "Hello.... Yes, she'll be there in a minute...." He watched Elzire start up the path to the hospital. "Thanks, I'll be in the shop if you need me. Keep your eyes open." He hung up and rushed back to the store.

A tall, slim nurse with an olive complexion and wavy auburn hair opened the door, smiling immediately when she saw that it was Elzire.

Elzire smiled in return when she saw that it was Nurse Monette who had answered. *Parise,* the French-speaking nurse had asked Elzire to call her. One of the new nurses hired by the board on Oliva's recommendation, Parise was a friendly, relaxed alternative to the brusque, dominating nurses previously brought in by Dafoe. Unlike so many of the others that had met Elzire at the door throughout the past seven years, Parise always had a smile and a few pleasant words for her and the rest of the family. At first, Elzire had attributed the nurse's sympathy to the fact that she had children of her own, but Elzire had soon realized that the kindness was not extended out of sympathy. Nor was it out of understanding, for that matter. It was a gesture of simple liking. Parise genuinely liked Elzire, and had from the moment they had met. It was a reflection of the way neighbours had taken to young Oliva's bride when he had first brought her around to meet them.

"Madame Dionne." Parise opened the door wide. "Come in."

"Thank you, Parise." Elzire was happy to see the warm face, but as she stepped through the doorway, she felt the same chill she always felt when she entered the hospital.

"The girls are getting ready for the show," Parise said, "but go ahead in. I'll tell the doctor you're here."

"Do you have to?" asked Elzire, mildly joking. She knew clearly that Parise had to report her arrival. Though she and Oliva had been given free access to the hospital, Dafoe had insisted upon being told when either of them were there, what rooms they wandered into, and when they left. He also wanted to know if they brought any of the other Dionne children along, and if any of them had a cold or "anything like that".

The two of them walked down the hallway that led to the large kitchen. At the end, they turned in opposite directions, Elzire right toward the girls' room, Parise left in the direction of the doctor's office.

As she passed the kitchen door, Parise looked in to see the cook spicing the pork for dinner.

"Anna," Parise called in politely. "Madame Dionne is here. Could you make her a cup of tea?"

"I'm busy right now," came the abrupt answer.

Another voice, equally abrupt, echoed down the hallway. "Did you say Mrs. Dionne is here? Now?"

Rapid steps approached.

Parise turned to greet Nurse Harper, one of the English-speaking nurses who had been with Dafoe from the time the hospital had opened.

"Forget it, Anna," ruled Nurse Harper from behind Parise.

"I wasn't going to make it anyway." The old cook bored a hole in the pork to insert another clove of garlic.

"What is she doing here now, anyway?" Nurse Harper asked. "It's almost time for free play."

"I'm sure a few minutes isn't going to matter," commented Parise.

Nurse Harper wouldn't budge. "But she never comes at this time of the day. The nurses have their hands full getting them ready. You know that."

The mother in Parise spoke out. "I don't see what difference it makes."

"The difference is she's never done it before. That's what we have Dr. Blatz's schedule for."

"I'm sure the schedule can bend a little."

"Since when?" Nurse Harper marched down the hallway to settle the matter with the quints' mother. "And why are you wearing that flower in your collar?" she called back, not even turning to look over her shoulder. "This is a hospital, not a nursing home."

Parise glared after her, then turned and continued down the hallway to Dafoe's office.

The door was closed. As usual. Most times, it was because he had company. The once-reclusive doctor seemed to always have a steady stream of visitors – reporters, photographers, corporate people, salesmen, celebrities – in and out all day long. But when he was alone, the door was normally closed too. Especially in the evenings. The nurses had grown used to hearing a door suddenly open, only to see the doctor walk out of his office long after everyone had assumed he was gone. *Business* he would say if any of them dared ask what he was doing. Parise, for one, wondered how much business was necessary to run a tiny hospital for five healthy inmates, especially when there were seventeen staff members doing all the real work.

Parise rapped hard on the door.

"Yes?" came Dafoe's little voice.

Parise opened the door and leaned in to see Dafoe sitting at his desk. He was smoking a pipe and reading the week-old edition of the

New York Times that he had picked up at the post office that morning.

"Excuse me, Doctor. I just wanted to tell you that Madame Dionne is in with the girls now."

"Um-hm, that's fine," breathed Dafoe through his pipe, barely turning away from Brooks Atkinson's latest review. "Thank you." He went back to his reading. Then, when he heard the door shut, he put down the paper and looked straight ahead, thinking. He was positive that no one, not even Nurse Monette, could find fault in "that's fine".

Ever since Hepburn had ordered him to open up the hospital, Elzire and Oliva had been coming over for long stays, sometimes bringing the other children with them. And though Dafoe had made a conscious effort to restrain himself from ordering them out, each visit had left him feeling less in control. He couldn't even trust his own nurses. A couple of them were still loyal to him, but most, like Parise Monette, had become friendly with the Dionnes. He had tried to solve this problem by looking for an excuse to fire any nurse who voiced too much sympathy for the Dionnes, claiming it was confusing for the girls to have too many attachments. But Oliva invariably objected to the board, raising language and education issues in an effort to keep as many hospital workers as possible under his control. And unlike Dafoe's objections, which were barely listened to, Oliva's were acted upon.

Parise was on her way back to the quints' room when Nurse Harper whipped past her without batting an eye. She headed straight for Dafoe's office, throwing the door wide open when she got there.

"Doctor, Mrs. Dionne wants you to take a look at Emilie. She says she has a fever."

"A fever?" He peered over the rims of his eyeglasses at her. "Did you look at her?"

"Yes. I didn't feel anything, but she wants you to examine her anyway."

"Can't you... oh, all right. I'll talk to her."

He rested his pipe in the ashtray and closed the newspaper before getting up.

Nurse Harper waited patiently in the doorway, then led the way down the hall.

Dafoe opened the door to the quints' room part way and looked in. Two nurses were busy dressing the girls in red taffeta outfits for the morning show. Another was taking the curlers out of their hair, and brushing the fresh curls. A fourth nurse was checking to make sure all the bows were straight.

"Don't you all look pretty," Dafoe beamed. The girls giggled and ran over to him with big hugs and kisses. Their bright smiles and affection momentarily cheered him. But the thought of that fat cow tickling and playing with his beautiful little girls ruined the moment.

"Good morning, Elzire," he said flatly. "Can we talk outside?"

"Good morning." Elzire joined him outside the room.

"Now, what's the problem with Emilie?" he asked, forcing a smile as he closed the door.

Elzire looked at Parise, who was standing to one side, then back to the keeper of her children. "I think she's getting a cold."

Dafoe was surprised. "She looked fine this morning." He had checked and weighed all of them at seven a.m., just before breakfast.

"She looks fine to me," added Nurse Harper.

"I think you should put her to bed anyway," Elzire suggested politely. "At least for a few hours."

Stay calm, Dafoe reminded himself. "I'll take a look at her after free play," he compromised.

"I'd like you to look at her now," Elzire requested, again looking to Parise, this time for support.

Dafoe looked at his watch. "Free play is going to start in a few minutes. I'll look at her right after."

She remembered Oliva's words: *"Don't let anyone stop you."* She raised her chin and looked the doctor straight in the eye. "The show can wait," she declared. "I'd like you to look at my daughter. Now."

"I said, later." Dafoe was getting annoyed at having to repeat himself. "Now, I'm sure it's nothing. Children get colds all the time."

Children get colds all the time – the words hit her like a bolt of lightning. How could he say that? Her mind spun like a wheel, from present to past, past to present, stopping wherever the hurt had been greatest. *You know how the doctor is about germs*, Nurse Harper had once said, trying to bar her from the hospital because of Daniel's cold. *You really should have come to the party*, Dafoe had said on the night of her babies' mock first birthday. *The babies aren't going anywhere. Not while I'm the boss*, he had told the world when Oliva needed someone to share the blame for the one thing he had done wrong in his life. The wheel spun harder, one degrading episode after another, until it stopped at the words she had just heard: *CHILDREN GET COLDS ALL THE TIME.*

She refused to walk away defeated. Not this time. "Right now!" she screamed, the force of her anger surprising even herself. "I want you to look at my daughter right now!"

Her voice reverberated down the hospital corridor, inducing the cook to stick her head out of the kitchen, and bringing two other nurses into the hallway. Even quiet Miss Vezina, the French teacher, wandered out of the classroom to see what all the fuss was about.

Dafoe stepped back. He looked to Parise, who stood dumbfounded; to Nurse Harper, who was in shock; to the other nurse and the cook down the hallway; and then back to the Elzire Dionne he had handled with relative ease all these years. He felt cornered. Everyone was watching him, waiting for him to speak.

"I'm telling you, Elzire," he warned, his squeaky voice rising higher than anyone had heard it before, "she's fine. I'll take a look at her after the show and not before."

Elzire fixed Dafoe with a determined, if not hateful, stare that for a moment seemed to frighten him. "There's going to be no show today," she said in measured, firm tones as she turned, opened the door, and went back into the room.

"Elzire," he called as the door slammed shut in his face. He turned to face the nurses. "What's wrong with her today?" he asked them. "I don't know why she's getting so upset over a little cold."

Just then, they all heard a shriek from inside the quints' room. It sounded like one of the nurses. Then the door swung open, and Elzire came running out. She was holding Emilie by the hand.

"Mrs. Dionne," cried Nurse Harper.

"Elzire, what are you doing?" Dafoe moved to stop her, but Parise was in his path. "Get out of my way," he shouted.

Elzire dashed quickly past, pulling a confused Emilie with her.

Nurse Harper ran down the hall after her and around the corner to the front door.

"Mrs. Dionne, stop!" she yelled frantically. "You can't take her outside."

But Elzire was already out the front door, holding tightly onto Emilie's arm. On the porch, Elzire stopped for a moment to assess the obstacles ahead of her. Their house was just across the road, but she first had to get through the gate, by the guards, and past the throngs of people making their way along the road. She was afraid, but she promised herself that she would plow through them if she had to.

Nurse Harper followed her out onto the porch, Dafoe a step behind. The cook and one of the other nurses also emerged, nearly crashing into the members of the tableau posed on the steps. Parise came out and observed the scene. Everyone looked like mannequins. None of them knew what to do. Even Nurse Harper hesitated to grab Emilie back, for Elzire looked prepared to strike anyone who came near.

Elzire and Emilie, mother and daughter, broke the rules and descended the steps.

It took only seconds before the sight of a quint hanging onto some fat woman registered with the people walking by on the other side of the fence. Even while hurrying to join the line-up, their eyes were naturally turned toward the hospital. When they noticed a little girl the same age as a quint, looking like a quint, and emerging from the log palace that was the quints' home, they knew it had to be one. What began as a stunned silence soon became a frenzy. Hundreds of bodies rushed toward the fence. Faces pressed against the metal. Noses poked through the small openings between the links. Voices called Emilie by the names of all the quints.

Another startling sight: famous Doc Dafoe rushing down the porch steps, followed by Nurse Harper, who grabbed Elzire's arm from behind.

"Mrs. Dionne, you let go of her right now!" ordered Nurse Harper.

"Elzire," Dafoe pleaded. "Please bring her back inside."

"Take your hands off me!" Elzire screeched at the nurse she hated the most. The words were met with an avalanche of voices and hoots from the crowd. The word that a quint was on the loose had spread like a brushfire. Now, more than a thousand people who had been in the queue were leaving their earned and valued places to see the new show that was going on inside the hospital gates.

Nurse Harper held on tightly as Elzire struggled to free her arm.

Dafoe became suddenly aware of the gaping crowd. "This isn't the place for a scene, Elzire," he exhorted.

Elzire broke free of Nurse Harper's grip and started to run with Emilie down the driveway.

Nurse Harper ran after her.

"Elzire," Dafoe called in vain.

Emilie buried her head in her mother's dress as they made their way toward the front gate.

"You're scaring her," Dafoe pleaded, looking at Emilie, then at the crowd. He was wondering what to do, wishing he could explain to the people that everything was fine, that they should all go back to their day at the fair. But they stayed. And, hearing the commotion, more were arriving by the second from all parts of Quintland.

"Oliva!" Elzire screamed, as she approached the gate.

"Elzire, bring Emilie back right now!" Doctor's orders.

"Mrs. Dionne!" Nurse Harper stopped running and put both hands on her hips. "I'm warning you!"

"Oliva," Elzire called out again, this time almost at the gate.

The people standing in front pressed closer to the fence, poking their fingers through in a feverish attempt to touch Emilie.

Elzire turned her daughter's face away from the crowd. "Open the gate," she called to the guards, who were prepared to do no such thing. Not without Dafoe's orders. After all, it was still his hospital, wasn't it? They just stood there, surprised as everyone else that Mrs. Dionne was stealing one of the quints from the hospital, and thinking that even if they could open the gate, the force of the rushing mob would crush them all.

"Call the police," one guard called to the other.

The young guard obeyed, rushing into the hut and picking up the telephone. "Get me the provincial police," he said, his hand shaking all the while. "Right away."

"Oliva!" Elzire continued to scream as loudly as she could. "Oliva!"

He came running, clawing his way through the crowd. "Out of my way," he shouted. "Let me through... let me through," he repeated in a panic. "Elzire!" he yelled above the clamour as he neared the gates. He could see her now, pulling at the gate as Dafoe stood by helplessly, pleading with her to return to the hospital.

Nurse Harper spotted Oliva coming and retreated to the hospital to call the police herself. Parise replaced her on the scene.

Oliva started to climb the fence. He was almost at the top, when the guard in the hut joined the other in tugging at his legs, trying to bring him down. The harder the guards pulled, the tighter Oliva held on to the fence. Finally, they were able to pull him down. He collapsed in a heap, both of his hands bloodied from his tight grip on the barbed-wire summit.

"Oliva!" Elzire screamed, seeing him fall.

"Please, Elzire," Dafoe coaxed. The click of a camera shutter sounded through a hushed moment in the din of voices. "I'll take care of her. Just come back in."

One of the other nurses joined Dafoe and tried to grab Emilie, who was now crying, her head hidden under her mother's arm.

"Don't touch my daughter," Elzire warned, hugging Emilie to her side even more tightly.

"Look at what you're doing to her." Dafoe stretched out both arms in front of Emilie to show Elzire how afraid the girl was. "You're scaring her half to death. Please, let her go back inside."

"No. Not unless you put her to bed right now."

"Okay, okay," Dafoe surrendered, almost in tears. "Just let go of her." As he pried Emilie away, Elzire finally let go, causing him to fall back. Elzire also rebounded backwards. Drained from the fight, she too fell to the ground.

The crowd grew still, silence rippling in wider and wider circles.

Dafoe got up and stood over Elzire. He reached for Emilie, who was sitting on the ground next to her mother, crying and pleading with her to get up.

Someone on the other side of the fence snapped another picture.

The gate opened a crack, just enough to let Oliva slip through. Then it closed again quickly, before the advances of the crowd could threaten them all. Oliva came running, his eyes darting in every direction: to Dafoe; to Parise; to Elzire; to Emilie, the little girl on the ground, whose face displayed a panic such as he had never seen before.

Emilie turned her frightened eyes from her father to the crowd. Terror spread across her face. She pulled her hand out of the doctor's, then picked herself up and raced along the driveway toward the hospital. Past the reaching arms and the cries of "Emilie" from the stunned nurses, the cook, and Miss Vezina. Up the steps as fast as she could. Through the open door without closing it. Down the hall to her room, where the sound of the door slamming shut behind her was the most welcome sound she had heard in the seven years she had lived there.

12

Victory

Dafoe stood nervously on Hepburn's doorstep, waiting for an answer to his ring.

He had been here once before, but it was in the evening for dinner. It had been too dark to notice the quiet street with its clean curb, the placid garden dotted with crocuses and forsythia, the still green pond, the neatly trimmed hedge that wove its way to the corner of the house. He had also been too excited about the invitation to notice much about the exterior of the building: its walls of perfect red brick, the elegant French windows sparkling in the sunlight, the white-painted iron mailbox, and the rich oak door with its curtained window – behind which lived the fiercest man he had ever known.

He wasn't quite sure why Hepburn scared him so. Perhaps it was his position – Premier of Ontario. It also may have been the way the big man gave orders to those about him with such ease. But it was most likely because Hepburn reminded him of his father. Both were men he had respected and hated at the same time. Both were men who had looked down on him, never pleased with what he could do. Good, to both men, had never been good enough. That was why he had left home in the first place.

But there was no escaping Hepburn. Not even in New York City. The telegram he had received last night had not been a friendly request, but a terse order: APRIL 20 1941 – DR. DAFOE – ALGONQUIN NY – MY PLACE ON WAY BACK – HEPBURN. Simple enough, but carrying with it the power to make him feel like a petrified child.

The door opened to Hepburn's uniformed young maid.

"Good morning, Dr. Dafoe," she smiled. "Please, come in. Premier Hepburn is waiting for you."

She led the way through the palatial foyer with its sweeping staircase, past the early-American dining room, through the big kitchen, and into the bright conservatory. "Sir," she announced. "Dr. Dafoe."

Hepburn put down the paper he had been reading. "Allan, good to see you." He grabbed Dafoe's little hand and shook it hard. "I'm glad you got my telegram before you left New York."

"Sounded urgent." He hoped that Hepburn wouldn't feel how cold his hand was.

"A drink, gentlemen?"

"Coffee will be fine." Hepburn looked up at the girl mischievously and winked. "It's a little early for anything else."

"Tea for me, if you don't mind?"

"Me too," Hepburn obliged.

"It won't be long," the maid said coyly, smiling at Hepburn as she closed the two glass doors on her way out.

"Sit down, Allan."

The two men sat opposite each other across the glass-topped patio table. Hepburn's hands were folded on the table; Dafoe's in his lap. They watched each other for a few moments, not saying a word. Then Dafoe, feeling very much the naughty boy for reasons yet unknown to him, broke the uncomfortable silence.

"Beautiful room," he commented, looking around at the decorative tables filled with plants, and through the windows to the garden of flowering almonds.

"I love it," Hepburn said easily, loosening his tie and lighting up a cigarette. "I can think and work and take in the sun – all at the same time."

"I'm sure," Dafoe said, noticing how relaxed Hepburn looked without his jacket on. It was the first time he had seen the officious leader resemble a human being. Men like Hepburn and his father had always appeared larger than life to him.

"How have you been, Allan?" Hepburn asked, looking concerned.

"Fine. All things considered."

"Good. Good." Hepburn leaned forward and moved his folded hands to the centre of the table. "I may as well get right to the point, Allan. Dionne's lawyer called."

"Oh?"

"Dionne is willing to drop all suits against you if you resign from the board."

Dafoe's face turned white. Up until that moment, he had held onto the foolish notion that he might have been summoned here for good news. "They can't blackmail us like that," he responded angrily, rebounding from the setback.

"They can, and they will," Hepburn declared with certainty.

"You can stop them, can't you?" Dafoe's trust in Hepburn as a fixer was still intact.

"Not without leaving ourselves wide open. Especially when they're ready to hit you with another suit."

"For what?"

Hepburn fixed his guest with one of his famous glares. "You tell me, Allan. What were you doing in New York this time?"

Dafoe was immediately defensive. "Nothing that concerns anyone. I have business there."

"Quite a lot, I understand."

"So? Why not?"

"Don't *why not?* me," the premier lashed out. "I'm not one of your fancy friends from the New York press, ready to eat up that kind of shit."

"What are you so upset about?" Dafoe asked uneasily, afraid of what the angry man might do to him.

"Just don't play innocent with me," Hepburn warned, levelling a finger at the doctor. "Now, I'll get right to the point." He reached to a magazine rack a few inches from his feet, and pulled out a copy of the *Toronto Daily Star*. He turned to one of the back pages, folded the paper back, and threw it in front of Dafoe. "You see that filler there," he said, almost poking a hole through both paper and table.

Dafoe adjusted his eyeglasses.

"It's about your endorsements with everyone under the sun. And, of course, your percentage of the quints' endorsements."

"I don't understand. You know all about this. It isn't news."

"It will be if we don't stop it fast. Dionne is ready to sue you for everything you've made off of his daughters if you don't resign from the board."

Dafoe got up and started to pace the room.

"I really thought you would have taken it easy with the endorsements," Hepburn lectured from his seat. "I thought that ridiculous *Doctor of Litters* incident would have taught you a lesson."

"I told you that was just a joke."

"Oh, I see. Then what do you call your nurse's little shoving match with Mrs. Dionne? A play fight?"

"It wasn't a shoving match. She fell."

"They have pictures."

"She was trying to take Emilie out of the hospital." He came to a stop at the far end of the room. "What were we supposed to do?"

Hepburn could see that Dafoe was nervously pulling at the leaves of one of the plants. "Come and sit down, Allan."

"I haven't done anything wrong," Dafoe stammered, panic carrying his voice higher than normal.

"Listen, my friend," Hepburn soothed, getting up to guide the doctor back to his seat. "Dionne is ready to push you to the wall for the endorsements. And he won't stop at you. He'll sue all of us, too – Clayton, Sharkey, even me. Anyone who was in on the guardianship, or who took cuts from the endorsements."

"Let him," Dafoe said defiantly, sitting back down. "You can fight it. It could drag on for years."

"Allan. These aren't idle threats." Hepburn sat too. "And you know they aren't groundless, either. Now, I'm not going to engage in a full-scale custody battle. They'll appeal to the Supreme Court and get an order to go through our files with a fine-toothed comb."

"We've got nothing to hide."

"Clayton's taking care of that right now, but they'll still second-guess every move we've made. I won't lay the Government open to that." He heard the maid approaching the room. "Now, keep a lid on this."

The maid opened the door and carried in a silver tea service accompanied by a vase with a solitary daffodil in it. "Here we are," she said, laying the tray down on the table in front of them. "Shall I serve?"

"We'll take care of it, thank you."

They watched as she closed the door after leaving. "You knew as well as I did that it was just a matter of time before the girls went back to their parents," Hepburn asserted.

Dafoe shook his head. "No, I didn't," he lied, sensing in Hepburn's tone that his worst fears were about to come true.

"It's inevitable. Everyone is saying that it's wrong to keep them away from their parents any longer. The newspapers, the psychologists, the Church." He poured the tea. "Sugar?"

"They're not ready," Dafoe pleaded. "Don't do this to them."

"To *them*, or to *you*?" Hepburn looked at Dafoe's bent head and sunken face. He felt pity for the man before him, but that didn't stop him from wanting to get down to the business at hand. "We'll release a statement," he said, trying to sound positive. "Make it seem like you stepped down voluntarily. It can be the end of a wonderful story. You can tell the press that you feel your job is complete. That it's time to send the quints home to live under the same roof as their parents."

"In that old farmhouse?"

"No, no. We've decided to build a big house for the whole family." He took a sip of his tea, giving Dafoe a few seconds to absorb that bit of news. "We can make the announcement together." He looked at Dafoe's untouched tea. "Come on. Drink your tea. And don't worry so much. Nobody has to know the real reasons. Dionne's lawyer, Poulin, has agreed not to leak anything to the press."

"I'll consult with Oliva more." He choked out the words in desperation. "I'll make it work."

"It's already done."

The doctor was silent.

"You're off the board," Hepburn stressed. "Now, in consideration, they've agreed to drop all current claims against the Government and to waive the right to take further action. And," he concluded happily, "they'll honour all the commitments we've made, including the Victory Bond Rally. It's a fair settlement, if you ask me."

Dafoe slumped back in his chair. "You've agreed to all of this without even consulting me."

"It's been almost eight years, Allan. It was a good arrangement for all of us. Can't you accept that it's over now?"

Dafoe stood up. "Arrangement?" Could he really mean that? "I'm their doctor," he faltered, stopping at that.

"Yes, yes. I know..." Hepburn continued for him in a sarcastic sing-song, "... and they're your patients... and you've only been taking your regular salary all these years to look after them."

Dafoe looked into his teacup, but there were no leaves to predict what words would be hurled at him next.

"I told you before. Don't lay that kind of rubbish on me. Do you really want to see your bank balance splashed across the front page of the *Telegram*?" Hepburn paused, hoping that the implications of *that* happening would sink in. "And don't be foolish enough to think that you can fight this. You've been losing one battle after another with Dionne lately."

"That may be true, but it's still my hospital."

"Is it?" Hepburn asked cynically.

Dafoe wanted to say yes, but the premier's look told him not to bother.

"You've still got your reputation," Hepburn pointed out. "And if you ease out carefully now, no one will be able to take that away from you."

Dafoe removed his eyeglasses, and rubbed his temples. "You sit there and tell me my time is up. What do you expect me to do, lay down and die?"

"You've got money," Hepburn said. "And I know you like to travel."

"But you *gave* those girls to me." He stood up and started to pace again, this time gesturing wildly with his hands as he spoke. "It was your decision to build the hospital, to set up the board."

"Yes, it was. And it was the right decision at the time. Now, come and sit down."

"And now it's right to take away the only things in the world that mean anything to me?"

"They're not things, Allan. They're people. They should never have been kept from their family this long."

The words stopped Dafoe again. He stared at the man who had never even wanted to hold the quints when they were babies. "You really do play with people's lives, don't you?"

"You're upset, so I'll let that comment pass. Why don't you sit down and drink some tea? It'll make you feel better." He reached under the table to lift his attaché case. "I have your statement with me. We can get it all taken care of right now, and then there'll be no more problems for any of us. Come and sit down. You'll just make yourself sick worrying about it for nothing."

Dafoe wouldn't sit. He watched Hepburn prepare the papers: putting them in order, marking Xs where he would be asked to sign, laying them neatly beside his tea, then asking him once again to sit. But he wouldn't. Instead, looking straight ahead, he walked out of the room, stiff as a puppet, though free now of the strings that had guided him for so long.

He left the house feeling a resurgence of strength. He was glad he hadn't signed the papers, and now no one could make him. He felt as he had half a lifetime ago, when he had refused to join his father's practice and walked out of the house for good. Then, he had gone north to become a country doctor. Now, he was going north to say goodbye.

He wouldn't stay in Toronto for the announcement. Not this one. He and Hepburn had shared the spotlight on many occasions over the years, beginning with the ground-breaking for his very own hospital, but he wouldn't stand at the premier's side for the last act.

What was he supposed to do? Smile for the reporters as Hepburn told them what was going to happen? Pretend that it was all for the best? That would be like parading one of his patients before a crowd, announcing that the man was terminally ill, and asking him to say a few happy words.

When he walked out of Hepburn's house yesterday, the premier had followed him and asked, then ordered, him to stay and sign the papers. But he just kept walking, silence the only answer he had to give. There was nothing more that Hepburn could do to him now.

The train ride to North Bay was the loneliest of his life. How different from the time, seven years ago, when he had returned home from New York after conquering all of Manhattan. He had stopped in Toronto then too, and had been greeted in the Ontario Legislature by a tremendous ovation. And when he had pulled into the North Bay station that day so long ago, it had seemed like half the town was there to welcome him. Late that afternoon, he had gone to the hospital to see his precious babies. When he had lifted them into his arms, each had given him a big smile. Everything had been so perfect then. Now, he was returning home, but to no great welcome. He would still go to the hospital when he returned, but only to bid his final farewell.

When he pulled up, Mrs. Henderson was outside planting gardenias. She looked up anxiously when he got out of the car. The sound of his voice on the telephone last night had told her that something was wrong. "Welcome back," she called out, trying to sound cheerful for his sake. But Dafoe had no salutation to return as he pushed through the gates and shrugged off her help with his suitcase. She took one look at his posture, and then at his pale face, and knew that whatever had happened had been bad. Very bad. She had seen that look on his face only once before, when she first started working for him, just after his wife had died.

She lowered her head as he passed, then continued her gardening, sparing him the concerned look that she knew he would not want to see. She looked up again when she heard the door open, just in time to see his bent figure disappear into the house.

Dafoe put the suitcase down and stood with his back against the door, hoping that Mrs. Henderson wouldn't follow him in. He couldn't face anyone just yet. After a few moments, he went into the waiting room and peered out the window to see what she was doing. Thankfully, she had kept gardening.

He walked through the doorway into the examining room that he had hardly used in the past eight years. Nothing had really changed since that remarkable May. In fact, nothing had changed since years before that. At the far end was his small desk, neat and organized as it always had been. Behind the desk were shelves filled with medical texts and journals. Along the other wall, the examining table. He looked at the table, wondering how many patients had sat on it while he told them to "open wide"? How many lollipops had he given to children to make them forget the pain? His eyes moved to the upright scale, old when he had bought it, and over to the drug cabinet, its white enamel badly chipped on the corners. He remembered how one of the early stories had described this same room as *dazzling* and *magical*. It was neither of those. It was just a simple GP's office. That hadn't changed in thirty-two years.

Dafoe looked at the two crayon drawings that hung on one wall. Their bright colours were a sharp contrast to the drab background. Mrs. Henderson had been urging him for years to help her wallpaper the room. He took a closer look at the yellow, pink, and blue in the drawings. He recalled fondly how the girls eagerly awaited their daily art period, and were always in a hurry to show him their latest masterpiece. He ran his hand over one of them: a naive drawing of a man distinguished by a huge bushy moustache and an oversized stethoscope dangling from his neck. He smiled, remembering when

Annette had given it to him. She had thought it a perfect likeness, and he had agreed, just to make her happy.

His eyes turned to the finger-painting next to it. All five girls had contributed to that one, and what a mess they had made. Not just their fingers, but all of their little bodies had been spattered with purple. They had come at him with their hands extended, pretending they were going to smear him, and had all laughed when he ducked away from them and ran out of the room.

He looked from one picture to the next, his misty eyes finally drifting to the only photograph on the wall. The three-year-old quints looked out from a brass frame, their eyes sparkling, each of them flashing a big smile for da....

As he left the room, he failed to see Mrs. Henderson, who was watching him from the telephone nook under the stairwell. He leaned into her shadow as he lifted his worn suitcase from where he had left it near the entrance, but he still didn't notice her. And she didn't say a word.

Up the stairs he climbed, pulling at his perfectly knotted tie until it unravelled and fell to the steps behind. When he entered his bedroom, he caught his likeness in the floor-length mirror in the corner. He closed the door and moved closer, looking deep into the mirror at the wrinkled reflection before him. He blinked a few times. This wasn't the man who had fallen victim to the quints. This was an old friend, the lonely man from Madoc – the one who had always refused invitations from his patients for fear of losing himself in their lives.

* * *

Martin Poulin walked into Oliva's souvenir shop, a big smile splashed across his face. He quickly put both arms behind his back to hide the long tube he was carrying. He passed two women who were busily selecting postcards from a wire rack, then spotted the salesclerk, who smiled at him in recognition before continuing with the man to whom she was selling a quint paperweight. Poulin looked at the customers and chuckled to himself. Get it while you can, he thought.

Oliva was standing at the far corner of the store, counting bronze key-rings from a small cardboard box. He had heard the bell ring when the door opened, but hadn't bothered to turn. He figured it was simply more customers who would announce themselves when they were ready to pay.

Poulin was practically breathing down his neck, when Oliva finally turned.

"Martin, what are you doing here?"

Poulin didn't answer. He just broadened his smile and wriggled his shoulders to make it apparent that he was hiding something.

"What are you so happy about?"

Shoulders shrugged again.

"Okay," Oliva obliged. "So we're playing a game. What have you got there?"

Poulin drew the long roll of paper from behind his back. "Oh, nothing," he said, laying it on the counter. "Just some plans for a new house that's going up in the area."

"Where?"

"Right over there." Poulin pointed through the window to the empty field beyond the west fence of the Dafoe Hospital.

Oliva peered out the window, then looked to Poulin anxiously. The plans. Poulin's smile. The empty lot across the road. "No?" he asked guardedly, not yet ready to believe the unbelievable.

Poulin nodded toward the plans.

Oliva fumbled with the papers, having to unroll them a second time when they rolled back up in his shaking hands. His eyes anxiously searched all corners of the paper for the caption. There it was, in the bottom right-hand corner, in blueprint blue and written all in capitals: *DIONNE HOUSE*. He absently scanned the plans, then looked up almost helplessly at Poulin, who just nodded and slapped him on the back.

Oliva grabbed Poulin's forearms tightly. "Thank you," was all he could say.

Everyone looked up as Oliva tore out of the store. They all looked up again when he flew back in, only to grab the plans from Poulin's waiting hands and dash back out again. They looked to Poulin for some sort of explanation, but he returned their stares impassively, then wandered out to meet the warm spring air. He turned, just in time to see the victorious father disappear behind the wall that separated his home from the carnival that would soon be leaving town.

Oliva ran through the house, unable to find Elzire. He called upstairs, then out to the back yard and down to the root cellar. Those possibilities exhausted, he decided to try the hospital, where she often took Oliva Jr. and Victor to visit with their sisters while the other children were at school. He picked up the telephone and called, in his exuberance telling the operator that he loved her while he anxiously waited for the hospital to answer.

"It's Oliva Dionne." He spoke rapidly, slurring his words. "Please tell my wife to come home right away." He hung up, then ran onto the front porch to wait for her.

He clutched the plans tightly in his hands and waved them in the air as Poulin climbed the steps to join him. They embraced, whirling around together in a mad dance, carelessly letting the plans crease between them. Then they looked across the road to the hospital, waiting for what seemed like hours until Elzire came out.

The moment Oliva spotted Elzire emerging from the front door of the hospital, he regretted not telling the nurse who had answered the telephone that nothing was wrong. For Elzire plunged out onto the porch alone, hastily descending the steps and hurrying down the driveway in an agitated run that spelled the anticipation of bad news.

"Let's go," Oliva said to Poulin, dashing down the path, and running through the obstacle course created by the crowd that filled the road. "I can't wait to see her face."

Elzire continued along the hospital driveway, slowing down a little as she ran out of breath. As she approached the gate, she saw on the other side of it two happy men: the husband she loved so much, and the lawyer he had hired to remove from their lives the sadness to which she had become accustomed. She took one look at the two grown men – dancing, throwing a long roll of paper back and forth between them, laughing – and knew right away that it was all over.

She stopped. Her body felt numb, her head heavy, her face flushed and immobile. She had no smile to offer. No tears to shed. No expression to tell a story. Nothing.

She noticed Oliva starting to come through the gate, and signalled him to wait. "I'm coming," she called, but when she tried to move, her feet were frozen to the ground. Emotions tumbled inside her, one over the other, fear leading the way. She bit her lip, it was trembling so much. Tears finally started to roll down her cheeks as a trickle of blood appeared on her lower lip.

Ever so slowly, she started to move forward. As she approached the gate, she could see the guard standing ready to open it for her. Not yet, she prayed, slowing her already slow walk to a crawl. She looked past her beaming Oliva and his proud Mr. Poulin at the tourists. Walking. Running. Determined to get that coveted place in the line-up before the next person did. She looked at them, the people who had come to see her children, and wondered if they could ever accept their darling quints as normal children, not on display for the public's amusement and delight, but at home with their real family.

Worse, she thought, as she stumbled through the gate into Oliva's arms: Could her darling quints ever accept it themselves?

Epilogue

They had not yet moved into the *big house*, when it came time for the Victory Bond Rally in Toronto. As promised by Hepburn, Oliva would take them, and Elzire would come along too. Elzire argued against the idea of parading her sheltered children in front of thousands of people once again, but Oliva was insistent upon sticking to the agreement he had made.

The quintuplets themselves were thrilled. They had talked about the trip for weeks. It was to be their first experience of the world beyond the gates of the Dafoe Hospital, and their enthusiasm was unbridled.

As soon as the train left North Bay, all five of them crowded around the window and pointed excitedly to each amazing sight along the way: the cows, the silos, the wide-open fields, the rooftops of the buildings in the distance, the industrial suburbs of the city. Everything was new to them except the cars. Those they had seen plenty of from the window of their bedroom in the hospital.

All along the way, the girls asked their parents question after question. *"What's that?"* they wanted to know. *"What's this?"* they pleaded. Eight years lost, thought Elzire, and so much to teach them, so much they didn't know. She and Oliva answered every question, only to see the girls gaze back out in wonder, or exchange private looks that only they themselves could understand. Elzire watched them worriedly. What could be going on in their heads? She knew all of her other children's thoughts almost as well as her own. But she had no idea of what these five were thinking, and it frightened her.

"Ladies and gentlemen, the Dionne Quintuplets." The voice of the emcee boomed out like that of a carnival barker. The crowd, which had squeezed into every available crevice of Toronto's Maple Leaf Gardens, cheered lustily as they awaited the arrival of the quints on the empty stage below. The loud, celebratory music that was playing grew louder. And then, an explosion of applause and camera flashes filled the air as the quints entered from stage right. Dressed identically, they rode oversized tricycles and followed each other in a circle, finally converging at centre stage under a huge banner that implored the crowd to *BUY VICTORY BONDS*.

The music stopped, but the roar of the crowd peaked only once the quints had gotten off their tricycles. The five of them lined up to face the eighteen thousand hungry sets of eyes that filled the stadium, as well as the dozens of photographers and newsreel cameramen that were there to record the historic first appearance of the quints outside the Dafoe Hospital. The emcee leaned down to Yvonne, prompting the applause to subside so that the little voices could be heard.

"And what's your name?" he asked.

"Yvonne," she responded shyly.

The applause thundered.

"And yours?" he asked, moving over one.

"Annette."

Once again, the avid cheers cascaded down.

"And who are you?"

"Marie."

"And which one are you?"

"Emilie."

"That means you must be...."

"Cécile."

He moved to one side, so that he wouldn't obscure the audience's view of them, then raised his arms in the air, extending them far apart. "Ladies and gentlemen," he shouted, in the split second before the noise of the crowd drowned him out, "the Dionne Quintuplets. Let's have a big hand."

No encouragement was necessary. The hockey arena now quaked with a force that shook the stage – the stage where stood five pretty girls, barely eight years old, each one as confused as the next by the magnitude of the adulation. People screamed until their throats hurt, and clapped until their hands stung, but the quints just blinked in the harsh glare of the stage lights. They knew the applause was for them, but they didn't know why.

They looked from right to left, desperately hoping to see some familiar faces. But there were none. They tried to find their parents, who were standing at the entrance of the tunnel beneath the stands, but the lights shining onto the stage were blinding, and all they could see were bright spots. So they continued to pose for the crowd, searching each other's eyes for an explanation, waiting expectantly for the cheers to fade.

Private looks continued to pass between them – almost telepathic looks that told each other they had already had enough of Toronto. *It was time to get back to the hospital.*

Aftermath

The Dionne Quintuplets were sent to live with their family at the age of eight. They had difficulty adapting to a normal upbringing, and came to resent their parents for taking them away from their idyllic life in the Dafoe Hospital.

After the quints returned home, Dr. Dafoe never saw them again. He died a year later. By that time, Mitchell Hepburn, who had been touted in a 1937 *Time* cover story as a future prime minister, had resigned as premier. He never again held public office.

As soon as the quints turned eighteen, all five moved away from home. Years later, they referred to the *big house* as the saddest home they had ever known. Three married, unsuccessfully. Two have died. The three surviving women live as virtual recluses in a Montreal suburb. They returned home when their father died in 1979, but left immediately after the funeral. Since then, they have rarely returned.

Elzire remained in Corbeil, a few hundred yards from the field that was once known as Quintland.